The Blonde on the Train

For Robin Hudler, who has made the writing life possible.

The Blonde on the Train

stories by

Eleanor Lerman

Mayapple Press 2009

Published by MAYAPPLE PRESS
408 N. Lincoln St.
Bay City, MI 48708
www.mayapplepress.com

ISBN 978-0932412-73-7

ACKNOWLEDGMENTS

Civilization first appeared in: *Turnrow*, Vol 5.2

Edison Park first appeared in: *Bridges*, Vol 10, No 2

Cover background courtesy Getty Images. Harpsitar image and cover design by Judith Kerman. Book typset and desgned by Amee Schmidt with titles in Tekton Pro and text in Californian FB.

Contents

Civilization

Person wanted to sweep up in harpsichord factory. That was the ad in the Village Voice that I answered when I was seventeen years and eleven months old and looking for a job so I could support myself in the city, where I was headed to join the revolution. It was 1972, I had already been out of high school for six months, working as a cashier in a restaurant near where I lived with my parents in the Bronx, and I had been planning my escape for a long time. It never even occurred to me to go to college. In the new world that was sure to unfold once we toppled the government and established a more equitable social order that would involve lots of decisions by committees that would probably be headquartered someplace like Bethesda Fountain in Central Park, I figured I already had all the skills I needed.

Well, those were the kinds of things people my age thought in those days. And those were the kinds of jobs that were available, the kinds of jobs that seemed like perfectly reasonable ways to spend your time.

So that's how I came to be walking down Charles Street, heading west of Sheridan Square into a landscape that no one would recognize today. There were mostly warehouses and truck depots; cobbled streets and cracked sidewalks stained with motor oil and littered with the remains of workmen's lunches. Oh, yes—and on the corner of Charles and Washington was a small, dusty lot where a man lived with goats, dogs, chickens, and a couple of ponies that local kids came to ride after school. A pony farm in Greenwich Village. I kept looking at the slip of paper on which I'd written the address I was looking for. Was I headed in the right direction? Yes, I was. And let me now repeat that from the distance of thirty years later: yes, surely I was.

I finally came to the last block—Charles, between Washington and West—where three elderly, Federal-style houses (one pink brick, one brown, and one fronted with a kind of gray slate that made it look like a jail) leaned against each other in a neighborhood that was otherwise occupied by buildings that looked like one iron slab had been piled on top of another and then hammered together with steel bolts in order to support the labor of heavy machinery. The gray building was where my job interview was supposed to be, so I rang a bell on the ground floor, which was answered by a man who introduced himself as Michael Edelberg, the manager of Edelberg Harpsichords.

He led me into a windowless, ground-floor workshop where a couple of girls were sitting at tables, doing what looked like craft work, which I later learned was actually the assembling of parts that went into Edelberg Harpsichord kits. Though of course, I didn't know it then, these kits were—and apparently, still are—world famous, and their sale is a steadily thriving business. At the time I walked into the workshop on Charles Street, the business was just beginning to expand, and that was part of the reason that Michael needed some help. The other part was that the business was really owned by his brother, Werner, who lived in Germany; Michael was supposed to stay here in New York and run the workshop. He had built all the machinery for assembling the parts himself—and he showed them to me proudly; odd little Rube Goldberg-type wheeled machines for cutting and winding the felt needed to pad sections of the harpsichord case and hitchpin rails; tiny hammers for tapping tiny gold pins into plastic frames that held the plectrum to pluck the harpsichord strings, which were really different strengths of gold and copper wire wound on bigger wheels stolen from old sewing machines and run by pumping foot treadles.

I don't know if there were even any other applicants, but I got the job right on the spot. It turned out that besides sweeping—which was a necessary task at the harpsichord workshop because among the integral parts of the instrument are rails and bridges that hold the tuning pins through which the strings are anchored, and drilling these produces a lot of wood chips and litter—I was supposed to be the backup person who could operate any of the machines if someone didn't come to work. And considering that the workforce was made up entirely of three hippie girls who were introduced to me as Sammie, Shandy, and Marceline—each of whom I soon figured out had loose affiliations to just about every aspect of their lives, including their jobs—I quickly learned to work all the odd contraptions with no problem at all.

Within a month, I had also learned just about everything else there was to know about Edelberg Harpsichords, including the fact that once

Michael had created all these machines, he had pretty much lost interest. He confided in me that he was really a painter; that he had a girlfriend named Rosalie who was the ex-wife of the brother of a popular black singer (it was important that the singer was black and the ex-wife white; it established all kinds of political identities and beliefs that we cared about in different ways than we do now); she owned a cottage in Westport, Connecticut, on the rocky shore of Long Island Sound and he much preferred to be there, smearing paint on a canvas. So, he told me one spring morning when I could tell he was itching to be far away from Charles Street, he would actually like me to manage the place. There wasn't much to it, he said; the orders came in, you filled them by putting the requisite parts in big, heavy cardboard boxes (that was one of Shandy's jobs; to assemble the boxes), filled out a label, called REA Express (now defunct) and shipped the harpsichords hither and yon. You wrote information on slips of paper, you kept records, you called Michael in Westport when you needed something and he'd sign a check or phone a supplier. It seems he had figured out quickly that for all my hippie dress, long black hair (which I ironed, in case it wasn't already straight enough), elaborate Cleopatra eye makeup, and professed affection for hashish, I was a responsible person. And he was right. I had been raised by immigrants who had used their wits to escape from some nameless, Jew-hating rural European backwater, which had imbued me with the idea that survival had a lot to do with paying attention to what was going on around you, making plans, and keeping your word. So that was me. Rebellious but reliable. I even called home once in a while to let my parents know I was okay.

When Michael had said, "manage the place," I thought he meant just the harpsichord workshop, but he meant the whole building, as well. It really consisted of just three apartments upstairs: his, which was the entire top floor, and two smaller ones on the floor below. There was a couple in the larger of the two apartments; nice, easy people who "went to business," as my parents would have said. The other apartment, a small studio with a tiny Pullman kitchen, was empty, and Michael was hoping I would rent it so even when I wasn't at work, I could keep an eye on things. He'd leave me a list of plumbers and electricians who could deal with emergencies, and of course, he could drive down from Connecticut if anything major needed to be dealt with. The rent, he told me, would be $100 a month.

Yes, believe it: he was giving me a break in return for services but still, $100 a month was not extraordinarily cheap. It was actually an added expense for me, since I had found an apartment in the East Village where two roommates and I each paid only $50 a month. But I couldn't resist the idea of getting out of bed and just walking downstairs to work, so I said sure, the arrangement was fine. And that's how I came to run Edelberg Harpsichords on Charles Street and live in an apartment upstairs. But the story I'm really trying to tell here hasn't actually begun yet; it's going to begin now, when Harmon Terry—who was in his late forties, nice looking, but with the kind of curly hair that men don't like to have anymore—walks into the harpsichord workshop. (Full disclosure: like Michael Edelberg, who has already literally and figuratively left the building, he isn't going to appear much in the following pages, but he will overshadow the story to come, since he's responsible for just about everything that happens next.)

Behind 161 Charles there was an old carriage house, built in the 1800s. It fronted on Charles Lane, a narrow, cobbled street that ran just one block, between Washington and West streets. The house on the Lane and the harpsichord workshop were separated by a small garden of brick pavers and colorful peonies; back doors from both houses led to the garden, so you could walk out the door of one house, across the garden and into the other. That was the route Harmon took to get to his car.

Michael had told me that Harmon was a movie producer who split his time between New York and L.A. When I came to work at Edelberg Harpsichords, he had just produced what turned out to be one of the most famous movies of the 1970s. He and Michelangelo Antonioni went out into Death Valley with a young, beautiful actress and her handsome co-star and blew up a lot of things. If you watch the movie now, it's kind of puzzling and you find yourself wondering, *What were they thinking?* But nobody thought that then, and the movie was called "haunting," "mythical," and "a confrontational portrayal of the violent, unsettled nature of our times."

Harmon, Michael also told me, owned a gun, was in the process of divorcing his third wife, and was known on both coasts and in a number of European cities as a very volatile kind of guy. Given that information and the fact that he was famous, I was a little afraid of him (I still very much thought of myself as a lower-class kid from the Bronx so I was both jealous and terrified of anybody living at a station so much higher than myself, and one that I had been conditioned to believe no one with my background could ever aspire to). I became more afraid one day when he walked into the harpsichord factory (as I sometimes thought of the place) and asked if he could use our phone, since his wasn't working. Sure, I said, and he proceeded to call Sophia Loren in Italy and actually had a nice chat with her. He left me a check to give Michael to pay for the call.

Actually, he was always perfectly nice to me. He said hello to me on those mornings when he walked through the workshop, taking a shortcut to get to his car, which was parked down the block, and hello to all the girls, whose names he had taken the trouble to learn. But one particular morning, instead of just walking by with his customary wave and *hello*, he stopped in front of a chalkboard that was hanging on a wall near the desk where we had our telephone, took our orders, and kept our paperwork for shipping the harpsichords. It happens that I had taken to writing poems at night, after work, and sometimes, if I liked one of them well enough, I'd copy it onto the chalkboard where we were supposed to write down what supplies we needed (which of course we didn't need to use for that purpose because I was so well organized about keeping whatever parts we needed in stock).

Now, it does seem like I just skipped by that part about *I had taken to writing poems*, didn't I? For the sake of this story, I suppose I should be a little bit more forthcoming. What actually happened was that about a year before I came to Edelberg Harpsichords, I had found a book in a drugstore rack called *The Spice-Box of Earth*, by Leonard Cohen. I knew him because he sang a song on the radio that I liked (that *everybody* my age liked) called *Suzanne*, so I bought the book and it did something to me. It was a book of poems, but not anything like any poem I had ever read before, since what they had force fed us in school was Robert Browning and his damn duchess, and fey little wispy weepings by Emily Dickinson, who—I don't care how lonely and admirable her life was—can keep her feathery hope all to herself for all I care. But when I read Leonard Cohen, I remember thinking something like, *Well, I could do that*, and it turned out that I could. So I'm being disingenuous by saying that I had "taken to writing poems." What had happened to me was that I had developed an addiction, an obsession, a desire to imagine things and describe them in a way that sort of conformed to a style that fit into uneven, unrhyming stanzas, so I suppose they were poems. Anyway, once I had started, I couldn't stop.

So this spring morning, in the harpsichord factory, where we had a record of whale songs playing in the background and three joints in the desk drawer that we intended to share after lunch, Harmon walked into the factory and stopped in front of the chalkboard to read what I had written there. I remember the poem well, particularly the line, "Vampires are happier when they're homosexual," which I am not even going to try to explain. After he finished studying the poem, Harmon said to me, "That's very good."

I was sitting at a worktable, tapping tongues into plastic jacks with a tiny hammer, so I raised my head and said, "Thanks."

"You're copying these down someplace, aren't you?" he said, which made me realize he'd noticed the poems even before he'd stopped to read this one today. "You're not just writing them here and then erasing them, are you?" He sounded surprisingly stern.

"I keep them in a notebook," I told him, which was true.

"Good," he said.

After that, whenever I had written a new poem on the chalkboard, Harmon would stop to read it. Once, he came over to me and said, "I really like that one today. That line about being a mental hermaphrodite? It's great. Do you think I could have a copy? I want to give it to someone."

"I guess so," I said. Until then, I don't think it had occurred to me that anyone would want to see these poems written down on a piece of paper. I kind of thought that part of their attraction—if they even had any—was that they made their limited public appearances on a blackboard, like messages from the underground, scrawled in the night. The *Village Voice* was always writing about "the underground," so the idea had some appeal for me. "Sure," I said. "I'll give you a copy tomorrow."

Some time later, on an evening at the beginning of summer when I was home watching TV, which is pretty much all I did in the evenings while I waited for the revolution to change the world (I thought I was doing my part by getting high whenever I could and in the colder months, wearing a pea jacket, purchased secondhand from an army/navy surplus store), Harmon knocked on my door. When I opened the door to him, I somehow thought what he wanted was going to have something to do with the poem, but that wasn't it at all.

He said, "Michael tells me that you've done a really good job managing the workshop and the house. I have to be away for the summer—I'm going to Europe to scout locations for a film—and I've rented the carriage house, but I'm wondering if you'd be available to help out the tenant if he needs anything. I'd pay you, of course."

I remember being flabbergasted, mostly because I had never, ever had anyone say anything to me that sounded even remotely like, *I'm going to Europe to scout locations for a film*, not even as a joke, so I wasn't sure how to respond. The words I eventually heard coming out of my mouth, though, were, *I guess so, sure*, meaning, his tenant could call me if he needed anything.

The next night, Harmon knocked again (I remember being annoyed because I was watching *Laugh-In*, which I liked a lot), and he had another person in tow. My first impression was of a big guy, maybe ten or fifteen years older than me, with dark hair and a bushy moustache—your usual hippie-looking-type person, in jeans and a work shirt. He appeared to be kind of embarrassed, like he felt he was intruding, so I felt embarrassed for him and stopped being annoyed.

"Maddy," Harmon said, "this is Neil. He's going to be staying in the carriage house this summer, working."

So here I'd better explain a couple of things: Neil is not this guy's real name, but it's what I'm going to call him in this story. Also, that's exactly how Harmon introduced him, by using only his first name, so I didn't think anything about who he might be other than some other artsy person, maybe connected to the movies, who had the luxury—and the money—to spend his summer in an expensive, rented house on a picturesque cobbled lane.

"Hi," Neil said.

I said hi back, and we shook hands. And that was it for a week or so. Harmon took off for Europe and I went downstairs to work every day. We took to playing the Band's *Music from Big Pink* a lot, though we often brought back the whales in the afternoon, if we'd gotten our hands on some particularly good grass and were feeling mellow.

It was late June, I think, the first time Neil called me. I remember it was just after five o'clock; the other girls had left for the day and I was just going to lock up the workshop when the phone rang. I answered and a voice on the other end said my name, Maddy, but I wasn't sure who was calling until Neil told me it was him.

"Look," he said. "I wonder if you could help me with a problem."

"Well, maybe," I said, thinking that if he needed a plumber or something, it was probably too late to call anybody. "What's the problem?"

"It's Corky," he told me. "He's staring at me."

"He's staring at you?" I repeated. This certainly had nothing to do with plumbing, but I wanted to be sure I'd heard him right.

"You got it," Neil said.

"Alright," I told him. "I'll be right there."

So I locked the front door and went out the back way, walking through the garden to the carriage house, where the back door had been left open for me.

I'm going to take a moment here to write down how much, over the years, I came to love that house. I lived on Charles Street for almost two decades, and there were many occasions, later, when I was invited to the Lane as a guest, and I always felt, that as someone who had been brought up in tenement apartments, where all the neighbors' water-stained walls and tired, boxy rooms of rump-sprung furniture looked like everybody else's, walking into the house on Charles Lane was like walking into the stage set of a kind of life that would have been beyond my imagining. The house itself was small, with arching wood timbers overhead and stone walls, and on the second floor, what would have been the doors to the hayloft had been replaced with panels of stained glass. In the kitchen, there was a trestle table and benches that looked like a place where monks would have eaten porridge. It's gone now—I heard that faulty wiring caused a fire some years ago and it burned to the ground—but in my mind, of course, all those welcoming rooms, the warm light from the lamps and the sun that reached down from the blue sky in the afternoons to spread a golden blanket on the tiny porch outside the kitchen—that's all still there, still accessible to me.

This June day, however, was only the third or fourth time I'd been in the house—Harmon had brought me over before Neil had moved in so I'd have an idea of what I was now in charge of. I spent a moment or two downstairs, just looking around, since Neil was nowhere in sight, and then climbed a short flight of stairs, which took me to the second floor. And that's where I found Neil, sitting in a wide, mustard-colored easy chair, looking across an old iron-riveted chest that served as the coffee table to the couch, where Corky, Harmon's cat, had established a position. Actually, as I understood it, Corky had belonged to one of Harmon's former wives, but when she had left, the cat had remained behind because he was something of an immovable object. He was a gray manx, with enormous yellow eyes that, startling as they were, still seemed in proportion to his body, since Corky must have weighed forty pounds. And he had an odd way of sitting, that I guess could make you feel like you were being watched—stared at—by some sort of all-knowing entity who was judging every move you made, since he tended to kind of sit on his well-padded rear, with his front paws resting on the round gray bowl of his stomach. He had the look of a pasha about him; like someone who had hidden resources he could call upon if he decided you were unworthy of sharing his personal space.

"See what I mean?" Neil said. "I was trying to work, but he keeps watching me." Neil gestured at a desk that was facing the stained glass doors and I saw that it held a typewriter; right next to that was what looked like a manuscript—really, a towering stack of white paper—along with assorted coffee cups, pens, an ashtray, and several packs of cigarettes. On the brick wall next to the desk, Neil had tacked more pages that were

Scotch-taped together to form a sort of continuous sheet that seemed to have names and dates on it, and lines that connected these from one page to another. It looked like a timeline of some sort (I remembered those; we had to make them in school) and I assumed all this had to do with some sort of movie script he was working on. What did I know?

"Okay," I said, trying to think of something I could do. Here was a man unnerved by a cat. How do you help such a person, if that is your job? "Why don't I put him downstairs?" I said, thinking of the small sitting room just off the garden entrance. Neil said that was fine by him, so I went over to the couch and hoisted Corky into my arms. Neil made no move to help me, but I hadn't expected him to. I remember that when I picked the cat up, he put his front paws on my shoulders, like an old man who has seen much that he prefers not to speak of accepting assistance from a witless handmaiden.

Installing Corky in a chair downstairs seemed to do the trick, though over the next week or two I received several more calls asking me to move Corky from one place in the house to another. I actually grew quite fond of the cat, and am pleased to be able to mention him in this story.

One evening, sometime later, Neil called again. I was expecting to be asked to perform another cat removal, but this time, he wanted something else. "What are you doing?" he asked.

I was home and I had actually been writing, but was thinking I might be finished for the night and was getting ready to turn on the TV. "I was going to watch *Hawaii Five-O*," I told him.

"I like that show," Neil said. "Maybe I could come over and watch it with you."

I didn't exactly think I wanted company, but I also still had the manners of a person who had been raised by polite people, so I wasn't really able to say no. He arrived about ten minutes later, just as the program was getting underway, so I offered him a seat on my couch, and poured a bag of potato chips into a bowl. At the time, that was about the extent of my ideas about being a hostess, but Neil seemed happy enough. He asked if he had missed anything important and I said no, Jack Lord had just gotten into his big, black Mercury and was on his way down to police headquarters, where no doubt, trouble was waiting to find him.

About halfway through the show, a commercial for Hostess Cupcakes came on, featuring a sharp-faced woman with what looked like lacquered black hair. She was wearing a poufy dress and walked around a shiny kitchen, carrying the cupcake package like a trophy she was proud to have won. I wasn't really paying all that much attention to the commercial, but when I happened to glance over at Neil, I thought he looked like he was going to swoon. "That's Ann Blyth," he said to me, in a choked voice.

"Who is she?" I asked.

I suppose he could have been offended that I didn't know who Ann Blyth was, since she seemed to mean something to him, but he was, apparently, too blissed out to care about anything like that. "She was a big movie star when I was a kid," he said. "I loved her, loved her, loved her. My mother used to buy movie magazines and I'd hide in the bathroom with them so I could look for pictures of her. And now she's on TV!" he exclaimed, as if the Hostess commercial was already an Emmy contender. "That's so great."

We missed a lot of the important plot points of *Hawaii Five-O* that came up in the next segment as Neil proceeded to tell me more about his Ann Blyth obsession, which had apparently begun when, as a young child his mother had taken him to see *Mildred Pierce*, in which she played Joan Crawford's rotten daughter. It would have been easy to interpret what he was saying as being very gay—I mean, Joan Crawford, *Mildred Pierce*; you might find yourself wondering—but I also had a brother, and I knew about boys and bathrooms and magazines with flashy pictures of women, so I took what he was telling me at face value. I was even sympathetic toward him and his Ann Blyth obsession, because I kind of had an obsession of my own.

I had a big bookcase in my apartment—I had built it myself with scrap wood from the workshop—and one whole shelf was taken up with books about T.E. Lawrence. I had seen that movie, *Lawrence of Arabia*, about two years ago and I remember thinking, when the movie was over, *There's something else about that guy*, and it turns out, there sure was: after reading everything about him that I could get my hands on (thank you, Gotham Book Mart), I realized that he was a brilliant, troubled, guilt-ridden man, an extraordinary writer (read *The Seven Pillars of Wisdom* sometime and you tell me that he wasn't a poet at heart) who had some serious masochistic and sexual-identity problems, but all that wasn't what made me feel, at that point in my life, a deep connection with him. Instead, it was his thing with costumes, which really hit home with me. If you look at a picture of Lawrence, as a young man, he's sort of wispy looking, delicate, with sandy hair—not your warrior type at all. But once he put on his white djellaba—his king-of-the-desert robes—he knew exactly who he was and what he was supposed to do. In other words, the right clothes helped a lot, and I understood that. It was, in fact, the failure of my ability to figure out what were the right clothes for me that kept me at home most nights, watching TV, when probably I should have been up at The Duchess Club on Sheridan Square trying to pick up girls.

I had known I was gay for a long time and really didn't have too much of a problem with that—when the revolution went down, I figured everybody who felt like it could be as gay as they wanted to be—but I had known a couple of gay girls in high school, older girls who were already out and about in the gay bars in the city, and they had explained to me the difference between butch and femme, and how important it was to signal which half of the equation you were by wearing the right clothes. I remember that shoes were particularly important (butch women wore shit-kickers of one kind or another, femmes wore high heels), as were haircuts and even what you drank in a bar: beer in a bottle, as opposed to a white wine spritzer, for example. I know these things are much less important now, but they meant a lot then, and unfortunately for me, I couldn't figure out which role I was supposed to play. I mean, I was me, I was basically a long-haired hippie kid who owned a couple of pairs of bell-bottom jeans and some go-go boots. What did that make me, other than confused? I was shy enough to begin with, so maybe I was using my problems with clothes as an excuse, but it did make me sensitive to Lawrence's craziness, and open to listening to Neil talk on for as long as he felt compelled to about how much he really, really still loved Ann Blyth.

We finally turned our attention back to the TV long enough to see the end of the show (a satisfactory conclusion, of course: McGarrett and his sidekick Danno always prevailed over their arch nemesis, Wo Fat), and then the ten o'clock news came on. The lead story, of course, was the latest bloody battle going on in Viet Nam, and the rising count of dead American soldiers. In May, President Nixon had decided to mine Haiphong Harbor and blockade the North Vietnamese coast, but the Viet Cong were fighting back fiercely, and the war, as the folkies sang in every other song on the radio, raged on.

Five minutes into the news broadcast, they showed a tape of Nixon giving a speech about something, and Neil reacted as if he'd seen a vampire. "Argghh," he said, or made some sort of sound approximating that. "Turn it off, turn it off! I can't stand that guy. I can't breathe when I see his sweaty face."

I could understand that, too. People today may think they have a problem with the president—they may even intensely dislike the guy, may want to punch him in the nose once in while—but I guarantee you that even the strongest reaction to any recent administration does not come anywhere near how we all felt about Nixon. Our fear and hatred of the guy was visceral, personal. He *did* have an evil, sweaty face with a weird nose and pin-sized eyeballs that always looked like they would rattle if you shook him. He had a file on all of us—every single one of us; we believed that sincerely—that made us all out to look like Communists or Weathermen armed at all times with homemade pipe bombs, and we knew he read these files in bed at night while his wife, Pat, was drinking in the White House kitchen, weeping on the shoulder of the black cook. I was relatively sure, however, that Nixon was not going to leap out of the TV and strangle me; Neil, on the other hand, apparently did not feel quite so safe. So I had to change the channel, but there wasn't a lot else on because this was in the dark age before cable, so we ended up watching baseball.

It took Neil about half an hour to recover from seeing Nixon, and then he said he thought he'd go home. I offered to unlock the harpsichord shop so he could walk through to the garden and get into the carriage house through the back door, but he said it was okay, he would just walk around the block to Charles Lane. After he left, I watched the end of the baseball game (the Yankees won, naturally), and I went to bed.

And then, in the middle of the night, I woke up with an epiphany: I knew who Neil really was, not that I thought I was wondering about that, but I guess my subconscious was. He wasn't a movie person—he was a writer, in fact, probably one of the most famous writers in America at that time, a man who had written a celebrated and remarkable book, a massive novel that I had once carried home from the library all by itself, because I figured it was going to take me the whole time I was allowed to keep it in order to read the whole thing. I had loved the book, though I hadn't understood a lot of it. (I've read it again since, and I get it a lot better now, though not completely.) It also occurred to me, that night, that what I had seen on the desk by the stained glass doors was another novel that he was working on, something just as big and complicated, from the size of the stack of manuscript pages and the timeline tacked to the wall. (This turned out to be true; when it was published, this novel, which was perhaps even more highly praised than the first, was equally complicated—characters shifted back and forth in time, scenes and locales changed without warning. It was a lot to take in.) Once all this dawned on me, you'd think, given what I said earlier about being jealous and fearful of successful, famous people, that by the morning I might have developed some sort of bad feelings about Neil, but I didn't. I fell back to sleep, and when I woke up to go to work, I thought about Neil and realized that, given the cat phobia, the Ann Blyth business, and his Nixon paranoia, he was not that much unlike me, really. He had problems and unreasonable fears—well, so did I, so I could go on dealing with him as just another guy, which seemed to be what he wanted, anyway. I knew that he had already developed a reputation as a recluse—for example, there were never any pictures of him published anywhere—and I imagined that was one of the reasons he was renting Harmon's house: he probably moved around a lot so no one would know where he was.

After the Nixon encounter, Neil kept to himself for a while. I didn't think about him much because we were suddenly surprisingly busy at Edelberg Harpsichords: some people in Pennsylvania had formed a clavichord society and ordered six kits to build together. We didn't often get orders for these odd instruments that are nearly silent when you play them (Michael described them as harpsichords for insomniacs who live with other people: you can play them all night and not wake anybody up); so we didn't usually keep these parts in store and had to create them from scratch. It meant getting some of Michael's other contraptions out of a closet in the back of the workshop—a special jig, a different-sized wheel for winding the felt stripping—and I changed the poems on the blackboard a couple of different times while we were doing all this.

Neil called toward the end of this week, when we were getting ready to ship out the clavichord kits. The other girls had gone home, but I was still in the workshop, sitting at the desk and going over some paperwork when the phone rang. I just knew it was him because to me, the ring sounded nervous.

"Can you come over here?" Neil asked. "Harmon left this list, and I've been ignoring it, but now I can feel it hanging over my head."

"What list?" I asked.

"You come see for yourself," he said. "It's the kind of thing that could kill a person."

Walking out the back door and through the garden, I was thinking that Neil was probably just overreacting to something—clearly, he did have a tendency to do that—but when he showed me the list, which I will capitalize the next time it appears, because it deserves that kind of recognition, I realized he was right. The List was murder incarnate. It was a Movie Producer's List of how to care for his house, and it required Neil to mobilize an army of hired help on what would probably have been a daily basis to not only wax, polish, wash, vacuum, and dust every surface on both floors, but also to set up and check half-a-dozen humane mouse traps—essentially, little wire cages—that were to be secreted around the house and whose prisoners were meant to be released down by the West Street piers. Cleaning of grout was also required, as was garden maintenance of all flowers, foliage, and pathways (the small course of brick pavers) along with inspecting and making any necessary repairs to weatherstripping, the fireplace flue, the roof, stairway treads, and tiling in both the kitchen and bathroom—and I know that there was more, that I'm only recalling some of the tasks that were mentioned. Neil told me that the only one being performed on a regular basis was the care and feeding of Corky, because the cat was attended to by one of the neighborhood kids who volunteered at the pony farm on the corner; Harmon had paid him in advance to come in every day after school and make sure that the cat's litter was changed and that his dish was always full of crunchies. (Corky was actually a modest eater; my guess is that he had a gland problem.)

"Well," I said, after I read over The List, "I'm sure we can catch up. We just have to get some people over here as soon as we can. Who do we call?"

"I don't know," Neil told me, sheepishly. "The names were on another list, and I can't find that one."

"Maybe we could try to call Harmon and ask him about the cleaning people," I suggested. "He left me a bunch of phone numbers."

"No, no," Neil said, sounding almost panicky. "He might get mad because I waited so long to do anything about this. He was really insistent about it."

I could see Neil's point. Although I didn't know Harmon all that well, he did strike me as the kind of person who *would* get mad if his instructions weren't followed to the letter, and since it was obvious to both Neil and me that neither one of us wanted to deal with an angry man on the phone from Europe (*What do you mean my mousetraps haven't yet been deployed?*), one of us would have to come up with another solution. Guess which one that was going to have to be.

Luckily, something did come to mind. One of my ex-roommates from my East Village apartment was a gay guy named Mitchie who wanted to be an actor; while he went on auditions and appeared in off-off-off-Broadway productions of *Zoo Story* and things like that, he made money by working for a company called Happy Hands that cleaned apartments. I said I'd ask him to come over with a cleaning crew as soon as possible.

"Just make sure they know how to treat a bombé chest with a French polish," Neil warned. I must have looked puzzled by this statement because he then showed me The List again. "See?" he said. "That's number 23."

I called Mitchie and arranged for Happy Hands to come to the carriage house twice a week for the rest of the summer. Paying them was easy enough, because Harmon had left me blank checks in case of emergencies, but there did turn out to be one problem with Happy Hands' services: having them in the house made Neil nervous. To begin with, he couldn't work with so many people around, and then every place he sat, within five minutes he had to get up or lift his feet so somebody could dust, vacuum, or use some handheld device that sucked up cat hair. (None of this bothered Corky, who just closed his eyes and refused to budge, so the cleaning people just worked around him.) So, what happened was that Neil started hanging around the harpsichord factory on the days that Happy Hands came to Charles Lane. And since he was there, I thought that I might as well put him to work (otherwise, he tended to sit at my desk, which was right across from where the blackboard with the poems was, which made *me* nervous). I sat him down in the back, at a drill press, where I showed him how to use one of the handmade guides Michael had designed for drilling harpsichord bridges; you just clamped the guide on a block of wood and drilled through the pre-existing holes. It wasn't hard work and Neil said that he actually found it relaxing.

On one of the days that he was there, REA Express delivered a shipment of cabinets. These came unassembled, since the kit maker was meant to assemble the harpsichord case as well as the instrument's inner workings, and were packed as flat planks of cherry wood or mahogany in boxes that were about seven feet tall and weighed over a hundred pounds. The REA deliveryman helped us get the boxes off the truck, but then we had to maneuver them into the harpsichord factory, which we did by walking them. What that meant was that one girl stood on either side of the tall carton, and first one, then the other, pushed her end forward, so the box "walked" with our assistance. It wasn't that far between the sidewalk, where the REA truck parked, and our front door, so the task, while sweaty, was manageable enough. The problem was that, as I mentioned before, we were in what was then an industrial neighborhood—for example, the truck depot of a furniture manufacturer was across the street—so whenever we had to move harpsichord cases into the workshop, we were subject to a lot of catcalls and comments. Some of them were of the "Hey, honey," variety, and some were a lot worse than that.

On this particular day, as we struggled to walk the cases into the workshop, the hooting and hollering from across the street was particularly unpleasant. *Hey, dyke boys,* someone yelled, and others took up the theme. *Lezzies, butch babes,* and other, more graphic remarks that I'll pretend I didn't hear were being sent our way from the other side of Charles Street. Sammie, Shandy, Marceline, and I were basically ignoring all this, trying to rise above it while at the same time attempting to get the harpsichord cases into the shop as quickly as we could so we could slam the door on the imbeciles who were hollering at us.

We had gotten two of the huge cartons inside and had six more to go when Neil suddenly popped out the door and onto the sidewalk. I thought that maybe he had come to help us out, but apparently, he had something else in mind.

I quickly saw that he had a camera in his hands—a big one, fancy looking, with a zoom lens. And he had another camera hanging from a strap around his neck, along with two other lenses. Plus, he was wearing sunglasses; the aviator kind that were supposed to mean you were a cool, no-holds-barred kind of guy. I could only imagine that all this gear belonged to Harmon, and that Neil had run back into the carriage house to get it. But why? To take pictures of us hauling harpsichord kits around? Nope, not at all.

As soon as he was on the sidewalk, he began snapping pictures of the truckers who were yelling at us. I don't know if there was even any film in either of the cameras he had, but he was certainly acting like there was. And he was running around like he was juiced up on something, crouching down to take up-angled shots and then jumping on the hood of a car to get overheads.

Finally, one of the truckers confronted him. "What the hell are you doing, buddy?" he wanted to know.

"I'm a photojournalist," Neil told him. "I just got back from Haiphong. And now I'm taking pictures to document how you're hassling these girls."

"Girls?" another one of the truckers snorted. "I see dykes."

"Well, I see girls," Neil said. "And I see you violating their civil rights. Hold it there, will you? I want to get a picture of you right under the sign with the name of your company."

I'll give Neil this: he certainly knew how to use code words. (He's a writer, so maybe I shouldn't have been so surprised that he had this facility.) In those days, photojournalists were people who ran around Viet

Nam taking pictures of atrocities that were then published in magazines or shown on television, embarrassing everyone who supported the war. Then, once they were back in the States, they immediately got on a bus and rode off to the latest civil rights demonstrations, where they took more photos that got lots of people in trouble and sometimes won the Pulitzer Prize. So, in less than a minute, Neil had managed to work two threatening terms into his exchange with the truckers: *photojournalist* and *civil rights*. It was an admirable and impressive effort, and much more useful than, for example, punching someone in the nose.

The truckers grumbled on for a while, but they finally drifted back to their truck-related duties, and we got the rest of our harpsichord cabinets inside without any further trouble. It was great.

Meanwhile, that summer, out in the real world, the civil rights movement was relatively quiet, but Nixon couldn't keep his mouth shut. He had sent his henchman, Kissinger, to Paris, purportedly to hold peace talks with the North Vietnamese, but things weren't going well, so Tricky Dick was threatening to step up the war. He was going to mine more harbors, launch more offensives, bite off the heads of little North Vietnamese children, if he ever got near them. Through July and into August, whenever Neil came over to watch TV with me, which happened pretty regularly, I had to be careful to change channels before the news came on because if he saw any of this, he became pale and agitated. If, by accident, we somehow happened upon Nixon, sweating and rattling his eyeballs on the television screen, I started asking a lot of questions about Ann Blyth to distract Neil while I got up from the couch (no, not everyone had a remote control in the Nixon years) to switch stations.

It was about the second week of August that Neil called with yet another request—something completely new: he wanted me to go out to dinner with him. I thought, for a brief moment, we were going to have some sort of awkward conversation in which I was going to have to explain that I didn't want to go on a date with him (and was taken aback that he was even asking; it didn't seem to me that anything like that was going on between us), but he must have guessed what I was thinking so he said, "This isn't a date."

"What is it then?" I asked.

"You're repaying a favor. Remember that I helped you out with those assholes across the street, right? So maybe now you can help me out. I've been invited to dinner with this guy and there's no way I can say no, but I don't want to go alone."

I asked *why* he couldn't say no, so he told me who the guy was and I suppose my jaw dropped or something like that: the man he named was another Famous American Writer, but more than that, he was sort of an icon, a literary lion. Neil didn't explain how he knew this person, but I could understand that if you were asked to dinner by such a figure and refused, he probably had the power to call up every major publisher in the world, if he was so inclined, and insist that no one ever publish anything you wrote, ever again.

"I can't go out with *him*," I said.

"Why not?" Neil said. "If I have to, why can't you?"

I started to get annoyed with him for whining at me like that, until I realized that he was treating me like someone who actually belonged at the same table as the icon, and therefore could argue about whether I really wanted to be there or not. Since I certainly didn't see myself that way, I ended up feeling complimented, so I gave in.

Which is how, a few nights later, I found myself struggling to keep up with Neil, who was loping along Bedford Street (he had very long legs), heading for East Houston and what he told me was an old mob restaurant also favored by the literati. We were late, in part because Neil claimed to be paralyzed by anxiety and had to smoke a joint before he'd leave the house, but also because I had experienced a paralysis of my own when I opened my closet and confronted my costume problem once again. Was I a hippie going to meet an icon? Was I a defiant queer determined to assert my identity in front of the rich and famous? (In which case, what *was* my identity? There was that butch-femme thing again.) Or was I just a kid with an unusual job in a harpsichord factory who hadn't had the sense to take her only lightweight pants to the laundry, so was going to have to wear a pair of black jeans on a hot August night?

Well, it turned out to be the black jeans, a black tee shirt and some sandals. Interestingly, Neil was dressed pretty much the same, so I guess, as we hurried along, we could have passed for either a pair of foreign insurgents on our way to a cell meeting or maybe two undercover narcs. In any event, by the time we got to the restaurant, the icon was already there, seated at a back table with his wife, a famous and beautiful actress with a face like a glowing cameo.

As we walked toward the couple, Neil pushed me in front of him so that I had to shake hands with the icon first, while Neil tried to fold himself into partial invisibility behind the dark screen of my tee shirt. Then we all sat down at the table and stared at each other.

We were given menus by an elderly waiter in a bow tie who also brought a basket of bread. Some of the bread had pieces of pistachio in it, a category of food that was unknown to me. But the whole restaurant was like that—an environment that I had no references for. There were white lace curtains on the windows, pulled shut so no one could see in, white linens on the tables, and, as advertised, groups of men sitting at the other tables who looked like they were in a very different line of work than, say, my father. Some of them had mean-faced women with them who looked like they could be the men's grandmothers. (Years later, when I saw *The Godfather*—specifically, the scene where Al Pacino has to go to a mobbed-up restaurant, get a gun from the bathroom, and shoot a corrupt cop—I remember thinking, *Ha, ha, Al. I was there first.*)

Both Neil and I asked for spaghetti; the icon and the cameo wanted more complicated dishes, which she ordered—and she did so in Italian. I looked over at Neil who was staring down at the tablecloth while nervously pulling at his moustache, and I knew what he was thinking, because I was thinking the same thing: how do we get out of here?

But then, just as I was trying to send Neil a message by mental telepathy (*We could just jump up and run*), the icon smiled at me across the table and said, "So I hear you're a poet."

I was extremely startled by this remark. Who had told him such a thing? Neil? Harmon? Did he even know Harmon? Maybe he did. Maybe all these famous people knew each other. Maybe they all belonged to a secret club. "No," I stammered. "Not really. I manage a harpsichord kit factory."

The icon laughed, as did his wife, but nicely. Gently. "Oh, I'm sure that's fine," the icon said. "All the best poets probably start out that way."

For the rest of the evening, I don't recall that Neil said more than ten words—and those in answer to direct questions, like, could you use an extra napkin?—but the icon turned out to be a really lovely man. He told a lot of funny stories about himself that I enjoyed: for example, he said that he had a habit of always saying the wrong thing. Once, he told us, he had been at an elegant dinner party whose guests included a man with only one arm, and all night he, the icon, felt compelled to talk about arms: *Arms and the Man*, disarmament, armed guards. He embarrassed everybody and, a few days later, got a nasty note in the mail from the hostess.

The spaghetti was wonderful, and for desert, we had tiramisu (my first time; the cameo had recommended it). We also had some hard, tasty cookies, and as we were finishing up with coffee, the icon leaned over to his wife and said something to her in Yiddish (I think I forgot to mention that in addition to his other credits, the icon—at least in print—was one of those sarcastic, outraged Jewish writers who included sex and psychiatry in almost everything he wrote). I understood him, because my parents had spoken Yiddish, so I knew he was asking the cameo if she had any quarters for him to put in the parking meter. (Another surprise: he drove his own car. I had been imagining that he had flown here in a helicopter or been driven in a limo by a toady.) She didn't, but I did, so I reached into my pocket and gave him some change.

When he came back from feeding the meter, he asked me how I knew Yiddish, which led us into a conversation that revealed the fact that his mother and father, like mine, had been driven out of Jew-hating wastelands by pogroms. (I had been born to my parents when they were older; his parents had produced him when they were quite young, which made them close in age, while the icon and I were certainly far apart.) "Well," he said to me, "that's a subject for a whole other conversation that I hope we'll have some day." He really was being very nice.

Half an hour later, I was once again struggling to keep up with Neil as he loped home. I didn't even ask if he'd enjoyed himself, because clearly, he hadn't; he had fulfilled what he must have seen as some sort of professional obligation, and had suffered every minute of it. I did get him to admit, though, that the spaghetti was exceptional. Mobsters, apparently, are fussy about their pasta.

The next-to-last phone call I ever got from Neil came just a few nights later—in the middle of the night, in fact. I was dead asleep when the telephone rang, and saw that my bedside clock read 2:15 a.m.

"Listen," Neil said, with great urgency in his voice, "things are heating up around here, so I've decided that I have to split." He named the literary figure who had invited us to dinner and said, "God knows who he's told where to find me now. And that Nixon...did you see the news tonight? He's going to do something big, maybe something nuclear, and I don't want to be around when that goes down."

At 2:15 a.m., I was having enough trouble relating to the idea that a renowned writer would have nothing better to do all day than get on the phone or send out postcards revealing Neil's whereabouts without even trying to figure out how what Neil apparently saw as a related problem—Nixon and his possible nuclear antics—might have an impact in the vicinity of Charles Lane. "Okay," I said, hoping I could go back to sleep soon. "Fine."

"My sister's driving down from Stockbridge to get me," Neil said and then suddenly stopped speaking. "Wow," he said. "Maybe I shouldn't have told you that. But you'll keep it to yourself, right?"

Well, why not? If it meant that much to him, I could keep a secret. "I never saw you," I said. "We never even met."

"See?" Neil said. "I knew you were that kind of a person."

We silently breathed at each other through the phone for a moment and then Neil cleared his throat and spoke again. "I know I'm kind of leaving you in the lurch with the Happy Hands guys and so forth, but I just can't stay another minute. I mean, once my sister gets here."

"Don't worry about it," I told him.

"The rent's all paid through September," Neil added. "Tell Harmon I'm not asking for a refund or anything."

"I'll tell him," I replied. And then, because I knew that I should at least say good-bye, I said, "Have a good trip."

"Oh yes," he said. "I will." And he hung up the phone.

But half an hour later the phone rang, and it was Neil again, this time calling from a pay phone. "Maddy?" he said. "My sister showed up and we were heading for the West Side Highway, but I made her pull over because I forgot to tell you something. Those poems you keep writing on the blackboard? You should get them published. As a book, I mean. And make sure you include that mental hermaphrodite one. That's my favorite." He hung up again, and then was gone for good.

In the morning, I walked through the harpsichord factory, out the back door and through the garden to the carriage house, where I sat on the couch with Corky, who blinked his eyes a few times, I guess because he was glad to see me. It was Saturday and I didn't have to go to work, so I just stayed put for a while, watching the sharp morning light puncture the stained glass windows as I thought about things. It's a long way back to reach, but I imagine the things I was thinking included, *How do you get a book of poems published? Should I try to get myself out of the house tonight no matter how I end up being dressed? And what about Nixon? How long is he going to let this unwinnable war go on?*

For a long time, I returned to these questions again and again, because they seemed important then, but of course, they don't matter much anymore. Which leads me to the conclusion that, given everything that's happened in the intervening years, I have spent much of my life worrying about the wrong things, and probably still do. What am I to make of that? I can only surmise that it's part of the process I'm going through—we're all going through—individually, collectively, perhaps even globally, of becoming better or worse human beings. And what a process—it's all so unpredictable! I mean, think about it: completely unprepared (as far as I can tell), we come into the world and we do things to it—and to each other—and then we're gone. In the meantime, danger arises in distant lands. What is fashionable in one generation is laughed at or pitied in the next. Rents rise, familiar buildings burn down, civilization remakes itself all around us, every minute, every day, all the time. Life enters us like a brutal drug and in brief moments of youthful enthusiasm, we think it will not seep away. And so we concentrate on what seems important in the moment, what we'll want to remember later, when we're trying to figure things out. What I've written about here are some of the things that I remember, some of the things I did. But notice what I didn't do, which I hope is one small contribution I have made as a human being: I kept my word. True, I did let slip that part about Neil escaping to Stockbridge, but that was a long time ago, and I'm sure that now, he's someplace else.

The Riddle of the Sphinx

The last time I got even remotely involved in politics was a long time ago, when I lived on Charles Street, in Greenwich Village. I remember that my apartment house, a nondescript, three-story survivor of what was then the past century, was on a block so far west—right at the edge of the Hudson River—that the only other buildings in the neighborhood were truck depots and warehouses full of office furniture. This was in the early 1970s; I was shy and on my own at an age when everyone else I knew was either in college or had gone off somewhere to live on a commune. But there I was, living in two cold rooms and working in a factory in Chelsea that made stained glass art objects, which was the kind of job you got in those days. I had no social life and I was lonely.

Probably because my father had been a devoted member of a labor union (he was a clothing cutter, and the one time they went on strike, the union gave him a weekly stipend, which I understood was the equivalent, for the working classes, of manna from heaven), when I read in the *Village Voice* that the Village Independent Democrats was holding a meeting one evening, I decided to go. Union members, like my father, were all Democrats, so it seemed to me that there was some connection there, which helped me talk myself into the idea.

The meeting was in another set of cold rooms above a gym for gay bodybuilders, just off Sheridan Square. I went that one night and then maybe once or twice more before I lost interest because the Village Independent Democrats turned out not to be what I was looking for, if I even knew at that age. They were mostly men, mostly a lot older than me, and they spent a lot of time discussing how outraged they were—outraged!—about Nixon, who was still around then. They were also outraged, as I recall, about the police driving around with packages of meat in the back seats of their patrol cars. Again, I'm going back to a time that seems remote even to me, but this was when the meatpacking district over by Little West 12th really was one big butcher shop during the day (no neighborhood-killing boutiques and boutique hotels there yet; not even one) and a lively meat market of another kind at night. Some of the meatpacking people were letting the prostitutes, both gay and straight, use their premises at night to conduct their dates, and then getting a percentage of the proceeds. I gather that the police let this go on as long as the meat people kept the steaks coming. The Village Independent Democrats didn't like this one bit, and of course, they were right, but I couldn't get very worked up about the problem. Then, after an hour or two of being pissed off about Nixon and the police and their meat payoffs, everyone would head over to the Cedar Tavern or the Lion's Head to drink the rest of the night away. It wasn't for me.

So, thirty years later—thirty years! It's unbelievable!—when my girlfriend came home and told me that she had joined the local Democratic club, I had quite a flashback. Unlike the much younger me, though, she had a very specific reason for getting involved with the Dems. All politics is local, right? And in this case, Lisa had a very specific local problem she wanted to do something about, and the Democratic Party was on her side.

Lisa is a nurse; she works in a hospital that's about ten minutes away from where I live now—where we live—on Long Island, in an ocean-side town called Barnum Beach. The hospital is built on a channel that connects to the sea; I suppose someone thought the view of sailboats and skidoos passing by in season would be uplifting for the patients. There are several restaurants on the other side of the channel, facing the hospital, and apparently one of them—the one directly opposite the hospital's nursing home annex—wanted to build an outdoor dock and create an area for al fresco dining during the spring and summer. *Dining my ass*, the hospital's head administrator had said to the local paper, or at least they printed words to that effect: *What they're going to do is serve drinks and play loud music until four a.m., and nobody in the nursing home is going to be able to sleep from April until October.*

So all spring, Lisa was going to meetings of the Barnum Beach Democratic Club once a week or so, and other nights, when she wasn't working, she might be stuffing flyers or calling people on a list of registered voters in the area to cajole them into voting no on a zoning proposition that would be on the ballot in the upcoming fall elections, because if the zoning change didn't go through, the restaurant couldn't build its dock.

In June, on a mild, foggy weeknight, while I was watching TV and Lisa was working a late shift, she called when she should have been on her way home to say the car wouldn't start. A friend had given her a jump but that hadn't done anything, so she was going to have the car towed to a nearby garage. She got home in a cab about an hour later, saying that the guy at the garage had declared that the something, something, something was broken; he had to get a part, but that shouldn't be too hard and the car would be ready on Saturday.

Well, that's great, I said, though I had no idea what she was talking about, and she probably knew it. I'm a city person, through and through: I was raised in the Bronx, on Mt. Eden Avenue near Yankee Stadium, and not only did my family never own a car, we didn't even know anyone who did. I mean, you live in New York, there are subways—why do you need a car? All you have to do is plan ahead, follow the subway map, and you can get anywhere. My father was great at this: you could give him an address in Manhattan, for example, and he could not only tell you what train to take from the Bronx, but which subway car to get in that would let you out closest to which stairway at the station where you'd need to change, and then all the shortcuts through the maze of interlinking corridors and walkways you'd have to navigate in order to get to the next train. When he gave people this information, he liked them to call him when they got where they were going to tell him how his directions worked, and they always worked well.

Barnum Beach is similarly navigable, with a little planning and consulting of schedules. There is, for example, a shuttle bus that goes round and round the town at fifteen-minute intervals, from early in the morning until past midnight, so you can get to the shops or to the Long Island Railroad station with ease, and from there, into the city, if you need to. Sometimes I need to, and with very little effort, in an hour, I can travel from the edge of the continent—the Atlantic Ocean, mysterious and deep, is right across the street, beyond the boardwalk and the beach, a sleepless neighbor always chewing busily at its own sandy shoreline, sometimes taking away, sometimes giving back—to just about anywhere in Manhattan.

There is also a perfectly reliable taxi service in town, and when Saturday morning came around, I thought that's how we were going to get to the car repair place, which was just over the bridge that connects Barnum Beach to the next town, but Lisa said that wasn't necessary,

"Alan," she told me, "is going to give us a lift."

Now Lisa, a small, pretty woman who you would never guess is in her forties, has lots of friends—men, women, gay, straight—and I can't keep track of them. I don't even try. But most of the time, when she mentions some friend, the name at least sounds familiar to me—but not Alan. *Alan* was not ringing any bells.

"Do I know him?" I asked.

"No," she told me. "I met him at the Democratic Club. He's a judge. His last name is Gorman."

Being Jewish—New York Jewish, in particular—Jewish geography is an inbred trait (when I was a child, watching television at night, black and white images that were bouncing, I believed, from aerial to aerial on the rooftops of the Bronx, my father always pointed out which performers were Jewish and which were hiding behind Christianized names), I immediately found myself wondering if Alan Gorman was Jewish, too. "Gorman" was tricky: it could go either way. Still, I kind of assumed that we were going to get a lift from some nice Jewish judge, a longtime member of the Democratic party, who would show up in his modestly outdated Cadillac and drive us to the garage where our little Honda Civic was waiting to carry us back home.

Well, not exactly. The person who showed up around ten o'clock was driving a black Grand Am with cat's eye lights, and when he emerged from this sleek car, he proved to be younger than me by about a decade (he was somewhere in his forties, I guessed), a slightly lumpy but pleasant-enough-looking fellow in a suit and tie. A suit and tie, on Saturday, in a beach town, going on summer. Guaranteed, he was the only man within a mile dressed like this.

Lisa and I came downstairs, she introduced me to him, and he shook my hand vigorously before we all got in the car and drove off. I was sitting in the back seat and intended to just drift off while Lisa and Alan Gorman chatted about Democratic politics or whatever, but instead, Alan immediately engaged me in conversation. He seemed to be very interested in what I do for a living—I gather Lisa had told him—and he asked me all kinds of questions.

So what do I do? I'm a ghostwriter—an "as told to" person, which is certainly not what I started out to be. I started out, actually, to be a lost and damned soul living in a hovel and using my pitiful wages from the stained glass factory to buy canned soup and hashish. I had been raised in the 60s on late-night FM radio and political rage—Nixon, the beatings at the Democratic Convention in Chicago, Kent State, all of that—and the message I got was, run away and hide because they're coming after you. Plus, I know I've made my father sound like a nice man, someone to remember fondly—and he was—but my mother died when I was twelve and the family took a very bad turn. Very bad. My father remarried quickly because he was not the kind of person who knew how to be alone, and he married badly, providing me with a stepmother whose face, when she looked at me, resembled a thin, deadly hammer just waiting to pound me into oblivion, which was her general attitude toward just about everything. My father didn't know how to handle this. He turned away.

And so did I. Shortly after I graduated from high school, I left home for good, intent on beginning my career as a Hippie Dropout from Society. I got the Charles Street apartment (for $100 a month, if you can imagine that; the building, which had only intermittent heat and electricity, also had walls so eroded that my neighbor's cat could walk into his closet next door and emerge from mine), was hired for the stained glass job, bought a thirteen-inch TV, a chair, a foam mattress, a pot to boil the soup in, and thought I was set. Screw you, world, was my general attitude: I don't have to participate if I don't want to. Jefferson Airplane said so. So did Arlo, sort of. I bought pasta made out of Jerusalem artichoke and lots of brown rice and beans.

But after a couple of years, when the counterculture was fading away or blowing up or giving up—whatever happened to it; let's discuss that another time—the market for chanting crystals and stained glass suncatchers collapsed, and the factory closed. Out of a job, I collected unemployment for a while, but I had enough of my father's work-ethic-trained good girl in me to know I needed to find another job. So I consulted the *Village Voice*, where I had found the stained glass factory, and saw an ad for a travel writer. I was still young enough to think thoughts like, *Well, why not?* Of course, the farthest I had traveled, so far, was from the Bronx to Manhattan—but on the other hand, if I was a travel writer I would probably get to go all kinds of places for free. "Free" was a good recommendation for trying anything. And I knew that I could write: it was the one thing I was good at in school, having produced stories and sheaves of gothic poetry about sex and drugs that my English teacher kept giving me good marks for but declined to let me read to the class, even when that was part of the assignment. He was a nice man—like my father, I guess, only a little more connected to the real world—and he told me my subject matter was too advanced for my classmates. He was probably right.

So, anyway. I remember walking uptown, to somewhere around Union Square, to an industrial building where most of the businesses seemed to be involved in the fur trade. Except, of course, for Vista Publications, which turned out to be located in a third-floor loft decorated with travel posters and dimly lit by orange-shaded lamps, so that you immediately felt you were already someplace else, someplace a world away from the center of a northeast corridor city.

There was only one person around that day, Bob Bright, Mr. Vista Publications as it turns out, and he read some of the wailing poetry I had brought as writing samples. Then he said he'd try me out on the travel writing, which, he explained, didn't involve any actual travel. What you did, he said, was go to the library, read a bunch of books about a place and then plagiarize a page or two for the quickie tourist guides that were his bread and butter. The trick, he said—which is why he was pleased to have snared what he described as a "creative writer" with his *Voice* ad—was not to sound like you were plagiarizing. My first assignment was Savannah, Georgia.

Well. I did just fine with Savannah (thank you, New York Public Library and your blessed pre-Internet picture and reference collection), so I got lots of assignments after that—Denver, New Orleans, San Francisco, all your major U.S. tourist destinations—and then graduated to Europe, Antwerp, Vienna, London, Paris, Amsterdam, Rome. I became quite the armchair tourist, and I enjoyed the work. But about a year after I'd written my way halfway around the globe, Bob Bright sold the company to another publisher, which specialized in unauthorized quickie bios of the rich and famous: movie stars, pop singers, astronauts. The owner of the new company thought my skills would be transferable to a new medium and he was right; it turned out that I was just as good with people as I was with places. But then the second company was bought by yet another publisher—this time a real one, an imprint of one of the major U.S. publishing houses—and one of the editors asked me if I thought I could do an "as told to" book. She was honest with me: she said she was desperate because they had a contract with a famous actress to write her autobiography, and she had already scared away three prominent ghostwriters. The actress was mean, she was bitter, she was disappointed in love and life and couldn't stand to look at herself in the mirror anymore because she was getting old. The publisher was worried that she would kill herself or die of some liquor-and-cigarette-induced disease that was surely creeping up on her before they got their promised book.

Well, they got their book, because the actress and I got along like best friends. After the manuscript had been turned in, the editor asked me how I had managed to bond with this famously difficult woman who demeaned everyone around her, and though I shrugged off this feat as simply practiced professionalism, I knew that much more than my own skill was at work here. Something else was, though I wasn't sure what to call it or how to explain it, though I certainly knew what had happened: somehow, I had been saved.

By accident, I had been saved from throwing away my life, though that had been my angry, vengeful plan. A child's plan in almost grown-up-hands: what could be more dangerous? At the tail-end of a generation that had either disappeared down the hippie trail or cleaned up, dived in, and straightened out (in every sense of that word), I had been pushed along by puffs of what seemed like chance and happenstance to arrive, somehow, across the span of a decade, at a safe and happy shore. I had survived myself and my times, and when I realized what had happened, I was no longer angry. Instead, I was grateful. I had survived the hammer face and the Nixon years. I had survived the waste-yourself suggestions of the music of my generation that led me to forgo even one extra minute of education. In that regard, I was probably the last person in the United States without a college degree to have a good job—in fact, I was probably the last person who even thought in terms of "a college degree" when nowadays, a B.A. and M.A. were the calling cards that got you where you wanted, but only in conjunction with the promise that you were studying for your Ph.D. And having survived all these pitfalls, I seemed to have a natural affinity for others who had done the same, though their circumstances might be extremely different. All the people I wrote with from the actress on—famous scientists, journalists, politicians, and more actresses, who became my stock in trade—were survivors, though, unlike me, their survival usually involved substantial conniving and strategic plans. It didn't matter; I found them all fascinating. I was like an acolyte studying the masters. I listened to them, I was sympathetic and nonjudgmental, and I wrote their stories with them, for them. I loved my work and it mostly went well.

And so, mostly, did my life. In my thirties, I met Lisa and we moved to the Long Island beach town where Lisa worked. We have lived here for almost twenty years now, and about ten years ago, I started to freelance. I work pretty steadily because lots of people want me to write their story. And I want to; I want to write them all.

I wasn't about to explain any of this to Alan Gorman, and anyway, it wasn't really my work that he was interested in. Mostly what he wanted to know was how you go about getting a book published, so I gave him the stock answer, since I get asked that question a lot: basically, you try to get published in literary magazines that also publish nonfiction, build up some kind of resume and reputation, and then get an agent. He thanked me profusely for this information, which made me feel a little bad—just a little—because I was hardly sharing any great insight. This is the same thing that any of those books you buy about how to get published will tell you. He then started talking about his children—he had a six-year-old boy and a four-year-old girl—which made me suspect that maybe he had in mind to write a children's book, since everybody always seems to be writing a children's book. Fewer words, I guess. I started waiting for the judge to tell me the story he had in mind: perhaps a rooster with a cold who can't stop sneezing? A frog who needs dancing shoes? I expected something like that.

Instead, when we finally got to the garage and Lisa went to retrieve our car and pay the bill, the judge, lingering behind, took my arm and guided me toward the back of his car. He opened the trunk and for a moment I thought, *No, he's writing one of those cops-chasing-a-serial-killer stories*, and assumed that he was going to show me items he'd collected for research: ropes, tape, gruesome magazines.

The trunk, however, was only full of books. Actually, dozens of copies of the same book, entitled *The Truth About Consequences: Tales of a Crime-Fighting Judge*. The cover of the book showed Alan Gorman, in his black judicial robes, standing in the front of a courtroom, with his arms crossed and one hand clutching a heavy wooden gavel. He had a big, friendly, notably un-ironic smile pasted on his face—not exactly the visage one associated with a crime fighter.

"So, Annie," he said. "What do you think of this?"

Nobody calls me Annie, but I let it go. I picked up one of the books and took a quick look at it. "Did you self-publish this?" I asked, though of course, it was clear that he had.

"I did," he said eagerly, as if proud of how ingeniously he'd solved the problem that I had implied involved a lot of work and probably loads of disappointment. Think of all the rejection slips from those elitist literary magazines. "Let me give you a copy," he said, reaching into the trunk but hesitating before he pulled out one of the books, as if he was picking through a pile of fruit, trying to find the best one.

I thought it would be insulting to refuse the book, so when he finally selected one, I took it and put it in my bag. It was a surprisingly hefty volume. Judge Alan Gorman, apparently, had quite a bit to say.

"I'm the first Criminal Court judge in Nassau County to write a book about his experiences," Alan told me. His pleasure in this accomplishment was evident.

"That's interesting," I said. "Really." I tried to smile at him. He kept looking at my bag, which was slung over my shoulder, as if he hoped I would remove the volume and start reading it right away.

Finally, Lisa came back and said we were good to go: the Civic had been revived and declared safe for the road. Alan kept asking Lisa was she sure the car was okay, did she feel confident about driving it now, and if so, was there anything else he could do for her, for us, any service at all he could provide? Lisa who, God knows, is a much kinder person than me, assured him that we could manage by ourselves now, and he could get on with whatever plans he had for his Saturday.

"You don't think he's a little odd?" I asked Lisa as we watched Alan drive off. "I mean, for a judge?"

"I don't know," Lisa said to me. "What's a judge supposed to be like?"

"Severe," I said. "Remote. Judgmental."

"They can't be like regular people?" she said.

"I don't think they should be the kind of people who self-publish their own books," I replied.

"Oh, did he give you a copy?" she said mildly. "He gives everybody one." Then she grinned at me. "I have two. Sometimes he forgets who he gave them to."

As I said, she's a very kind woman.

So life went on. I basically forgot about Judge Alan Gorman until sometime in the middle of July, in what was turning out to be a scorching summer. Again, it was Saturday; Lisa was working a weekend shift and I had spent the morning on the beach, under a sunny blue sky, going over draft chapters of the book I was currently working on, the memoir of a spy. He was the real thing: a lonely man with a forgettable face who had slipped in and out of European capitals for thirty years, tinkering with history. He lived in a sparsely furnished house on Long Island Sound, watching out the window for boats that might unexpectedly appear beyond the breakwater. *Always on alert*, he said. It was a lifelong habit.

By the time I left the beach, at noon, the weather was changing rapidly. I had lunch, sat down on the front porch to continue reading, and when I looked up sometime in the afternoon, it was as if the sunny morning had itself been erased from history. The sky was now a kind of dangerous green that looked like it had been boiled in lye; the horizon was a thin silver slit at the edge of the ocean, beyond the dunes.

The wind was coming up, too: clearly a storm was on the way. Those who had stayed on the beach throughout the deteriorating afternoon—mostly day trippers who took the Long Island Rail Road out from the city for an afternoon of sun and surf—were now streaming away from the beach entrance across the street from our condo. Some were carrying babies who bobbed around in their parents' arms, interested to see what was going on. Some were pulling small children behind them or carrying radios and suntan lotion or hampers of food. As I watched the beachgoers heading for shelter, I suddenly realized that something else was happening, as well: the stragglers at the back of the crowd had stopped, and were now turning back to look toward the beach. A few of them were pointing at something in the distance.

The dunes blocked my view of the shoreline, but I quickly figured out what the growing commotion was about, because fire trucks and an ambulance were now racing down the street, heading toward the beach entrance. One of the fire engines was followed by a flatbed truck with the Barnum Beach logo on the side; in the back were a dozen or so lifeguards that had apparently been picked up by the driver as he careened along the road that ran beside the beach. I had lived here long enough to know what that meant: someone was in trouble in the surf, and the fire department was going to carry out a water rescue. If necessary—meaning, if someone had drowned in the waves and a body couldn't be found—the lifeguards would form a human chain and walk through the water, searching for the submerged human form.

It began to rain. Cold, green, hard-driving rain that seemed to descend in undulating sheets. Curtains of rain, rivers in the street. But the rescuers were undeterred—they kept running back and forth between the beach and the trucks, bringing more equipment, and were soon joined by even more lifeguards who were answering a siren that was the town signal for disaster. I don't know how they knew to come to our beach, but they did, and they ran through the streets without shoes, soaked to the skin, determined to save a life.

As I watched this human drama playing out on my block, I heard my phone ringing inside. I didn't want to leave the porch to answer it, but

I did, in case it was Lisa. In fact, I hoped it was Lisa so I could tell her what was going on.

I picked up the phone and before I could even speak, I heard, "Hello. This is Judge Alan Gorman. Is Lisa there?"

"Alan?" I said. I just couldn't bring myself to call him Judge Gorman. "It's Anne. Lisa's at work today."

"Oh," he said. "Well, I just wanted to let her know that I was nearby."

"Nearby what?" I asked.

"Near your house. Near the scene of the rescue attempt. I'm in my car, but I'm standing by, just in case I'm needed."

What would they need a judge for? I almost blurted out. *They need lifeguards and firemen. They need people who are ready to dive down into the ocean and pluck some poor soul from Davey Jones' locker, that's what they need. Not someone lurking "nearby" in a sporty Grand Am.*

"I'll tell Lisa you called," I said finally. And then I hung up the phone.

By evening, the storm had blown away and the sky was decorated with bright lariats of stars. Two fourteen-year-old boys from Brooklyn had been swept far past the rock jetties by a wicked undertow, but had been rescued; a younger friend had drowned. His body had been recovered by the lifeguards and carried off the beach, wrapped somberly in heavy blankets.

When Lisa came home, she told me that she'd heard about the day's events at the hospital, where both the rescued boys had been transported. I let her talk for a while, half listening to her describe the hubbub at the small hospital when the ambulances came screaming in with the two terrified teenagers who had to be told over and over again that they could breathe normally now, there was no need to go on gasping for breath.

When I thought I could finally get a word in, I said, "You mean your friend the judge didn't show up at the hospital?"

"You mean Alan Gorman?" Lisa said. "Why would he..."

I was so eager to tell her about his weird behavior that afternoon—*I'm standing by*—that I didn't even let her finish. I reported my conversation with Alan to her word for word, and I was sure that I had left nothing out because I had repeated our exchange to myself several times that evening so I would be sure to get every nuance, every detail right. What I didn't say at the end is, *Your friend is a whack job*, but I didn't have to.

When I finally stopped talking, Lisa looked at me with narrowed eyes. "What have you got against Alan?" she asked.

"I haven't got anything *against* him," I said. "I just think he's a little strange and I don't understand why you seem to like him, which you do. Seem to, I mean."

"Do you know why *you* don't like him?" Lisa asked me, and this time, it was me who didn't get to say anything. "Because," she told me, "Alan is not your kind of Jewish person."

I can't stand it when anyone who isn't Jewish—even Lisa—says Jewish person. But because it was Lisa, I was trying very hard not to go into my usual response to that phrase, which is acidic sarcasm.

I think I succeeded, but not completely. "So," I said. "He is Jewish."

"Yes, detective," Lisa replied. "He mentions that in his book."

"Well, good for him," I said. "Now tell me, what is my kind of Jewish person?"

"Either artistic," Lisa told me, "smart, or deadly."

"Like who?" I said. "Give me some names."

"Easy," she said, and I could hear in her voice that while I was struggling not to get angry, she wasn't bothered by this conversation at all. "Bob Dylan. Albert Einstein. Your spy."

I didn't realize that she knew my spy was Jewish, which he was, and which just made him—and the book I was helping him write—more important to me, personally. He was an extraordinary man who had crawled out of the concentration camps as the only surviving member of his family and who, after arriving in the United States and being recruited into what he called the espionage trade, had put his life on the line time after time. He didn't have to do that. And now, he knew that when he published the book we were working on, he was probably going to spend the next decade or so in court, fighting the various national security agencies that were going to attack him for telling secrets. He didn't seem to care about that, and I couldn't imagine where he got his courage. It seemed like a deep vein that ran through his entire life, a constant, uncontestable and unyielding certitude upon which he stood, had always stood, and would not be moved. In his empty house, looking out beyond the breakwater. He would not be moved.

"Bob Dylan," I finally responded, "is only sometimes Jewish. According to him."

"According to *you*," Lisa said to me, "you can't defect."

This was true. She had heard my Hitler-as-evil-Santa-Claus rule a number of times, which was based on the belief that even if you were only part Jewish or had formally converted to Christianity, Hitler would still know you were a Jew and shove you into an oven. I don't think that this conviction is unique to me: I assume that many people my age, descendents of the shtetls, think this way. It's what their parents—or their grandparents, if they had any—always told them.

It was probably about ten days later that I ended up once again answering calls meant for Lisa. This time, though, the calls were from people who, like her, were involved in the fight against the restaurant. There was a hearing scheduled for the following night, at city hall, and the Barnum Beach Democrats were organizing themselves so they could show up in strength and testify. People were looking for rides, people were checking the time they were supposed to meet, people were wondering if they were supposed to make signs and march around. Lisa, it seemed, had become a leader in the anti-restaurant movement, and everyone wanted her advice. I called her at the hospital to tell her this and give her all the messages that had accumulated in the morning and she took down everyone's phone number with a kind of calm seriousness that I knew meant big trouble for anyone who set themselves against her. She's a lovely woman, kind, as I've said, and funny, but she has a side to her that is a kind of sorting machine for right and wrong, and when called upon to name what's right, there is no hesitation in her. Not for a second.

Even with all the phone calls, I made good progress in my work, but stopped in the early afternoon when my friend Robert came by. It was a surprise to see him: he runs the housecleaning service we use, and I was expecting our usual cleaning person, Kevin, who always comes on Wednesday afternoon. Instead, there was Robert, who came up the stairs dragging an assortment of mops and cleaning products.

"Well, hi," I said, as I let him into the condo. "Where's Kevin?"

"You know they all disappear this time of year," he grumbled. "Check the Fire Island ferry. Call the Crown and Anchor in P-Town."

Robert's cleaning service mostly employs young gay men—actors, dancers, musicians—and they do tend to kind of drift away as the summer glows its way from one golden day to another. (There hadn't been another storm, or even a drop of rain, since the afternoon of the water rescue.) When they do show up, though, Robert's employees do an exemplary job, so much so that Lisa and I, walking around our gleaming, dust-free home after Kevin has left, really have to put some effort into not making the kinds of jokes that gay women make about gay men and how assiduously they clean.

As Robert pulled our vacuum cleaner out of the closet and got himself set up to tackle the living room, I asked him, without thinking that I was going to, "Have you ever gotten involved in politics?"

"Not really," he said. "I mean, not for a long time. There was Stonewall, of course."

"You know," I said, "every gay man I've ever met claims he was around for Stonewall, even if he was in Iowa at the time. Even if he wasn't born."

"Well, I wish," said Robert, a thin, handsome man with a small moustache and an equally modest diamond in his left ear, "that I could claim to be young enough to have been holding a wedding for Barbie and Skipper in my playpen at the time but I was living in a studio on Greenwich Street and spending every night I could at the Twelfth of Never. So I wasn't anywhere near the Stonewall at the time—the truth is, it wasn't that great a bar, anyway—but I did go to a lot of marches after that. Demonstrations. I even got on a bus once or twice and went to Washington in the big AIDS days. All of which was hard for me, actually, to put myself on the line like that. I mean, to be political—or at least to feel like that's what I was doing. Because at the time, all I wanted was to have fun, fun, fun. But then everything started to get shoved in our faces, so to speak. So there didn't seem to be any choice but to get on the bus and ride off to storm the Bastille. And now look at me," he said, as he wrestled with my old Hoover, which was holding up quite well even after the many years I'd had it. "Now I'm vacuuming. And all my employees are living it up in the Pines."

Robert cleaned and cleaned while I worked in my office in the back of the condo, and then he stayed around for a while, having a drink with me on the porch while we waited for Lisa to come home, so he could say hi. But then she called to say she would be late and he had someplace to be back in the city, so I spent an hour or so waiting for her by myself, watching the sun go down over the dunes.

When Lisa finally did show up, I could tell there was something wrong the minute she got out of the car. Her face looked angled, unhappy, and she fumbled a lot with her purse when she was putting away her keys. None of this is characteristic of my cheerful, organized—well, they haven't invented the word yet, so I'll use one I don't like. My partner.

"Did you see the news?" she asked as she walked up the stairs to the porch.

"No?" I said. "Why?"

"I'll bet it's on the news," she said, pulling open the front door and marching inside.

I followed her. "Okay," I said. "Please. Tell me."

"Alan's been arrested."

"Alan?" I said. "Alan the judge?"

"I heard about it at the hospital," she told me, "but I just couldn't believe it, so I drove over to the Democratic club on the way home, and it's true. For money laundering. Can you believe it?"

"I don't understand," I said.

She asked, "What are you drinking?"

"I made margaritas. Robert was here and we..."

"Give me one," Lisa said. "They've got him on tape."

"Saying what?" I asked.

"I don't know. Saying sure, I'll launder your money. Whatever they say."

"I don't think they say..."

"Anne. I know they don't."

Before we went to bed, one of Lisa's anti-restaurant colleagues called and we got more of the story: some petty mobster who had appeared before Judge Gorman in court must have seen a gleam in the judge's eye or something like that, because he later approached the judge in a diner with a plan to use cash skimmed from an off-shore gambling boat to buy Cambodian rubies, which Alan would hold onto for a while and then sell, splitting the profits with the mobster. It sounded more like the plot of a bad movie than a criminal enterprise, but apparently the mobster was looking for a break from a federal prosecutor who was about to file charges against him under the RICO Act, so he offered Alan up on a plate. Tied with ruby-red ribbons. He taped his conversations with Alan at subsequent meetings, in which the judge is heard eagerly agreeing to accept the cash and buy the jewels. And now Alan Gorman was in a lot of trouble. He was going to be suspended from his job and indicted on felony counts. This, indeed, was the Truth about Consequences.

Later, I woke up in the middle of the night because a rage against Judge Alan Gorman seemed to have sprung up in my dreams, which were inadequate to contain it. I didn't want to wake Lisa, so I started wandering around the house, thinking about how angry I was. I knew that the way I felt had something to do with his being Jewish and that was somehow tangled up with some unresolved feelings about my father. (Remember, I'm from *that* generation: obsessive self-analysis is second nature to us.) My father died years ago, but I'm still mad at him, and love him, too. The part of me that loves him—and probably the other part as well, if I am going to be honest—is still influenced by a lot of the values I was raised with, which include work hard; do your job well because you should, not because your boss wants you to; and don't disgrace the Jews. My father was not an armed-Israeli kind of Jew; he was the kind that was still trying to prove we didn't deserve the Holocaust.

Alright, fine, I thought, I'm mad at Judge Alan Gorman because he disgraced the Jews. But why did he do it? For money, certainly—but we all need money. Lisa and I need a new hot water heater and it's going to eat into our savings. Plus, since I work as a freelancer now, much as I enjoy that, the cost of my medical insurance, which I have to pay myself, is enough to break the bank. And in a couple of years, Medicare is on the horizon and I don't understand it one bit. I mean, Part A, Part B, Part D? And I knew I'd better figure it out because the next thing that was coming at me was illness. Some big, serious illness. I don't fool myself about that. Life is up and down, I know that, so sure, I've been going along quite nicely for a long time now, but still, like everyone else, my insides are probably just waiting to let loose whatever genetic time bombs they've been hoarding all these years, never mind how many soy products I include in my diet. I'm five years away from sixty. My good luck can't last.

I did finally get back to sleep but I woke up feeling gloomy, which is unusual for me. The feeling stayed with me throughout the day and kept me from focusing on my work. As a consequence, I didn't get much done, which made me feel worse. By the end of the day, I was restless and bored, and unhappy with myself. So when Lisa called from the hospital to remind me that she was going to the town meeting after work, I volunteered to go with her. Surprised, she asked me why, so I told her. I had to get out of the house, I said.

"I don't know that this meeting will make you feel any better," she told me, "but I'll stop by and pick you up."

The meeting started at seven and was held in a small auditorium with a low stage and rows of uncomfortable wooden chairs. The eight members of the city council sat at a table on the stage, flanked by an arrangement of flags: a large American flag, and a smaller New York State flag accompanied by the flag of Barnum Beach, which featured a mermaid, breaking waves, and seashells. In addition to her fishy tail, the mermaid was wearing a kind of modest tube top and also a slight scowl.

By the time Lisa and I found a parking spot and made it to the auditorium, the place was packed to the rafters. The supporters of the restaurant expansion were on one side of the auditorium, the opponents on the other, with the center aisle running between them like an uncrossable chasm. It was immediately clear which side was which, because the two sides were so clearly divided, not only by which part of the room they were in but also by appearance and age. The pro-restaurant people were young, lively, and dressed in shorts, Hawaiian shirts, and the like. Most of them clutched sports drinks or bottles of water imported from countries with fjords. On the other side, the crowd included doctors and nurses from the hospital but also a fair number of folks in wheelchairs, or using canes and walkers. Some of them must have been nursing home residents; the middle-aged men and women with them were, I assumed, their children and maybe other relatives. Some idiot had put the auditorium's air conditioning on an arctic setting, and while the cold only seemed to invigorate the bunch in the cute summer clothes—they were joking around with each other and sucking on those water bottles to beat the band—members of the other group were shivering in their hard chairs or pulling on the bottom of skimpy sweaters, trying to cover their knees.

Eventually, the debate got started—if you could call it that. There was a microphone near the stage, facing the council members, and people lined up to make a statement. Some of those "statements" went on and on. The case for both sides was easily summed up: basically, it was either, *We're young, it's summer, and we want to party*, or *We're old, we're only going to get older, and we need our rest!*

After a while, my attention began to drift. I finally noticed a couple of coffee urns at the rear of the auditorium, so I whispered to Lisa that I was going to stretch my legs. I made my way through the crowd to the back, near the doors where the coffee was set up, and poured some for myself into a paper cup. Surprisingly, for coffee that had probably been boiling inside these big silver vats for hours, it wasn't at all bad. Someone had also set out cookies on paper plates, and I had some of those, too.

I stayed by the coffee table as I munched on the cookies, watching the goings-on. From the back of the auditorium, I could see straight down the center aisle, which gave me a clear view of the stage. The city council members—five men and three women, evenly divided between Democrats and Republicans—were all looking grim, which was probably their way of trying to appear interested in what the parade of speakers had to say. But the truth, of course, and everybody knew it, was that their main concern was getting re-elected in the fall (campaign signs were already posted all over the town) so it wasn't hard to imagine what was really going on in their minds: *What choice do I make that will be better for me? Do I vote the way the old farts want me to or go with the kids? The old farts have more influence in the town right now, but the kids will be running it in a few years, so what do I do? Can I abstain?*

In the end, they decided to do what people almost always do in these situations—especially people in a small town faced with an upcoming election: the council members voted to commission a study, which the chairman said was a masterstroke of bipartisan cooperation. They were roundly booed by both sides of the divide who didn't know what to do after that (no storming the Bastille in Barnum Beach), so everyone ended up just slowly filing out into the mild summer night. A full moon, as bright as a lantern, presided over the dispersing crowd. Some people were heading for their cars, others, who lived closer, were beginning the stroll home.

"Jerks," Lisa said, as we got into our car and started it up. "Every one of those council members is a jerk. They're all afraid to take a stand."

"They'll have to, eventually," I replied. "After the election. They'll have the study done, it will recommend some kind of compromise they can endorse—like an enclosed deck, with soundproofing; somebody mentioned that, right?—and then everyone will be happy."

"I won't be happy," Lisa said as she nosed our car into the line to get out of the overcrowded parking lot next to city hall. "I wanted them to make a decision. Everybody did."

"So nobody got what they wanted, but also nobody got what they didn't want," I pointed out.

Lisa turned to look at me. "Suddenly," she said, "you're being philosophical?"

"I've been feeling kind of depressed all day," I reported, "but now I feel better. Maybe it was the cookies. I love a good lemon snap on a warm summer night."

She sighed. "Often," she said, "I don't understand you."

Then—out of the blue—something occurred to me that I hadn't thought of in years. "Lisa," I said, "I'm going to ask you a question. What walks on four legs in the morning, two legs at noon, and three at night?"

"I have no idea," Lisa answered, as we finally made it to the parking lot exit and she was able to ease the car out onto the wide boulevard that bisects the beach side of the town from the bay and the channel that connects them both.

"Man," I said. "And to update the story so it's politically correct, woman. So let's say, human beings. Humans crawl on four legs as an infant, walk upright on two in the prime of life, and hobble with a cane in old age."

"And you thought of that—why?" Lisa asked.

"I don't know," I said. "Maybe it was the people in the auditorium—the way they were divided. The younger crowd on one side, the bunch with the canes and walkers on the other."

"I think you're missing something from your little story," Lisa said.

"It's a riddle," I told her. "The Riddle of the Sphinx."

"Well, whatever it is, it needs infants, right? Babies. But there were no babies there tonight. Nobody brought any kids or any babies."

There I had her, because she was wrong of course: there were actually babies everywhere. Being carried off the beach in a summer rainstorm, for example. Or being born in Lisa's own hospital—one after another, night and day. Our town, in fact, was full of babies; in the summer, parents pushed them in strollers on the boardwalk. In the winter, they dressed them in warm clothes and took them outside to see the snow. Which is something that I always remember about my father: from the time I was very small, he was always the one who got me dressed and out of the house, who took me to the park, to the playground; he was the one who carried me down the street on his shoulders, heading somewhere, bouncing along.

And come to think of it, he was the one who first told me the Riddle of the Sphinx. Just some Jewish guy from the Bronx, some mid-century, working-class, nobody-in-particular kind of person walking along Mt. Eden Avenue with his daughter, who somehow grew up to be me. How did he know that particular story? More importantly, whatever made him decide, one day—out of the blue, as I recall—to tell it to me? It's amazing, when you think about it. Human beings. How can you ever predict what they will do?

The Blonde on the Train

My phone rang while I was in O'Hare Airport, in Chicago, waiting to change planes. Even though I knew the call was coming—I had been anxious about it when I left New York in the morning, and worried about it all through the first leg of my flight—when I felt the phone vibrate in my purse, and then begin chiming like a tiny bell, I had some sort of delayed reaction about answering it. It was because of the airport; the unreality of it, the sense of being caught between here and there that always overtakes me at these stopovers, when I'm sitting in a plastic chair in a glass building on the flattened outskirts of some city I will likely never see. There is no weather in these places, no season, no straightforward progression of the hours, just soft music to ease you along, to keep the river of traffic flowing toward arrival or departure; that's all you are here, that's all you need to know. Coming or going, with a coffee and a Cinnabon. Take off your shoes and fly away.

When I finally connected to the idea that the chime meant I had a call, I dug into my purse and pulled out the cell just before it would have switched to voicemail. I opened it quickly and said, "Hello?"

"Lynn?" It was Donna Peasey, my best friend Mary's sister, calling from St. Vincent's Hospital in Manhattan. I knew what the call was about, but I still felt myself begin to shake inside.

"It's me," I said. "So was it...?" I just couldn't bring myself to say the word.

So Donna said it for me. "Yes, it was cancer," she told me. "The doctor was right. But it was early and they think they got it all—they just did a lumpectomy. She'll have to have chemo, but they think she's got a very good chance."

"Alright," I said, meaning, more than anything, that I should have been prepared for this, so I should gather myself together. If I was about to go anywhere near despair, I should turn around and go the other way, immediately. I should calm down. "Can I call her later?" I asked.

"I think so," Donna said. "She's in recovery now, but they said they'll start waking her up soon. By this evening she should be able to talk to you. And you'll be back tomorrow?"

"Late afternoon," I said, though at the moment—the airport thing again—I was confused about time. Somewhere I was going to lose an hour, somewhere I would gain it back.

"Okay," Donna said. "She'll be here a day or two and then they'll send her home."

"We'll work out a schedule," I said. Donna and I had already agreed that at least for the first week or two after Mary's surgery, if the suspicious lump on her mammogram turned out to be cancer, we would leave her alone in her apartment as little as possible. But we hadn't gotten much further than that, since the diagnosis and then her doctor's decision to put Mary into the hospital and get her into surgery had happened in such a blurry rush that I hadn't even been able to reschedule this trip, much less sit down with Donna and figure out what we were going to do after. *After.* There just better be an after, I found myself thinking—and then quickly made myself stop.

"I'll call you if anything changes," Donna told me. "But let's hope this is it for now."

We said good-bye and I put the phone back in my purse. Adrenaline had washed through my body when I had heard the word *cancer*, and it was seeping away now, leaving me feeling poisoned. I got out my ticket and studied it to make sure that I still remembered where I was going, what plane I had to make. The numbers printed on the piece of paper I had received from an electronic kiosk looked faint and smeary, but confirmed that in half an hour, I had to board a flight to Indiana. To Indianapolis, actually. There, I would catch a cab to the headquarters of Jennifer Juniper, a cosmetics firm, where I had an appointment in the afternoon.

Eventually, my flight was called and I got out of the plastic chair. I boarded the plane, ate the sandwich and the cookie I was given and drank a can of Diet Pepsi. This was a business commuter flight, and I noticed that all the other passengers in my row had asked for spring water. Going with the pure stuff, gearing up for the big business fight ahead. I always mean to do that, but I forget. Besides, I like soda better.

The terminal at the airport in Indiana was cool and comfortable, but once I stepped outside, looking for the taxi ranks, I could feel summer in the dry Midwest baking all around me; the cloudless blue sky was sizzling with heat. Thankfully, I was soon able to find a cab and was back in air conditioning before I melted. I told the driver where I was going and then retrieved my notes from my shoulder bag in order to review what I needed to know for the meeting.

I've had some version of the job I'm doing now for almost twenty years. I work for *Jane Street*, a magazine that started out as a gay literary quarterly (named for the street in the Village where there was once a famous gay boys' bar, now long and sadly gone) but has evolved, with its audience, into a serious, glossy, lifestyle publication that still publishes fiction but also attracts notable journalists, both gay and straight, who write about issues that affect the community. Our subscription readership is a mix of gays and lesbians, though on what we still call the newsstands—more and more, now, that means bookstores like Barnes and Noble—more copies are bought by women than men. To serve both audiences, which also includes the transgendered community, we also have gossip, health, beauty, and travel columns—and of course, a horoscope. Everyone, everywhere, wants to know what the stars have in store for them.

I started out with the magazine as the one-person subscription department, having got the job because, in the long ago and far away, I answered an ad in the *Village Voice* for a responsible person who could type. The ad attracted me for a number of reasons: I thought I had a responsible nature, relatively speaking, the only thing I was good at in high school was typing, and besides, I was sick of what I'd been doing in the years since then, which was working as a secretary for a maniac who owned a tool company. The plant that manufactured the tools was in New Jersey, but the maniac had an office on Columbus Circle in Manhattan, where I typed up tool orders all day and then he yelled at me when I handed them to him, just because he could. (Six dozen needle nose pliers, four dozen allen wrenches; eleven bell hanger drills; there are brain cells in my head that will never let go of the names of those damn tools. Never.)

As the times changed, and the gay community became more mainstream, the magazine changed ownership—the writer who started it sold it to a young business type and his lawyer boyfriend—which is when it started to become surprisingly successful. When we began, in earnest, to solicit advertising, I moved from subscriptions to ad sales, a department that I now run under yet another management setup; six years ago, the company was bought by a media conglomerate, which, aside from installing some executive's gay daughter—a woman named Laura Kennedy, who had at least worked in publishing before—thankfully, has kept mostly a hands-off attitude. Still, I should probably admit I'm making the situation sound grander than it really is, since along with managing our ad sales, I am also the only member of the department. When I'm not in the office, an assistant on the editorial side answers my phone.

There were years when I spent much of my workday compiling research so I could go to client meetings armed with facts and figures aimed at getting potential advertisers to understand that the gay community was an important consumer market for their products because, as a demographic, gay people skew toward the middle- and upper-middle class; in other words, gays have money, and they spend it. They buy the same things everybody else does—clothes, cars, and houses that need furniture and fixtures, including televisions, computers and whatever is the latest, coolest electronic hookup for blasting music—but they also buy lots of health and fitness products, lots of special food and grooming aids for their pets, and they go on lots of vacations. They are, in fact, as American as apple pie—just maybe a little hipper—so my spin, always, was that if an advertiser would recognize this to be the case, whatever it cost them to advertise in our magazine was an investment in reaching a receptive audience. Sometimes that worked and sometimes it didn't, but interestingly, I don't often have to do the hard sell anymore. Now, the clients I deal with have done the research themselves: anything I could tell them, they already know. Now, they tend to call me before I find them, because they've analyzed the demographic, they've run the numbers, and they've figured out how to position their products, when they want to, for a wide variety of niche markets. When one of those markets is the gay community, sooner or later they find *Jane Street*, run *our* numbers, and then they call me.

What hasn't changed though is that while yes, now they call me, and they are open, cordial, and perfectly appropriate in all they say and do, when I finally meet my potential advertiser's representatives (and I always do, I always visit, always establish a personal, albeit professional relationship with our clients), I still often feel like I am a visitor from another planet. Or maybe I mean, another tribe, another culture, another race? Like in the morning, in front of the mirror, they rehearsed how to speak to me: what words to say or not say, what questions to ask, even which sports, entertainment, or other newsworthy figures they should reference. I even know what kind of person they are expecting me to be:

someone thin and sharp-edged, with spiky hair and rubber bracelets. I guess I could look like that if I wanted to, but I don't. Twenty-five years ago, I wanted to look like the twenty-five-years-ago version of that (bell bottoms and bat-wing blouses, purchased in East Village boutiques hung with black light posters of Janis and Jimi), but now I go to the department stores, like everybody else, and buy business clothes. Some cruise line ad rep might think I should look like I spend my time on the ramparts, fighting the culture wars, but I think that I should look professional.

The headquarters of Jennifer Juniper was near the campus of the University of Indiana, in an old elementary school building that had been converted to offices. The woman who had founded the company was married to a tenured professor, which I gathered was why the business operations of the company were located here; most of the very expensive products, which were unabashedly retro (pale lipsticks, eyeliners dark as paint, shadows in Nile blue) were actually manufactured in Europe.

When I got out of the cab, I found myself in a leafy neighborhood, washed with sunlight and remarkably quiet. I marveled at the idea that this could be a city—even here, at the suburban edge, shouldn't I be seeing some kind of foot traffic, hearing human voices, car engines, wheezing trucks? Maybe, but the reality was that I was standing alone, among the lush summer greenery, on a street with just the one red brick building flanked by dandelion-spotted lawns and dogwood trees. I walked up the paved path that led to the schoolhouse door, which had been replaced with a sheet of smoke-colored glass, and went inside.

The interior of the building was sort of Indiana schoolhouse meets downtown New York: the old wood floors had been retained but wore gleaming coats of varnish, which reflected the bright crayon colors that had been selected for the angled bits of minimalist furniture in the waiting room (a couch shaped like a sharp-edged cup, an armless chair looking back-tilted and yawning toward the floor). At the reception desk, a cheerful young woman found my name in an appointment book, buzzed upstairs to tell Malcolm Morris, the company vice president I'd come to see, that I had arrived, and then sent me to an elevator at the end of the hall.

Malcolm, whom I had spoken with on the phone many times since he'd first called Jane Street to talk about advertising with us, but whom I'd never met, was waiting for me in a conference room on the third floor, where a wall of windows showed endless blue sky slicing toward the horizon. I expected there to be other people with him—assistants, people from the ad agency; usually these meetings involved dealing with a team of players—but he was by himself, sitting at the head of a free-form table, also glass, this time smoky bronze. As I stepped through the door, Malcolm rose to greet me, and I saw a thin, handsome man with a stylish gray crew-cut, wearing expensive jeans and a black tee-shirt under a black linen jacket with the sleeves pushed up toward his elbows. He moved toward me and instead of shaking hands, he gave me the two-cheek European kiss, which meant a lot of things including, *Well, hello there, you did guess we were playing for the same team, didn't you?* As well as, *This may be Indiana, darling, but I'm East Coast all the way.* I nodded to underscore the fact that I got the message, and sat down near the head of the table, where he had dozens of proof sheets laid out for me to review.

After a few general pleasantries, we got down to work. Usually, my first visit to a new client is just a meet-and-greet, but Malcolm Morris already had his ad campaign mapped out. First he showed me the proof sheets, which were glamour shots of an aging but attractive blonde in a variety of suede and silk outfits; lots of fringe, lots of lace, all very retro chic. The more I looked at the photos, the more the model looked familiar to me: she had a kind of chipmunk-cheeked cheeriness about her that, hard as she was trying, radiated an almost desperate desire for whoever it was out there looking at her picture to regard her with sympathy and affection rather than projecting the cold aloofness usually required of the women in these shots.

"The theme of this campaign is 'Girlfriends'," Malcolm told me, "which will help launch our new Jennifer Juniper II products, including a line of skin refreshers, exfoliants, collagen-enhanced creams, and moisture-enriched foundations—in other words, all the anti-aging goodies. The age cohort we're aiming at should remember rock royalty and their ladies, like our friend Pattie here, and hopefully relate to how fabulous she still looks."

"Pattie?" I said, though I knew I should know who she was. "Pattie who? I mean, who is she?"

"She's the blonde on the train," Malcolm said, with evident fondness. "That, my dear, is Pattie Boyd. Or should I say, Pattie Boyd Harrison Clapton."

"Oh my gosh," I said, and along with that asinine exclamation, I'm sure my hand flew to my mouth, as well. "*A Hard Day's Night*," I said, confirming out loud all the mental connections I had just made. "In that first Beatles movie, she's the blonde teenager in the schoolgirl outfit, chatting up Paul when they're all on that train ride. When they're escaping from the fans, right?"

"The very one."

"But she's a wife," I said. "I mean, she married George Harrison. And then Eric Clapton."

"Well," Malcolm responded, "yes, technically, she was a wife. But she had to be a girlfriend first, right? And besides, she's just the first model in a series, and most of them were girlfriends." He took a quick breath and then rushed on. "We've got feelers out to people like Prudence Farrow, Anita Pallenberg, the Shrimptons—both Jean and Chrissie—they dated *everybody* you know, including Mick Jagger—and even Jane Asher, Paul's old flame before he married Linda, but I'm sure she won't do it because she's an *artiste* now, an actress on the London stage and she won't even talk about the Beatles. But I'm sure we can get Jenny Boyd—she's Pattie's sister, and she was married to Mick Fleetwood for a while. I guess that would technically make her a wife, too, but we'll certainly bend the rules for her because she's the company namesake. Donovan wrote the song *Jennifer Juniper* for her, did you know that?"

"I think so," I said.

"Randa just *loved* Donovan," Malcolm Morris told me, and it took me a minute, amidst all the names that he had just poured into the heavily air-conditioned atmosphere of the conference room, to figure out who Randa was—but then I remembered that she was the professor's wife who had created the Jennifer Juniper line of beauty products. The slogan, which they had begun using in their print ads, was *Cosmetics for Coming of Age*. Though I had made a point of looking at their ads before I came out here to Indianapolis, I hadn't really registered what the slant of that particular tag line was getting at. But now, along with Malcolm's earlier comment about who might remember Pattie Boyd, I clearly understood that the age of the customer they were aiming for was over thirty. Over forty, even. In other words, they were aiming for me.

"Of course," Malcolm continued, "there are some of those ladies we couldn't possibly even think of using. I mean, they've just gone to seed, and our point, of course, is that you can look fabulous even if you aren't a sweet little pouty-faced babykins anymore. Like, have you seen Cynthia Lennon lately? Or Marianne Faithfull? Maybe she's singing up a storm all of a sudden but come on—how do you let yourself go like that?"

I murmured some words of agreement—part of the gay creed, at least on the boys' side, was that you never let yourself go (dyke culture, on the other hand, sometimes seemed predicated on letting yourself go as far as possible)—and then we went on to discuss which of the print prototypes Malcolm was showing me might work best in *Jane Street* and what kind of a deal he could get on our rate schedule, which I had already e-mailed to him but which also was, of course, negotiable, depending on the space he wanted and the length of contract he was willing to commit to. All the while, I kept glancing back at the photos of Pattie Boyd. She had to be sixty, I thought, but all the long, straight blonde hair, the Jennifer Juniper retro-pale lipstick coupled with the Egyptian eye makeup and updated Stevie Nicks leather-and-lace gypsy gear looked great on her, somehow age appropriate and subdued, in a chic kind of way, rather than showy. I spent a moment—while half listening to Malcolm recommend a restaurant to me for dinner, later, if I didn't want to eat in the hotel—wondering how Pattie could pull this off, and decided it was because of her face. Not that she was all that beautiful, though she was pretty enough, still: it was, as I had first noticed, her expression—that wistful cheeriness that she projected. It was disarming.

Malcolm Morris and I talked for a while longer and agreed on the details of a deal to carry the Jennifer Juniper ads in the next six issues; after that, they were planning to launch a perfume line and might want to do scratch-and-sniff inserts, which would have to be printed separately and bound into the magazine. The company could clearly become one of our biggest advertisers, and I was pleased to get the contracts signed.

But when I was back in a cab, heading for my hotel, which Malcolm had explained was somewhere on the other side of the sprawling University of Indiana campus, I allowed myself to feel the worry that I had kept in the back of my mind all through the afternoon. Mary. How was Mary? I'm very good at dissembling—meaning, even if something terrible is going on, I can pretend it isn't happening for as long as I need in order to do something else that can't be put aside—but that brief vacation from reality was over now, and I was concerned about my friend. I called the hospital, and was told that Mary had been moved to a semiprivate room, and there was a phone at her bedside. The switchboard transferred me, but it was Donna who answered. She told me Mary was sleeping, and I said I'd try again later.

Back at the hotel, in a room on a high floor with a view that could have been anyplace at all (trees, that vast, flat blue sky with a slice of early moon floating low on the horizon), I stretched out on the bed, thinking I'd watch TV for a while, but soon fell asleep. It was that time problem again; just shift my internal clock by an hour or two and apparently, I'm lost.

When I woke up, it was evening. Out of nowhere—well, out of some connection to Jennifer Juniper that had apparently suggested itself while I was sleeping—I found myself thinking of an old Donovan song: *When the sun goes to bed, that's the time you raise your head, that's your lot in life Leleana, can't blame yeh, Leleana.* It was a sad lyric and I tried to banish it by turning on the radio, which started singing something nicer to me. Anne Murray, I think. The Canadian songbird made me feel a little better.

I remembered the restaurant that Malcolm Morris had suggested, and decided to walk there. That's something I like to do when I'm visiting a new place: take a little tour. Something short, not too adventurous, but just enough to make me feel like I can say, somewhere down the line, *Well, yes, I visited there once. It seemed like a nice enough place.*

The desk clerk gave me directions and I walked from the university area toward downtown Indianapolis, where every department store and office building seemed to be closed, though it was only around seven o'clock. Sunset blazed behind me, and in the glass-fronted buildings the light became a fiery glare. No one else seemed to be walking in my direction; the few people I passed were all hurrying away, toward some suburban home.

Finally, I reached a residential neighborhood—old houses, painted the color of green apples, with vine-covered porches and flowery yards. The restaurant I was looking for was in the only brick building I'd seen for a while: three squat stories with tables on two of the floors and open-air dining on the roof, which is where I asked to sit. I marched upstairs behind a young waiter and then found myself the only patron seated beneath the Indiana sky, which now held both the sun and the moon on its evening horizon, both looking small, modest: two minor actors passing each other as one arrived onstage and the other departed.

It had been a hot day and remained so, at dusk. And again, I noticed the silence. I had never visited a quieter city, where street noises and the ambient sounds of human habitation seemed so absent. Even when a couple finally joined me on the roof and sat nearby, they seemed to address each other in hushed whispers.

The waiter brought me a glass of wine I'd asked for, and then I tried to call Mary again, but this time the phone rang and rang, unanswered. I called back, dialing the hospital's main line, and asked for the nurse's station near Mary Peasey's room. When someone finally answered there, they told me that Donna had left and Mary, who had been awake only briefly, was asleep again and since they had medicated her, she probably wouldn't be up again until morning. So I ate my dinner and then called a cab to take me back to the hotel because I didn't want to walk through the silent, empty streets again. I expected to sleep well, since I'm used to hotels and unfamiliar beds, but I didn't: I woke up around three a.m. feeling anxious and worried, but I wasn't sure about what. I listened to the air conditioner hum and looked out at the moon, which seemed to be looking in on me. It was as a big as a plate now and finally alone in the sky, here in the middle of the middle of the night.

The next day, my journey back to New York was a nightmare. The first leg, from Indianapolis to Chicago, was fine, but twenty minutes into what was supposed to be a forty-five minute wait at O'Hare for a connecting flight, there was a bomb scare and the entire airport was evacuated. Along with thousands of other hot, weary, and eventually angry passengers, I stood outside the main terminal for two hours, watching uniformed police officers, firemen, and bomb sniffing dogs come and go, all of them (except the dogs) constantly talking into radios and telephones and to each other, but never to us, the traveling public. Some people in the crowd had CD players that also got AM/FM reception, so we were able to get information from a local news station that explained what was going on, and that's how we heard—on the radio, not from any official of the airport—that a bomb threat had been called into one of the airlines, but all the terminals had been searched, nothing had been found, and flights were finally due to resume in another hour. Eventually, we were all let back into the terminal but of course, everything was chaotic and it was another two hours before I actually got on a plane back to New York City. By the time I landed at JFK, it was almost evening again and, besides being totally confused about the time (I only knew it was dusk because the sky was darkening in the east, where night was zooming in across the Atlantic), I was exhausted.

But I had to see Mary. I had tried to call her from O'Hare but couldn't get cell phone reception, probably because everyone that afternoon was trying to call everywhere at once, and the lines to get on a hard-line phone were impossible. So, at JFK, carrying my small overnight bag, I got in a cab, and told him to take me to St. Vincent's Hospital, north of the Village in Manhattan.

It was past the dinner hour when I finally got there. At the information desk, I was told that Mary's room was on the fifth floor, so I took the elevator upstairs and tried to follow the signs on the wall to her room. Down this corridor, up that one: hospitals, especially at night, are nothing like what you see on those TV medical shows. To begin with, there is not a handsome doctor in sight—in fact, there are very few doctors around at all, either male or female, though at night, hospitals do seem to be run by women, aides and nurses, mostly, all of them underpaid, ill-tempered, overworked, and walking around on aching feet. And the atmosphere in the halls is sour with anguish: the elderly and demented, in their wheelchairs, are parked in the hallways like dying plants abandoned on a doorstep; televisions cackle from their bolt-mounted perches above the beds of the suffering; and nothing, from the stiff sheets piled on carts outside the patients' rooms to the scuffed floors and gray walls, seems clean. When I found myself back at the elevator bank where I had started, I thought I would never locate Mary's room, but after another few minutes of searching, I finally did.

She was in a two-patient room, in the bed by the window, which looked out over the low rooftops of the West Village toward the new skyscraper condos that stood like knife-edge towers along the banks of the Hudson. The room was dark, the dinner trays pushed off to the side of the beds, waiting to be collected. The patient in the other bed was asleep; Mary was sitting up in bed watching a rerun of *Judge Judy* on a local station.

I gave her a long hug and then stepped back to take a look at her, though I tried to pretend that wasn't what I was doing. Mary and I have been friends since we were in our twenties, and I know we both look different than when we first met, but she has changed less, I think. She has always been long-boned and athletic, a woman with an open, attractive face and short, light brown hair that she has a habit of using her fingers to rake back from her forehead. Tonight, she looked smaller, somehow, reduced; seemingly pinned back against her pillows by the drip tubes snaking from a beeping machine by the bed into her arm and by the bandages that formed a mound inside her hospital gown. And like almost everything else in the hospital, the gown looked like a used rag, gray and faded.

"I'm sorry it took me so long to get here," I told Mary. "I've been traveling all day."

"I'm just glad you're here now," she said and reached out for me again. She winced when we embraced, but still didn't let me go for a long minute.

Finally, I pulled a chair toward her bed and sat down. "How bad is it?" I asked her. "I mean, how do you feel?"

"Right now, I'm doing okay," she told me. "Actually, I'm pretty stoned, if you want to know the truth. They've been giving me morphine and it's a very floaty drug, I mean, it makes me feel floaty. And itchy. Mostly," she concluded, "I've been sleeping."

"But you're going to be fine," I said. "Donna told me that's what your doctor said."

"They think so," Mary agreed. "But Lynn," she said, her voice suddenly cracking, "I have to go through all that awful stuff. All that patient stuff."

I knew what she meant. On the afternoon that she'd gotten the diagnosis of breast cancer, Mary had gone back to her office—she's the financial officer of an engineering firm—closed her door, and spent the afternoon on the Internet visiting medical web sites which, she told me, more often than not offered two ways to search information: *Click here if you're a physician; click here if you're a patient.* So she kept clicking "patient" and found out every awful thing that could possibly happen. Even if the surgery was successful, as hers apparently had been, she was going to have to go through a powerful regimen of ingesting drugs that would make her sick, weak, and miserable. She would lose her hair, possibly bloat up like a toxic balloon and probably miss weeks of work.

"Let's talk about something else. We can think about all the bad stuff tomorrow," Mary said. Making an effort to lift the arm that was not pierced by tubes and needles, she tried to press the back of her hand to her forehead in a Scarlett O'Hara kind of vapor-y gesture, but she couldn't lift her arm far enough without a stab of pain. When she had composed herself again, she said, "Tell me about Indianapolis. How did your meeting go?" Mary closed her eyes then and seemed to fall back even further into her pillow. "Jennifer Juniper," she said. "Mellow Yellow. An Epistle to Dippy."

"Well, yes," I said. "I mean, sort of." I opened my bag, pulled out some of the proof sheets I'd brought back with me and laid them across the bed. "Look," I said.

Mary's eyes fluttered open—how quickly, I thought, she had almost fallen asleep—and she focused on the ads. "Who is that?" she asked. "She kind of looks familiar."

"Do you remember *A Hard Day's Night?*" I asked.

"The Beatles movie?" Mary said. And then, for the first time since I'd arrived, she smiled at me. "I even remember where I saw it: on the Grand Concourse, in the Bronx. At Loew's Paradise Theater. I couldn't have been more than what—thirteen?"

"Me too," I said. We looked at each other and laughed.

"Jesus," Mary said. "Was anybody really ever thirteen?"

"When I saw the movie," I told her, "I screamed my brains out. I was so in love with Paul. I still am."

"Oh God," Mary said. "Those droopy eyes he has. Anybody would switch teams if you could look into those eyes every day." She peered at the pictures again. "That's not...what was her name? His old girlfriend?" "Jane Asher," I said, remembering that Malcolm Morris had mentioned her. "No, she had red hair. This one was the blonde on the train. She had on, like, a school outfit, a jumper and a white shirt..."

"Pattie Boyd," Mary said. "Wow. Back from the dead."

"Not exactly," I told her. "Malcolm Morris—the guy I met with at Jennifer Juniper—told me she's actually kept pretty busy. Apparently, she's a photographer. There have been quite a few exhibitions of her work."

"Of course she's a photographer," Mary said. "That's some life she's had. Probably everybody she knows is worth a photo shoot all by themselves."

"Hey," I said, knowing what direction the conversation was drifting off to, "your life hasn't been so bad—I mean, it will be okay again. And what about me? I've mostly been alright."

"Do you like living alone?" Mary asked, and I think regretted it right away. It sounded like a challenge, meant to wound.

"I can bear it," I said. I had broken up with my last girlfriend a year ago, but it had been by mutual agreement. I sometimes still missed her, but I didn't regard her loss as the end of my life. "I mean, I'm forty-eight years old. There's still hope, right?"

Mary sort of looked at me sideways and tried to grin. "Well," she said, "you are still sort of cute. I guess you've got a shot at hooking up with someone...maybe." I thought, then, that our conversation was lightening up a bit, but another cloudy thought had occurred to my friend, the patient in the hospital bed looking out at a cityscape darkening in the blue evening. "Linda McCartney died of breast cancer," Mary said.

"Well, she probably didn't go for enough checkups or something," I replied. "We know they found your cancer very early. You're going to be absolutely fine."

But she wasn't really listening to me. "Can you believe we outlived that marriage?" Mary said. "I remember their picture in the *Daily News* on the day they got married: Paul and Linda, outside the city office where they had the ceremony. It was someplace called Marylebone. Linda was holding her daughter's hand. What was her name"

"Heather," I said, because I remembered the picture, too. I imagined that every woman my age did. "Look," I said, "we've outlived a lot of people. We're going to outlive a lot more, I hope. It doesn't mean anything important. It's just...well, I don't know what it is. Fate. Luck. Mammograms."

"You make us sound like old ladies," Mary grumbled. "Boobless, almost—at least in my case. Toothless is next." She closed her eyes again and almost immediately, they began to flutter behind her eyelids. Again, she had floated across the barrier between sleep and wakefulness as if no crossing point actually existed. Laying back against the pillows she looked pale; her skin translucent. I kissed her forehead, whispered that I'd be back tomorrow, and left her room.

I was headed downtown, toward the ferry terminal at Battery Park, so I had to catch the subway first. But when I got outside, I felt momentarily confused, not sure in what direction I should walk. I think I was unnerved by our conversation, me and Mary—maybe because there had been too much cancer in it? I knew we were going to have to talk about cancer and it wasn't that I was afraid of the subject—it's just that I'm better at dealing with trouble when I can avoid thinking about the fact that it's real. I mean, I think I could handle poisonous snakes if I had to, as long as I could pretend that they were stuffed toys or garden hoses. *Old ladies with cancer.* Jesus.

In order to get home, I didn't have far to go—just across the river to Jersey City. I lived in a building that had just been constructed a few years ago, a tall tower in a neighborhood of towers; the area had been industrial in a different age; ruined waterfront and dumpsites in recent decades, but had been bulldozed, flattened, and built upon in order to attract young and, like me, no-so-young professionals from the city who were willing to invest most of their income on rent in exchange for a quick ferry commute and a view of the Hudson River. I had moved to Jersey about two years ago, after having lived in the Village from the time I was in my early twenties, in a one-room, rent-stabilized studio—the kind of place that *The New York Times* real estate section told you people would kill for. But *The New York Times* doesn't have to come home every night and sleep on a pull-out couch in an apartment facing the street where the music from the after-hours club three doors down—not to mention the fights, noisy sex, and occasional gunshots on the pavement below my window—could be counted on to keep me up most of the night. And these were straight people; queens used to act like this, when the Village was gay, but they, at least, stayed home and tried on outfits or did their nails once in a while. I mean, you got a night off from the noise now and then—but the twenty-somethings down the block (the girls unknowingly, I guess, having cast themselves in the image of the Village queens, all sparkles and stilettos, while the boys had adopted the posing and bad attitudes) went on drinking and drugging themselves into oblivion every single night to the accompaniment of the loudest music I have ever heard.

So that's where I was headed now, to my eighteenth floor apartment with its view of the river, the bay; stars, moon, bridges, ferries, yachts, and barges. When I got home, I sat on the terrace for a while, in the warm night, watching the boats drifting by on the dark, calm water. Having watched every Japanese monster movie that ever played on TV when I was a child—which meant I had seen Godzilla, Mothra, and the like over and over again on shows like *The Million Dollar Movie*—I could never look at deep water without waiting for the moment when a huge, scaley behemoth would suddenly rise up from beneath the black waves and start stomping toward the shore, breathing fire. So I waited for Godzilla for a while, and since it looked like he wasn't coming tonight, I finally went to bed.

Mary got out of the hospital a few days later and soon had to begin chemotherapy. Donna and I planned to take turns going back and forth to the hospital with her, which meant I was going to be taking time off work with some regularity over the course of quite a few weeks. That was fine, I thought, I would just use my vacation time and break it up into half days. We were able to take three full weeks and a couple of personal days, so I didn't expect any problems. At *Jane Street*, the procedure for arranging vacation time was to hand in a memo to the office manager, and that was that, unless your schedule conflicted with someone else's; since the magazine operated with a small staff, we all tried not to be away at the same time that someone else was. So I was surprised when Beverly, our office manager, came to see me the same afternoon I'd handed in my vacation memo and sat down in the chair opposite my desk, as if we were going to have a long conversation about something.

"Listen, Lynn," she said, "about the way you want to take your time off? In half days? You can't do that."

"Why?" I said. "Since when?"

Beverly, like me had started working at this magazine a long time ago—long enough to remember when most of the ads were for escort services, bath houses, and bed-and-breakfast places in Key West and P-Town. She had been in charge of our subscription list, which meant she hand wrote information on file cards which were kept in a couple of long, skinny drawers near her desk. I remembered her as a young kid, always in black, always wearing scuffed Frye boots, hunched over her desk, her left hand curled around those blue-lined, three-by-five cards, as she scribbled away. These days, she had a kind of pouchy look about her: she had gained some weight and wore big tee shirts to hide that fact. The one she had on today was mint green; since her short, cropped hair was dyed dark red—

the color, I thought, of a poisoned lollipop—I was having trouble taking her seriously. She just didn't look like anything she said had to be paid attention to. But it did; she made clear to me that I had a problem.

"Since Laura became publisher," she said. "After the magazine was bought by Redrock Media. Don't you remember we gave everyone a new handbook with new company policies?"

"Laura is fourteen years old," I told Beverly. "What does she know about anybody being sick?"

She sighed, because she knew where I was going: back to the black days, the black plague, when everyone here knew someone who had AIDS and half the time half of us were spending our days in hospitals or hospices. The unwritten rules, then, were that you did what you had to do, you went where you had to go when you had to go, and you got your job done in whatever time was left. But now, the attitude seemed to be that AIDS was something you could take a couple of pills for and get on with your life; or else it was some foreign scourge that killed people in Africa if war and starvation didn't get them first. The issue was actually a sort of quiet source of tension around the magazine, between the editorial staff, who tended to be older, and the administrative staff such as Laura, our publisher, who tended to be younger and who didn't seem particularly interested in shining a spotlight on the fact that the disease was still out there, still doing its deadly work. Why? Maybe because they didn't think it was likely to affect them, or their generation. Maybe because they didn't think it would sell magazines.

"Is that what this is about?" Beverly asked. "Someone you know?"

I nodded. "My friend Mary," I said. "Cancer."

"Oh God," Beverly whispered. "I guess now there's that, too." Then she shook her head, a gesture that seemed almost superstitious; like she was paying her respects to the power of all ill fortune. "Well, for the record," Beverly told me, "about Laura. She's twenty-nine—and a dedicated activist."

"Sure," I said. "She goes to all the right fundraisers. She says all the right things."

"Lynn..."

"I'm sorry," I said, because there was no reason for me to be curt with Beverly. "What should I do?"

"What should you do about what?" she said, standing up, closing the folder she had been holding on her lap all this time—it contained, I supposed, my memo. The details of my problem. "We just discussed the fact that you're going to have a lot of meetings outside the office for the next few weeks, which is fine. Just check in with me—or with someone in editorial—if you're going to be gone for more than a few hours. If something comes up, we'll call your cell."

"Thanks," I said. "Really."

"Listen," she said, "you do your job. You always have done your job. There's no question about that." She ran her hand through her lollipop hair and shook her head again. "Twenty-nine," she said. "Fuck." And then she left my office.

So for the next few weeks, I arranged my time around Mary's chemo schedule. She lived in Brooklyn, so usually, I'd work in my office for a few hours in the morning, then ride the subway to her apartment building, pick her up, take her to the hospital in Manhattan by cab, and back home by car service. I'd spend the rest of the afternoon with her then, and stay the night, because sometimes she was very sick. At first, I worried that it was embarrassing for her to have me see her retching in the bathroom, crying and vomiting until her bones seemed to rattle. She was always such a strong person, proud of being able to take care of herself, but now there were times when she could barely get herself out of bed. And then her hair began to fall out, so sometimes, as I half-carried her into the bathroom, I thought that she looked war-ravaged, almost, like someone who had been radiated, cursed, maybe driven mad in the aftermath of some unimaginable Armageddon. I asked her once, was it better for her that I was with her through these nights or worse, and she said, *Just stay with me. Sometimes I feel like I'm going to die.*

There was a night toward the end of summer when I heard her trying to make her way down the hallway to the bathroom long after midnight. I got out of bed to help her, and ended up sitting beside her, on the side of the tub while she hung over the toilet bowl. After a while, she slid down and sat on the bathmat, with her head against the wall. The room was like an aquarium; a school of orange and yellow fish as wide as fans swam across the shower curtain and next to the medicine chest was a framed poster of lime and lemony colored cartoon fishies, swishing their tails in bowls of blue water.

I was counting these fish—it was a habit I had gotten into, these nights in the bathroom—when Mary said, "Did I ever make a pass at you, Lynn?"

I had to run the words through my mind once or twice to make sure I understood her. Suggest a list of a hundred questions that I thought my friend Mary might ask me during the course of our lifetimes and I guarantee that one wouldn't have been on it. "No," I said. "At least I don't think so. Why? Do you want to make a pass at me now?" I knew I was smiling, and even if I shouldn't have been, I couldn't help myself. "I have to tell you, honeypie, it's not going to work."

"Don't be silly," Mary said. She looked at me, and I thought that her eyes weren't really focusing: she was here with me, but at the same time, she wasn't; not really. "I was just thinking about that bar we used to go to. Where we met."

"Oh God," I said, "I know where you mean. Cookie's, on Fourteenth Street in Manhattan. It was in the middle of the block, between a driving school and a place that sold vitamins and yoga mats. You're talking about a hundred years ago."

"We danced," Mary remembered.

"We did," I agreed. "And we started talking, and that was that. We've been friends ever since."

"Good," Mary said. "I just wanted to be sure."

She tried to pull herself up then, but quickly sat back down and shook her head. "Not yet," she said.

"Okay," I told her, though I didn't think she was really listening to me. "We can wait."

She was quiet for a while and then, suddenly, she said, "I should probably move out of this apartment. I mean, when all this is over. How could I go on living here?" She waved her hand. "All these fish."

"Where would you like to go?" I asked her.

"Maybe where you are."

"The towers of nowhere? Let's try to think of someplace better."

"I know," Mary said, almost seeming to brighten. "Let's both move down the shore. By next summer, we could be spending all our weekends at the beach. We could just walk down the block and the ocean would be right there. Wouldn't that be nice?"

"Sure," I said, but Mary had already gone someplace else; she had turned her head and looked off somewhere that I couldn't see.

"Where do you think Pattie is now?" she asked me.

"Who?" I asked, because it was late and I wasn't following the odd jumps from here to there that Mary's thoughts were making.

"Your Pattie," she said dreamily. "The blonde on the train."

"Oh, I don't know," I said. I hadn't thought about Pattie Boyd for weeks now; the deal with Jennifer Juniper was done and I had gone on to other things. "Swanning around on a boat in the lake district, wherever that is. Maybe in the Apennines, in a chalet, smoking a cigarette with someone who's much too young for her. Why?" I asked. "Where do you think she is?"

"I think she can't sleep," Mary said, answering some other question of her own. "She just can't settle into her own skin. From the outside, it seems like she should be just fine, you know—I mean, that's what I thought. What a life, right? But then, if you think about it some more, you have to admit that she was really just a lesser light, and that must bother her. Everything good that ever happened to her was because of somebody else, so now she tries too hard. Those snaps you told me about...the photos? The English call them snaps. Well, they probably mean a lot to her—the fact that she has something of her own. Something she can do all by herself, no matter who comes and goes in her life. I bet Linda felt like that, too. She was a photographer."

I was able to follow the conversation now; fragmented as it was, it made sense to me. I knew who Linda was. I suddenly remembered a picture I'd seen of her once, a black-and-white photo like one she might have taken herself, I imagine. It's taken from behind, and she's walking down some sunny street, on a warm, breezy day, with one arm around Paul and the other encircling one of her children. In the photo, she's looking back, over her shoulder, smiling at the camera: a young, happy woman, with the perfect life. On a perfect day.

"Do you think Pattie knew Linda?" Mary asked me.

"They probably all knew each other," I said. "Long ago and far away."

I managed to get Mary back to bed after that, but I didn't sleep well because I kept getting up to check on her. At seven, when I should have gotten myself up off the couch to go to work, I couldn't move, so I dozed for another two hours or so and finally got to my office at ten, which was late for me. I spent the rest of the day at my desk, getting things done that I had neglected for weeks: I made phone calls to people I had been avoiding, I did expense reports and paperwork that our accountant usually had to cajole me into turning in. I wrote memos, made plans to see clients. I was an absolute whirlwind, and when Beverly left at around five-thirty, I made sure to wave at her when she passed my office, so she could see that I was staying late. I don't know why that seemed important to me, but it did.

It was then that I finally got around to opening my mail. Among the correspondence and advertisements, I found a stiff, see-through envelope with a tinge of golden ink around the edges. Inside was an invitation from Jennifer Juniper to a party they were having in New York to officially launch the "Girlfriends" campaign for the Jennifer Juniper II line of beauty products. Their first print ads were already running in *Jane Street* as well as in a number of high-end women's magazines, but the billboards and TV spots were yet to come. With the invitation were a couple of inserts that were meant to look like those strip photos you used to have taken for a quarter in an amusement arcade, each showing a row of small black-and-white photos of a woman making exaggerated faces: pouty, grinning, swan-eyed, and sultry. There were three strips, and I had to read the captions on the back to recognize two of them: Angela Bowie, still looking remarkably dangerous, and Alana Stewart, showing off a great tan. But when I picked up the third strip, I had the sensation of gazing, suddenly, into the face of an old friend: there was Pattie, with her desperate-to-please smile, trying to change her expression for each different frame, but without much success. In each little black-and-white box she was looking straight out at the camera, and I could imagine someone standing just out of the frame—someone quite like Malcolm Morris—saying *kissy, kissy, darling; show us your glam face*, but she couldn't quite manage it. Something else was coming through in those photos, some fragile quality of disappointed hope that you couldn't help feeling sympathy for. At least I couldn't. I took the Pattie photo strip and put it in the pencil cup on my desk. I didn't think I was going to keep it there forever, but it seemed like a good place for it, for now.

I picked up the invitation again and noted that there was a phone number to RSVP. The area code was the same as for Jennifer Juniper, which meant it was a number in Indianapolis. It was after five now, in New York—what time was it in Indiana? As usual, I couldn't figure it out in my head, but since I was sitting by my computer, I was able to click on an icon that I had long ago downloaded onto my desktop; a bland, round clock face that actually linked to the web site of the atomic clock, which is maintained by the government and hidden away in the U.S. Naval Observatory in Washington, where it ticks away ceaselessly, perfectly, calibrating time, space, the rotation of the earth, and the procession of the stars from the time before humanity on into the infinite in order to report, in chiseled, blinking, atomic-colored knifepoints of computer-generated light the absolute, unquestionable time at any place on earth. It also, amazingly, has a voice, this clock: if you have a radio with a weather band, you can turn to a certain frequency and find it intoning the time in a deep, somewhat threatening and definitely nonhuman voice. You can't listen to it for more than a minute or two, though; after that, its indifferent certainty that relentless time must be precisely counted off, moment by moment, becomes unbearable.

The online clock told me it was only four-thirty in Indianapolis, so I called and told the secretary who answered the phone to put me on the list for the reception, and that I was bringing a guest. Then I called Mary and said, "Want to go to a party?"

"You have to be kidding," she replied.

She sounded weak, but I plunged on. "I am not," I told her. "It's a big bash being held by our anti-aging friends at Jennifer Juniper, and it might be fun. Free drinks, free cheese, free samples."

"I don't need that stuff," Mary said, and I was glad to hear at least a whisper of her fighting spirit remember it could growl. "Maybe you do."

"Oh, I do, absolutely," I said. "But I don't want to go myself. So in three weeks, when I know you'll be feeling better, you and I will take ourselves to a place called Plum on Little West 12th Street..."

"In the meatpacking district?"

"Yeah," I said. "Remember that? The cops used to pull up to the back door of those warehouses and drive away with their trunks full of steaks."

"I remember girl boys in hot pants," Mary said. "Or were they boy girls?"

"Whatever, they were making money," I replied. My apartment in the Village had been only blocks away from the neighborhood that had traditionally been where dozens of meat packing and processing businesses had been clumped together on narrow streets near the river; by night, when the warehouses were closed and the industrial freezers slowly bled ice and blood into the gutters, the streets belonged to the working girls of various genders. But no more: hotels were being built there now, with heated pools on the roof and Europeans sitting at the bar. Celebrities bought the multimillion dollar apartments in the condo towers being erected along these old streets and used them as bicoastal bedrooms.

"Oh, for the good old days," Mary said, and then she laughed. "Okay," she told me. "I'll try."

So a couple of weeks later, on a warm Friday evening after work, with the moon rising and the sky stippled with stars, I took the subway out to Brooklyn and arrived at Mary's apartment, ready to take her back to the city, to the "Girlfriends" launch party.

"That's what you're wearing?" she said to me, smiling away when I walked in.

"What's wrong with this?" I asked. I had on black jeans and a black pullover with beaded sleeves; an effect that I thought was sort of dressy casual. Gone were the dangerous days of leather pants and a hundred silver bracelets; maybe not gone for good, but gone for now. Gone until I could at least figure out what I was supposed to look like these days, when I was not buttoned into one of my Macy's-bought business suits.

Before Mary could answer me, I took a good look at her and said, "Wow. You look great."

And she did; for the first time in weeks, she did not look death haunted. She was still pale, still kind of wavering around the edges of being a human being, but this was, at least, definitely a good day, not a bad one. Donna had brought her a wig as a kind of joke—a silvery-blonde pageboy that she'd seen in the window of a store that sold magic tricks and costumes—but on Mary, it had the effect of creating a look, an attitude, that she had deliberately set out to achieve.

"Heroin chic, right?" she said, pulling me over to a mirror on the wall so we could both examine the silvery tendrils of hair that framed her face. Her eyes, still dazed with the lingering poison of killer drugs, looked like blue rays that were not quite burning at full power. "Is that still in? It better be, otherwise I don't think I can get away with wearing this in public." Then she shrugged, and turned away from her reflection. "Oh well," she said, "I guess anything is better than looking like a bald egg. If there is such a thing."

Since she was always chilly these days, Mary wrapped herself in a purple Pashmina and we headed for the subway. It was a short ride to the Christopher Street station in the Village, where we exited, amid a crowd of people, into the Friday night frenzy of a destination neighborhood for knowing young urbanites in ultra expensive clothes.

"Yikes, yikes, yikes," Mary said, as we headed west, passing one exotic restaurant after another; each dark interior, seen through windows tinted like the eyes of aliens, exuding mood, glittering with the light of tiny candles, hidden lamps. "Everybody's straight. When did that happen?"

"While we weren't looking," I told her as I guided her along. She held onto my arm, still a little unsteady on her feet, and that made me remember something I'd read in some guilty-pleasure gossip magazine I'd been leafing through in the supermarket: Paul said that his new wife—Heather, the one who had followed Linda—always held his arm when they walked along because she was an amputee, and for someone with a prosthetic limb, the surface underfoot should always be considered treacherous and untrustworthy.

When we turned the corner from Washington Street onto Little West 12th, narrow and cobbled, the red brick buildings I'd remembered, hung with carcasses to be processed and stacked with beef bones, had metamorphosed into high-end bars that had sprouted outdoor tables serviced by waitresses dressed in silk rags, with hair like long silk curtains. These hot spots were nestled beside the downtown outlets of uptown designers; the clothes in the windows made me think of kitty-kat fashions: sharp, sleek, designed to be worn by something with claws.

We knew where we were going because outside one of these buildings was a line of limos and a clutch of large men in sunglasses, glaring secretly into the night—these were the bodyguards, probably hired for the evening by Malcolm Morris and his Indiana minions to produce the effect of a high celebrity quotient inside. We approached one of the guardians of the velvet rope, who found our names were on the magic list that allowed us to enter Plum Bar, which turned out to be all steel surfaces lit by an orange glow, like a smoldering factory fire. Music was being blared at an inhuman decibel level, but after a few moments I was able to make out Tom Jones' booming voice wanting to know, "What's New, Pussycat?" It was inevitable that Petula Clark would be next, declaring the virtues of going downtown.

"We're back in the 60s," Mary said to me, shouting in my ear. "They're probably going to force us to eat brown rice."

"Can you have a drink?" I shouted back. "Because if you can, that might be a good idea."

"A spritzer," she told me. "As long as they don't make it with Boone's Farm."

Waiters, dressed in tie-dyed tee shirts and bellbottoms, were circulating among the crowd, but we couldn't get near them, so we made our way to the bar. As we squeezed through the chattering throng, we passed a clutch of sub-supermodels posing for photographs with three long-haired men who had creased faces, long hair, and wore sunglasses even darker than the ones displayed by the bodyguards outside.

"I think that was Steppenwolf," Mary said to me.

"I think this is all an illusion," I said, wiggling my fingers like a swami in the scented air; Jennifer Juniper fragrances, no doubt. "All Wavy Gravy."

"Cherry Garcia to you, too," she said, as we continued to try to push our way toward the mob of serious drinkers grouped around the bar.

When we had finally gotten two glasses of white wine, one liberally dosed with sparkling water, we decided to find out where they had stashed the celebs. The girlfriends. I assumed there had to be at least one or two of them here, and at events like these, they usually keep the stars of the show safely tucked away on a banquette somewhere, guarded by more of the sunglass brigade. We found them, eventually, at the far end of this steely space, a circle of three golden blonde heads and more than enough pretty boy escorts nodding, murmuring, glittering with their special, secret light. I recognized Malcolm Morris among the circle, although he was standing off to the side; basking in the pleasure of the company he was keeping, though, apparently, not quite important enough to slide right in among them.

I couldn't place two of the blondes—minor girlfriends, I imagined; some rock stars' old flames not quite famous enough to have reached photo-strip-in-the mailer level—but the third woman, who was wearing a ribbony dress and a long necklace of sea-colored stones, was, to me, instantly recognizable.

"Mary," I said, "that's Pattie Boyd."

Mary pulled herself up on tiptoe in order to see above the crowd. "You're right," she said. "Wow. All the way from England. The poor woman will probably go anywhere for a party." A moment passed as we tried to stand our ground amidst the press of noisy, jostling people and then, suddenly, Mary turned to me with what looked like tears in her eyes. "That was a mean thing for me to say," she told me. "I'm not like that, really. I don't say things like that."

"I know you don't," I told her, trying to sound soothing. "It's okay."

But despair immediately turned to determination. "I want to say hello to her," Mary said. She reached into her purse—an envelope-shaped handbag that I remembered her buying from a midtown street vendor two summers ago—and pulled out a black-and-white photograph; a glossy print of a movie still. "Where on earth did you get that?" I asked her when I saw what it was.

"I bought it on eBay," she told me. "Twenty-five dollars plus shipping." And then she was off, pushing her way through the crowd.

I followed after her, thinking that if she actually wanted to speak to Pattie Boyd, I might have to do some negotiating with Malcolm Morris, since you never actually get to talk to the celebs at a product launch, just admire them from afar. But maybe there was something about the way Mary looked with her silvery page boy framing her shining, wasted eyes—something fashionably retro, especially for this gathering—that gave her the air of someone who belonged among the golden blondes, because the beefcakes in sunglasses didn't stop her as she approached. I saw Malcolm glance at Mary with some concern, but then he recognized me, and once I smiled at him, he just smiled back and stayed where he was.

Standing just behind her, I saw Mary touch one of the blondes—*our* blonde—on the shoulder. "Miss Boyd?" she said.

Pattie turned around and I saw that face: thinner than I would have thought but still pretty and resolutely cheerful; a sweet girl's face grown older, still etched with dreams.

"Yes?" she said. And then, focusing on Mary, she reached up and touched her wig. "Oh, I like that," she said. "Very Carnaby Street, yeah? Maybe Mary Quant?"

"I had cancer," my Mary blurted out, and then looked shocked when she realized what she had said.

But Pattie's face was immediately shadowed by what seemed like real sympathy. "Did you, darling?" she said. "It's after everyone these days, isn't it? Horrible. Just horrible. Are you going to be alright?" Before Mary could begin to even form an answer to that question, Pattie noticed the photograph Mary was holding in her hand and, pointing to it, said, "What have you got there?"

Almost reluctantly, Mary showed her the glossy still—maybe she was embarrassed, now, to have brought with her this leftover bit of Beatlemania. Maybe Pattie didn't exactly need strangers offering her talismans of her old life at a party for her new one.

But again, Pattie's reaction seemed neither censored by a need to mask her feelings nor tempered by any sense of surprise or offense at how easily reminders of passing time and old identities could simply be thrust before her eyes. In fact, once she took a good look at the photo—*that* image from *that* film: a seventeen-year-old blonde girl in a school uniform, with long wisps of blonde hair falling into her eyes as she chats up Paul McCartney in a train car, a million years ago—she simply giggled. It was as if the golden girl in the photograph was an old friend, long gone but still fondly regarded and gladly met again. "My goodness," she said cheerfully. "Just look at me."

"Would you sign it for me?" Mary asked, and then told Pattie her name.

Mary produced a pen from her black bag and Pattie signed it, handing it back with a big, sweet smile. Mary thanked her and then turned to me to show me her prize.

"Look," she said. "*To Mary. Best wishes from Pattie Boyd.* She really did seem very nice. And still so pretty. Do you think she'll ever get married again?"

That's what she does, I was going to say, but remembering how upset Mary felt about the unkind remark she herself had made earlier, I refrained. Besides, Pattie had done nothing to earn that kind of cattiness from me; whatever her life was—easy, difficult, suffused with love or empty of it—she'd had the good grace to stop and share a pleasant conversation with a fellow traveler on an uncertain road. I probably should have been ashamed of myself for expecting something different.

In the moments it had taken me to look at the photograph and then back at Mary, her whole demeanor had suddenly changed. Fashionably pale had turned to pallor; something, suddenly, had gripped her and appeared ready to turn her inside out.

"Lynnie," she said to me in a gasping voice, "I don't feel well. I mean, I *really* don't feel well. It just came on so quickly..." She shook her head, as if she were angry with herself, but whatever resistance she was contemplating seemed to immediately collapse. "I think I'd better go home right now. Can you get a cab?" she said. "I don't think I can manage the subway."

It was a bad hour to try to get a taxi to take us to an outer borough, but I was already mapping out in my mind which street we should head for to try to track one down. Then I took Mary's hand and started leading her through the throng of people. *We're going to be alright*, I wanted to tell her, *we're going to make it*, but the bar was too crowded now, too noisy; she'd never hear me. Maybe, if Mary wasn't so sick, it was something I could turn back to tell Pattie—to ask her?—but I could see that the someone else was talking to her now; someone was handing her a glass a champagne as the sunglass brigade closed ranks around her. There was no way, now, that we would ever get near her again.

Woodstock, Again

In the early morning, Kay is in the kitchen, drinking coffee, as her dog watches her. Zero. He'd like some coffee, too, and she's thinking about giving him some. It's her fault that he's developed a taste for it—she's too quick to let him share whatever she's eating or drinking—but if he wants it, why not? He's a big dog; how hyper can he get from a few slurps of caffeine? It's morning, anyway; a little extra pep will help him get through his day. Kay pours some Mocha Java into the dog's bowl, just as the back door opens.

"Hey," says Sandy as she walks in. She's pulling a bag of golf clubs behind her. The bag has big rubber wheels for rolling across the greens. It's very eco-friendly.

"Morning," says Kay, who means nothing by it, just hello. At least, that's what she thinks she means, but Sandy's got her number.

"You're still mad at me," Sandy says.

"About what?" Kay asks, holding onto the fiction that she is fine, just fine.

"Last night," Sandy says.

"I was never mad," Kay tells her, though she's not sure whether or not that's completely true. "Just surprised. Astounded, actually. You're such a bright woman, so smart. How can you believe a nutty thing like that?"

"It's not nutty," Sandy says. "It's true. Nobody ever landed on the moon; the government just faked it all."

"In a hanger, on a set, in...where was it?" Kay says. "Hollywood?"

"Nevada," Sandy replies.

"Where they keep the crashed UFOs under wraps, too?"

Sandy is not backing down on her side of the argument, but at the same time, she's smiling at Kay. If Kay was in the mood, she might assume that Sandy's smile could lead to a truce, but instead, she simply sees it as a character trait which, on a better morning, she would appreciate: Kay's view of Sandy is that she is a true, sunny, California-bred blonde: swimming, hiking, golfing, anything done under the sun makes her happy, keeps her happy for hours. So fine, she's been out playing golf in the autumn sunshine, so maybe she feels light and breezy, but Kay feels as crazy as she did last night when, out of the blue, Sandy announced that she did not believe human beings had ever actually landed on the moon. Well, not completely out of the blue; they had been watching a show on PBS about the 1960s, which featured the usual grainy frame-by-frame of Neil Armstrong's foot landing on the cold gray surface of our nearest neighbor in the sky. Our friend, our nightlight, that shining orb of green cheese.

"I don't believe in UFOs," Sandy says.

"I know," Kay tells her. "We went through this last night. You don't believe in UFOs, you're as horrified as I am about the intelligent design loonies, you're sure Oswald killed Kennedy, and you don't for a minute believe that 9/11 was an inside job. So why this? What's so appealing about this particular conspiracy theory?"

"I've read about it. They built a set. They wanted to scare the Russians into thinking they couldn't possibly win the Cold War."

"It seems impossible to me that you're serious about this," Kay says.

"It's not just me," Sandy mildly replies. "There's a whole online community."

Kay can't listen to this anymore; it's just too much. It's illogical, it's wacky, it's way out there. But then, she reminds herself, they're living in the capital of way out there; they're living in Woodstock, New York, U.S.A.

Any way, why are they here? In this place that Kay doesn't think she really likes, though she thought that she liked the idea when Sandy first proposed it: to sell their Brooklyn condo and move up here, to the country, to this old hippie enclave where Kay's friend Barb lives—Barb who runs a gallery where Sandy, a photographer, exhibits and sells her work—and where they could live inexpensively in a little house on an acre of meadow and wildflowers. Kay, who had actually been to the Woodstock festival a million years ago (*Three days of peace and music! They've closed the New York State Thruway, man!*) when she was a teenager and had to explain to Sandy that it didn't really take place in Woodstock but in Bethel, a nearby town, hadn't minded coming up here on weekends now and then. But living here for real, day and night, summer, winter, spring and fall, had turned out to be something else entirely. The Woodstock Festival had been mud and drugs and dancing in the rain—all fine when you're fourteen and your parents are going to kill you when you get home because they said no, you can't go, but you went anyway. But now? Kay was born in the Bronx; she'd lived in the Village and later (a big move, in her mind, like voyaging to foreign shores) in Park Slope, with Sandy. In other words, she is a city girl. (A city middle-ager? What do you call yourself when you're fifty-five?) No way had she been prepared for life in the boondocks, no matter how hip the tiny, artsy town at the center of the community still was.

Still, here she is, back in Woodstock, again, probably for a long time. Possibly for good. Living in a manner that can only be described—in Kay's mind, at least—as *rural*, a word that she is beginning to associate with other words like *spooky* and *cold, cold, cold.* Come November, she'd already be wearing two sweaters under her parka and those ridiculous boots with laces and snaps and what looked like tire-tread soles that she'd bought at the Minnetonka store. *Rural*: there are bears in the woods and the mountains often seem to lean down on her like witch's hats. Like those cyclopean beings H.P. Lovecraft wrote about in his crazy horror stories: big pyramids of earthy goo. Plus, she's a little worried about serial killers out there on the roads (she's seen enough slasher movies to know that the real danger of being a victim of bodily harm isn't in a well-lit city but in some backwoods cabin surrounded by fields of stunted crops), which is why Zero, a big shepherd mix, is now a member of the family. Sandy thinks that Kay just likes dogs—and she does, but she's secretly hoping that Zero has a little wolf in him; that he'll foam at the mouth and bite anyone who might approach her with an axe when they're out for a walk.

Why is she out on the roads, anyway, on foot? Because she hates to drive. The house is close enough to Tinker Street and the Village Green so that she can walk back and forth to the local stores when she needs certain things like coffee or a bottle of wine. (She could also get incense, handmade jewelry and sandals, fringed jackets, artworks, geodes, vintage posters of rock concerts at the Fillmore East and West, candles and tarot cards, some of the things that the tourists who flood the town on the weekends stuff into their cars and drive away with.) If, however, real groceries—including big bags of dog food—are required to keep the household running smoothly and Sandy, the driver in the family, happens to be out taking pictures or playing golf, then Kay has to drive to the next town, Phoenicia, where there is a sort of supermarket. Not super-sized, actually, but it carries the basics. Phoenicia is an even smaller town than Woodstock, but Kay usually doesn't have to parallel park, which is her biggest problem; she can just kind of glide the car toward the curb near the end of Main Street, carrying out an action that she thinks is probably something like docking a boat. The town always seems almost empty to Kay, but Sandy has told her that the surrounding roads winding up into the mountains are studded with houses built at great expense, cantilevered over chilly lakes and wrapped in winterized decks with clear-day views of the great white north. Who lives in these houses? Screenwriters resting from their travails in L.A., celebrity stylists, dress designers recovering from the launch of their latest line of vampire glam. Sandy meets some of these people on the Woodstock golf course, a surprisingly proper place, considering its locality (no tank tops, no short shorts, no sweat pants allowed) which rolls over an expanse of grassy acres near their house.

"I'm going to do some work," Kay says to Sandy.

"Me, too," Sandy says. "After I take a shower." Leaving the bag of golf clubs near the kitchen door, she turns to leave the room and head upstairs, but stops after a few steps. "Think about Capricorn One," she says to Kay.

"That was a *movie*," Kay says, "And besides, it was about a faked landing on Mars, not the moon."

"Well, they couldn't use what really happened," Sandy says. "But so many people know that Capricorn One is based on the staged moon landing that the movie has been suppressed."

"No it hasn't," Kay says. "You can get it on NetFlix." She actually hasn't had time to look up whether or not that's true, but she's willing to bet it is. Besides, she's sure she remembers seeing Capricorn One in the cable movie listings some time back.

"With important parts edited out," Sandy says. She walks swiftly back toward Kay and swipes a quick kiss across her check. "If you don't want to think about Capricorn One," Sandy says, "think about how much you love me." And then she heads for the shower.

Now Kay is wondering again—as she did last night—whether or not Sandy is serious about this. Maybe she's just enjoying teasing Kay and will eventually admit that of course man walked on the moon, planted a stiff American flag and said that thing about one small step.

Or maybe not. As Kay leaves the kitchen, exiting by the back door, she thinks about how impossible it is to live with people. Men or women—she's lived with both—and thinks they're equally crazy. They think and do crazy things, and when you ask them why, they give you crazy reasons. Or they start drinking too much or taking drugs. Sandy, Kay knows, suffers from neither problem. Can she really, in every other way, be a sane, creative, and sensible person and still hold such a contrary idea in her head as this moon business? Apparently, anything is possible.

Kay leaves the kitchen, followed by Zero, and walks across the yard to the small, one-room studio that sits at the edge of their property. This little building, cooled in the summer by breezes wafting across a reedy creek nearby and warmed in the winter by an overhead space heater, is one of the reasons that Kay allowed herself to be talked into moving here. It's an inviting place: she likes the way the sunlight slides through the windows and makes wavy puddles on the floor; she likes the paint splatters left by the artist who preceded her. And it's a perfect place for her to work. Kay builds harpsichords from Edelberg Kits. They are remarkably high-quality instruments and in great demand. Long ago, after Kay finished high school, she had lots of jobs: she worked in a stained glass factory, she cut hair, she typed invoices for a tool company. And, for many years, she had worked for Edelberg Harpsichords, carefully packing the handmade pieces that a buyer used to build an instrument. Edelberg sold kits for harpsichords, spinets, and clavichords. Sometimes, someone who had bought a kit but couldn't manage to put it together (it did require some woodworking skill and an ear capable of tuning strings) sent it back to have the company complete it for them. Once, when there were too many of these projects on hand, Kay was asked if she'd like to try her hand at finishing one of them off. It turned out she had a talent for building these instruments—both rescuing botched projects and later, putting together instruments from kits she bought herself, at a discount, and then sold—and she liked doing it. Making harpsichords from Edelberg kits and selling them had become a way to make a living; the company even listed her contact information now on their website so buyers could get in touch with her directly.

The instrument parts and the tools she needs are arranged neatly on shelves in the studio, which also houses a table saw, a grinding wheel, and a drill press. Zero stretches himself out in a favorite corner and drifts off into dreamland. Kay turns on the radio—a local station is playing deep album cuts from the English invasion—and spends an hour assembling jacks for a Flemish single harpsichord she's working on. While she works, she feels peaceful and content.

But she's not really planning to spend her day in the studio. Around nine, she wakes her dog and leads him back to the house, where he finds another favorite place to continue his morning nap. Kay tries to call Sandy, who's left a note saying she's out taking pictures, but cell phone reception in this mountainous area is notoriously poor and she can't even get voice mail. So she leaves a note, too, reminding Sandy where she'll be today, and heads back out the door.

She's going into town to catch a bus to the city. The walk takes only ten minutes and it's not a route that worries her in terms of armed loonies coming out of the woods. True, she's walking a country road, but it's a bright morning, just on the edge of fall, and her path takes her past a number of her neighbors' houses. Everybody seems to have put out flags this season, the kind you buy in garden centers: rainbow flags, peace signs, smiling pumpkins saying *Welcome, Autumn!* are flapping from just about every front porch.

She enjoys the walk. The cool morning breezes feel like scarves floating by and the mountains, colored by the turning leaves of the trees massed all along their slopes, from earth to sky, seem to be keeping their distance. They are undeniably beautiful; the kind of scenery that will crowd the town with tourists again this weekend. Fall foliage and old hippies: Woodstock's stock in trade.

In town, she stops in the bakery to buy more coffee and a newspaper. Since everybody knows everybody here, Kay exchanges greetings with Meggy, the woman working behind the counter this morning, who is another California refugee, a surfer girl who spent the psychedelic years traveling the world chasing waves and boys and who, fifty pounds heavier and decades past her adventures, has landed in Ulster County, New York, hunkered down with the last of the tribe in their mountain enclave. Meggy introduces Kay to the only other customer in the store this morning, a small, nut-colored man in saffron robes whose name Kay doesn't quite catch, but it sounds something like Tenzig. He is a monk from Thailand, visiting the nearby Karma Triyana Dharmachakra monastery on Overlook Mountain. When Meggy tells him that Kay is a harpsichord maker, the monk engages her in a surprisingly informed conversation about the development of the clavichord, which must be played with skill and is almost silent; savoring its whispered music is itself an art form. Afterwards, standing on the street in the sharp morning sunshine, Kay wonders about the fact that a monk from the edge of Asia would know so much about the historical antecedents of a 14th century European keyboard instrument. But then who can predict, Kay thinks, what people will take an interest in.

The bus is on time and Kay naps for part of the two-and-a-half hour ride. She's a good traveler; she can sleep anywhere. In particular, the act of travel itself—being carried along a road, over the rails, or even through the sky in a plane—lulls her into a deep doze. She wakes up when they're closing in on the New York City skyline and has the reaction she always has, no matter where she's coming from, no matter how long or short a time she's been away: *Home*, she thinks. *Home*.

Which is why she's on the bus in the first place. Her destination today is the workshop of a man named Shimmel Epps, who makes hand-tooled soundboard roses. She has ordered two of them from Epps; one for the instrument she is working on now and one for a kit that someone is sending her to finish for him. That customer wants an ornate rose made from contrasting black walnut heartwood and lighter-colored sapwood, figured around the initials of his name. Kay could certainly have these items shipped to her, but it's an easy trip back and forth between Woodstock and New York, so why not come in person, just so she can be in the city for a few hours? Once in a while, she thinks, you can just have enough of nature. Taxis and skyscrapers can be good for the soul, too.

The bus lets her out at the Port Authority terminal. She makes her way to Seventh Avenue and then walks downtown, to what was the old fur district of the city but now, like every other corner of Manhattan, is slowly turning into upscale condo buildings surrounded by stores selling pricey clothes and fancy food. Here and there, however, a block still looks pretty much as it was decades ago, when shirt-sleeved men sat at the ranks of sewing machines on the sagging loft floors of these soot-stained brick buildings, piecing together pelts for coats and stoles. The furriers are gone now, of course, replaced by other small business enterprises and some residential conversions, but these are still old streets, hard streets, where making a living still seems like it might be a day-to-day gamble.

The building Kay wants is a narrow structure with a gritty coffee shop on the ground floor and the chutes-and-ladders of a rusted fire escape zig-zagging across the upper floors. There is a freight elevator in the building, but no one to operate it and it's not for passengers, anyway, so Kay walks up seven floors to Mr. Epps' workshop. She knocks and he lets her in—a small man in a vest and cuffed pants, with an egg-colored yarmulke on his head. His workspace is also small: one room, with an ancient desk, a workbench, and a few tools. The light is sparse, leaking through a window of what seems to be gray glass. Whenever Kay is here, she always finds herself thinking that she's in a different century than the one in which her studio exists, back in Woodstock. Maybe even a different continent, a whole other world.

Mr. Epps greets Kay in Yiddish and her secret—a secret only because no one would expect it of her except Sandy; this is something Sandy certainly knows—is that she can reply in the same language. In fact, though not with great fluency, Kay can carry out most of her conversations with Mr. Epps in Yiddish. It was the language of her grandparents, and, though less reliant on it, her parents spoke it as well, which meant that Kay absorbed it. Much of it remains in her memory, like a box of words carefully packed up and preserved for use when needed, as it is now.

Epps gives Kay one of the roses, the more traditional one carved of fruitwood in a Florentine style, which she will use for the kit she is assembling, and then shows her a pencil sketch of the one he's yet to make, which will include the intertwined initials. Kay takes the scrap of paper on which Mr. Epps has done the sketch and puts it in the padded envelope she has brought with her to protect the fruitwood rose. She thinks the design of the more elaborate—and expensive—rose is perfect, and intends to send the sketch to her customer. In her experience, people like to see things like this, the odd bits and pieces that go into making their harpsichords, and they like to keep them as souvenirs—evidence of the eccentric creativity that has made their instrument, though built from a kit, both special and unique.

As Kay is writing a check for the roses, Mr. Epps excuses himself to use the men's room, which is outside, in the common hallway. He's back before Kay has even closed her checkbook, and he looks wild-eyed, frightened.

He runs over to the window and struggles with the ancient sash, which probably hasn't been lifted for decades. Taking a putty knife from his workbench, he stabs at the paint-encrusted edges of the window, trying to set it free from the grip of time. Kay is so surprised by all this that as she fixes her gaze on his thin hands, balled together as they grip the knife, it hardly even occurs to her to try to figure out what he's doing, or why.

Finally, she realizes that he's muttering something about the office next door. Once, Epps had mentioned that it was a diamond showroom, of sorts, a place where one of the 47th Street diamond merchants could bring customers who wanted privacy, to view diamonds the seller didn't necessarily want anyone else to see. In other words, nobody is supposed to know that the showroom exists, but somebody obviously does because, if Kay is hearing Epps right, he's trying to tell her that the diamond dealers next door are being robbed—and by men with guns.

Still, what is he trying to do? Kay is frightened herself now, but there's nothing in this room that anyone would want to steal. The best thing for them to do is make sure the door is locked and then stay quiet, but that plan is clearly not the one they're going with. As Epps continues to hack away at the window, Kay thinks to pull her cell phone out of her shoulder bag and dial 911; speaking softly, she tells the operator that there's a robbery in progress and gives her the address. The operator tells her to stay on the line, but she can't; unbelievably, Epps has pried the window open and is now lifting it open as far as it will go. There is, it seems, just enough room for them to jump out into space.

"Gey, gey," Epps says to Kay, gesturing frantically. *Go, go.* He's clearly trying to make her go out the window.

She walks over to him, thinking that maybe she should try to pull him away from the window and—what? Tie him to a chair until he calms down? But as she approaches, Kay sees that there is another fire escape here, fixed to the back of the building. Quickly, Epps pull himself up on the window ledge and begins to climb the metal stairs to the roof.

Kay follows him—what else can she do? Epps is an old man—at least Kay thinks he's old; it's hard to tell. He could be just a little older than Kay; he could be ancient. But she can't leave him alone, not when he seems to be terrified, even panicked. More, she thinks, than the situation calls for. This isn't TV; she doesn't think whoever came to rob the diamond merchants would choose to top off their day by chasing the neighbors up a fire escape. And now across the roof, because once they get there, Epps does not stop; he sprints across the tarry surface of the building they've just escaped from and heads for the brick parapet. In the distance, Kay can hear the wail of police sirens, coming closer.

The buildings here are all the same height and so close together that it's just a matter of a stretched-out step to get from one roof to another. Epps crosses these divides—one after another—without hesitation and Kay, though she does stop for a moment to consider the consequences of a misstep (probably none, she doesn't think there's even enough space between the buildings to allow for a fall) finally sprints after him realizing that now they are in full escape mode. With his vest flapping in the breeze, Shimmel Epps seems ready to run across all the rooftops of Manhattan.

As they keep going, Kay becomes convinced that Epps can't have taken flight just because he got a glimpse of a robbery—they've got to be at least a block away now from the scene of the crime. Then what are they running from? The usual demons that come to mind: Cossacks? Nazis? Or some more recent nightmare? Because it must be a nightmare that's at their backs now. But just as Kay can't pinpoint Epps' age, she has no idea where he's from, so can't guess at whether his fear is rooted in some European or Russian vision of torment. Or perhaps it's rooted in South America, or the Middle East. The fact that he speaks Yiddish means nothing; Yiddish traveled wherever it was chased. He could have spoken Yiddish in Shanghai or Buenos Aires. Kay's own grandparents spoke Yiddish and she never got a straight answer about where they came from: the old country, a bad place, a land of monsters. *We're here now*, was the clear message. *This is where we're from.*

Finally, Epps stops running. He hunkers down beside the steel-banded leg of a wooden water tower and puts his head in his hands. He's breathing hard, but is otherwise uncommunicative; to Kay's repeated question about whether or not he's alright, he answers nothing

She sits down beside him and decides to just wait a while before suggesting that maybe it's safe to go back. Which she assumes it must be; how long would your average diamond robbery go on for, anyway? Surely, the men with guns will have gotten what they want by now and be gone.

But in the meantime, she thinks, as she finds herself calming down, it actually isn't bad up here on the roof. In a way, she thinks, it's like a vacation. Like a song: in her mind, she can hear the Drifters trilling away: *Up on the roo-oo-f.* Perhaps this relaxed point of view is so readily available to her because there was a time when city rooftops were, for Kay, just another playground. She remembers being on the roof of the building where she grew up, in the Bronx: that was where her mother hung the laundry to dry; that was where she accompanied her father on his many trips to wrestle with the television aerial. There were often kids and parents on the roof, carrying out some part of their lives. The blue sky overhead, tar paper underfoot; often enough, that was the scenery of just another ordinary day.

The sky is blue today, too: it looks crisp and snappy, presenting itself as a nice topper to a brisk fall day. Even the moon is in view as it sometimes is in the afternoon, a pale preview of the bright disk it will become in the evening hours. *You*, Kay finds herself thinking as she spies this moon's round face peeping into the world before the hour when it is expected. *Troublemaker.*

Just then, her phone rings. She doesn't recognize the caller ID but answers anyway, and finds herself speaking to a policeman who identifies himself as Officer Cabey. They have, of course, gotten her number from her 911 call and now, says Officer Cabey, he'd like to talk to her about the robbery she reported.

"It wasn't actually me who saw anything," Kay tells the officer. "It was my, uh, friend." That seems like the easiest way, at the moment, to describe Mr. Epps, who now seems to be talking to himself, mumbling softly. Maybe, Kay thinks, he's praying.

"Well then, we'd like to talk to him," says Cabey.

"That's a little complicated," Kay tells him. "We're on the roof. We sort of ran away."

"That was probably a sensible thing to do," says Cabey, "though I don't know if I would have headed for the roof. Anyway, it's safe to come back. The place," he says theatrically, possibly hoping for a tension-reducing laugh, "is crawling with cops."

Kay, who considers herself a New Yorker through and through, thinks that she knows cops. All New Yorkers, she believes, think this, because they're everywhere, and because during the course of your life in the city, you're going to deal with them in one way or another. Traffic tickets, noise complaints, bar fights, neighborhood spats—get involved in anything like that and you're going to get to know a cop. Like anyone else, they're heroes and villains, good guys and bad. This one on the phone, Kay thinks, is a good one—and funny, humorous. Probably he thinks she might still be scared and he's trying to make light of the situation to put her at ease. She is at ease though, now; it's her new "friend" who seems to need help.

"I think we have to wait a little while," Kay tells Cabey. "My friend is an older gentleman and he's a little out of it right now."

"Do you need a paramedic?" the officer asks.

"Maybe later," Kay tells him. "I think, right now, we should just sit here for a while."

"We could have some guys climb up the fire escape," Cabey tells her.

"Well," Kay replies, "it might not be so easy. We're definitely not on the roof of the building where we started, but I'm not sure where we've exactly ended up. Actually," she says, looking around her at the ledges and chimney pots that seem to stretch from horizon to horizon, "we could be on the Upper West Side for all I know. Let me call you back in a while."

"You have my number," he says pleasantly, but then adds, "I'll give you fifteen minutes and if I don't hear from you, I'll give you a ring."

There you go, Kay thinks as the call snaps off, that's the police for you. Even the nice guys have to show you who's in charge.

She waits a while longer, watching the clouds drifting by, big cottony puffs heading west toward New Jersey, the Continental Divide, the deep blue ocean on the other side of the map that pops up in her mind. Checking her watch, she realizes that a lot more time than she thought has gone by and probably, she'd better call Sandy and tell her what's going on and that she might be late. But she can't get through—it's like there's a force field around Woodstock, which is lacking in cell towers, anyway. Still, when Kay's phone rings a few minutes later, she imagines that somehow, it's Sandy calling her. Why not? They've lived together a long time—there is the possibility of telepathic communication. There is also, of course, the possibility that Sandy is not answering the phone because she's decided to be mad at Kay for being so cranky this morning, when the fight—if it was a fight—should have been over last night. This possibility makes Kay feel much more anxious than she would have if she were on her way home to straighten things out instead of marooned on a rooftop. In any case, it's not Sandy on the phone, it's the police again, though this time, nice Officer Cabey is not on the line. Instead, it's someone who says he's Sergeant Davis and he is decidedly unpleasant.

"Look, Miss Lomann," he says in a voice growling with aggression, "we want to talk to Shimmel Epps and we want to talk to him now. We want to make sure he's alright."

When Kay made the 911 call, she gave her full name but never mentioned Mr. Epps, so she knows the police have been doing some checking. Fine. So they probably know she's a harpsichord maker from Woodstock—what do they think, that she's gone crazy and has decided to hold this frail old fellow hostage on a roof? Because she is getting the distinct impression that in fact, that is what they think. Ridiculous as it is, Kay figures that she'd better try to appear cooperative, so she turns to Mr. Epps and tries to hand him the phone. But he's still praying—Kay is convinced now that must be what he's doing—and he doesn't acknowledge her.

"He doesn't seem to want to talk right now," Kay finally says to Sergeant Davis.

"I think we're going to have to come up there and see for ourselves," warns the sergeant. Kay finds herself envisioning him at the head of a posse, with six-guns drawn—obviously, she thinks, she watched too much TV as a child. Or maybe it's just Woodstock kicking in: she's trying, she's trying, but how seriously is she supposed to take that threat?

"You know what?" Kay says, losing patience. "I sort of wish you would. This was fine for a while but now I'm getting cold. And I've already missed the bus that I planned to take home so sure, please, come find us. We'll be the two people sitting under the water tower. My friend seems to be talking to God, but I'll be the one waving hello."

The phone call ends, and Kay spends the next few minutes watching the far rooftops as if they were the ridges over which the bad guys will soon come riding. But no one appears. A couple of pigeons land nearby, coo at each other as they peck around for a while and then fly away. Overhead, the bright sun and the more modest moon are keeping their distance from each other, but still sharing the same sky.

Kay tries Sandy again, but still has no luck, so she decides to call her brother, Joey, who lives in Vermont. For whatever reason, the Green Mountains are much more forgiving about cell phone calls.

Joey is Kay's older brother, by three years. When they were both teenagers, he was the one who originally decided to go to what the posters in all the headshops actually called an Aquarian Festival taking place at Max Yasgur's farm and let her tag along. He was a hippie through and through and now runs an organic food collective in a small town where many of the residents were once members of the same commune. Long ago, in the days when the revolution was winding down, Kay tried living there, but she only lasted about three days; there was a little too much togetherness for her, too little privacy. Still, they like each other, Kay and Joey, and they keep in touch.

When Joey answers the phone in the far north, Kay says, "It's me. And you'll never guess where I am."

He guesses Panama, which he claims is the first thing that came into his head, and after Kay says no, she fills him in on what's going on. "The worst part of it is," she says, "I can't get Sandy on the phone."

"But she knows where you are," Joey says. "I mean, not exactly, but generally."

"We had a fight," Kay tells him. "I thought it wasn't bothering me, but it is."

"What did you fight about?" Joey asks.

"It was stupid. She doesn't believe that we've been to the moon."

"We haven't."

"Don't you start with me, too." Kay says. "I don't mean *us*, I mean humans. Men. Astronauts."

"Why does she have to believe that?" Joey asks. "Everybody's allowed at least one eccentricity, aren't they? That's yours, by the way," Kay's brother tells her. "You can't stand eccentricity. If the counterculture had survived, you would have been crazy."

"That's not true," Kay says. She's offended, but she's not sure why.

"Okay," her brother says kindly, "Maybe not entirely crazy. Just a little."

Ignoring him, Kay says, "You don't think she would have turned off her phone, do you? Because she's mad at me?"

"Of course not," Joey replies. "The Woodstock Nation is still open to messages of love and forgiveness."

"Tell that to Sergeant Davis," Kay says.

"You aren't really in trouble, are you?" Joey asks, sounding worried.

"I don't think so," Kay tells him. "But I better see if I can do something about getting off this roof."

Just as Kay concludes the call with her brother, she feels a hand on her arm. It's Mr. Epps, back from wherever he had decided to retreat to for a while. "Miss Lomann?" he says. "I think I'm alright now." His eyes are blurry, but not, Kate thinks, with tears.

They sit together companionably for a few minutes, shoulder to shoulder beneath the moving clouds. Finally, Mr. Epps stands up. "We should go back?" he says, and while, of course, they have to go back, Kay thinks she understands the question in his voice.

"The police are probably there," Kay tells him. "They're going to want to know what you saw."

"What I saw," Mr. Epps says with a long sigh. "What I saw. Better they should ask, what didn't I see."

Kay thinks she understands that, too—maybe not exactly in the way Shimmel Epps means it, but that's okay. She helps him up and then follows him back over the rooftops, retracing their steps. Mr. Epps seems to know exactly where he's going, which leads Kay to think that maybe, this is an escape route he already had prepared for himself. Just in case.

When they pull themselves back through the window into Mr. Epps' workshop, there are, in fact, several policemen there, and more next door where the robbery actually took place. None, however, seems to be either Officer Cabey or Sergeant Davis. Perhaps those were pseudonyms; perhaps they don't exist. Perhaps they are elements in some good cop/bad cop ruse written down in some manual, somewhere. In any event, Shimmel Epps is quickly swarmed by both the police and his neighbors, the robbery victims—three orthodox Jews in long black coats—plus their employees, who are chattering in both Yiddish and Russian, along with assorted family members (women, more men, children) who have been summoned to the scene and have brought with them plates of food wrapped in tinfoil, bottles of flavored water and, Kay can tell from the snatches of Yiddish she overhears, cash and their checkbooks, just in case the robbery is some sort of harbinger of worse to come: you never know when the authorities might have to be bribed, tickets purchased for cross-border escapes. In this atmosphere, even the police officers quickly calm down about their witnesses' rooftop adventure and though every time Kay gives her name and address and they get to the part where she says, *Woodstock*, she gets a suspicious look even from those cops who are too young to really understand what they're reacting to (something from ancient history but definitely anti-establishment, troublemaking, involving uncontrollable crowds), they quickly sort out that she saw nothing, knows nothing about what happened, and simply kept their real witness company while he spent a couple of hours absorbed in prayer. That's what she says, that's what he says, and it all seems to make sense to the kind and sympathetic neighbors who keep apologizing to Mr. Epps that their misfortune has caused him so much distress. These conversations (*What did you see? How do you feel? Can you describe the man who had the gun? Would you like a chicken sandwich?*) seem destined to go on for some time, but Kay is finally told that she can leave. Mr. Epps, with whom, up until the point they both climbed out his window, Kay has had a rather formal business relationship, actually kisses her good-bye, and then she is released into the golden fall afternoon. Already, though, the edges of evening are darkening the horizon; this is the season of short hours, when the curtain collapses on daylight before anyone expects it.

Kay walks back to Port Authority, but has to wait a long time for a bus headed back up the New York State Thruway. When she's safely aboard, and she sees the signs for Sloatsburg, which means they really have left the city behind, she dozes off again, waking only as the bus turns off the main road, heading into Woodstock. She alights from the bus near the Village Green, where someone is sitting on the grass, quietly playing the guitar. A few people are standing around, listening to the notes drifting up into the night sky.

Kay is expecting to walk home, but then she hears a dog barking, and turns to see that Sandy is just rising from a bench across the street, and is waving at her. Zero, who has already announced his presence, is sitting at her side.

"How did you know what bus I would be on?" Kay asks Sandy once they are together.

"Joey called to tell me where you were," Sandy replies. "So I guessed. Actually, I met the last bus, too."

Apparently, Kay decides, the force field is only blocking communiqués from New York City; the channels to Vermont are clear. Those jealous mountains must grant each other some sort of mutual right-of-way.

Sandy suggests that since neither of them have eaten, they might as well have dinner in town. They go to a local restaurant on Tinker Street that has a menu heavy on tofu, but that's alright, Kay actually likes tofu. In most places, dogs, of course, are not permitted in restaurants, but this is Woodstock and hey, rules are made to be broken—except, of course, on the golf course—so Zero is welcomed into the tofu place (which is actually somewhat famous; it is a locale that has appeared in numerous songs and memoirs over the years) and winds himself around Kay's feet, under the table. All through dinner, she feeds him the extras that come with her meal: cherry tomatoes, sesame sticks, rice. So does Sandy.

"So," Sandy says, before their food is served, "you had an adventure today."

"You wouldn't believe it," Kay answers.

"Yes I would," Sandy says. "Tell me everything."

And Kay does, in great detail, leaving out only the part about how, when she was on the bus nearing New York and saw the skyline, she thought, *home.* That would only hurt Sandy's feelings, and Kay doesn't want to do that, especially right now, when nobody seems to be mad at anybody anymore, about anything. Last night has been replaced by tonight.

Sandy has not brought the car, so after dinner, she and Kay do have to walk back to their house. It gets so dark up here at night, on these country roads, that even if you know where you're heading, some of the time you're really going on instinct. Kay and Sandy do alright though, finding their way, partly because they can follow the dog, who, in his heart of hearts, believes that he can navigate his way around Woodstock with a blindfold on, and partly because it's a bright night: the sky is lit up like a highway of stars. In its own corner of the sky, the moon—which intends to rise quite high tonight; it's round and full and feeling feisty—looks on at these two earthbound women and their dog, just as it looks on at almost everyone, with friendly interest. It probably does have a human footprint on its surface, but just one—or two, or three—is not enough. It likes visitors. It wants more.

Photographs

Keller! Keller! Keller, Keller, Keller!

She hears her name called, but incorporates it into her dream so that she is being summoned by her old boss in the Post Office, who wants her to sort packages in a dark room, on a cold morning, and the packages are heavier than the union rules say she has to handle. And then the scene changes and she is out on the street, in a bleary dawn, and someone she can't see is calling her from a woods. Of course, there really is no woods across from the postal substation in Brooklyn where she used to work, but she doesn't think about that, in the dream.

Again, *Keller! Keller!* and finally she wakes up, still tired, trying to focus her eyes on the clock beside her bed. Nine a.m. She could have slept for hours more.

Keller!

At last, she realizes who's calling her: Yudi, the man who lives downstairs. Old man, crazy man, disabled man: she's not sure. He's thin and grizzled looking, and sometimes asks her for help with small things: sometimes he seems to have trouble reading his mail, which occasionally brings Social Security checks but little else, and sometimes he wants to use her phone, because he doesn't have one. The only place she has ever heard him call is the drugstore, which he always argues into delivering his blood pressure medicine even though he could walk there himself. What he has never done before, not in the entire year and what?—one year and two months—that she has lived in this building, is scream her name the way he has been for the past five minutes. Or more.

Jane Keller gets out of bed and grabs her raincoat, the first thing that comes to hand because it's hanging over a chair near the door, and goes out onto the first floor landing. There's Yudi, standing in the tiny lobby below, huffing and puffing.

"What's the matter?" Jane calls down to him. Normally, she would have better manners than to shout in the hallway, but there's no one to disturb: there are only two other apartments upstairs and one other next door to her, all occupied by immigrant families whose adult members seemingly work all the time; at this hour, the children of these families are in school. There is no one home in this small building except herself and Yudi, who lives on the first floor in what must have once been some kind of commercial space. It has its own entrance and two small windows facing the street, which have been occluded by frosted glass.

Jane begins making her way down the stairs, and realizes that she is wearing socks, but no shoes. Yudi is still semi-hyperventilating in the hallway, but has not answered her. So again, she asks, "What's wrong?"

"There are people outside!" Yudi finally calls back to her, though she is only a few steps away from him now. There's no need to shout. "They want to come in!"

"What kind of people?" Jane asks as she begins advancing down the stairs.

"Dopes!" Yudi tells her. "Two dopes!"

What can he possibly mean? Jane wonders. Dope fiends? Is he from a generation that would describe people that way? And *could* there be dope fiends outside at nine a.m. on a weekday? Well, there could be *somebody* dangerous. There have been a number of home invasions around here lately, so it's best to be careful.

Just as Jane reaches the ground floor landing, Yudi pops himself back into his apartment and closes the door, leaving only a crack through which he continues to shout at her.

"Tell those dopes to vamoose!" he says to Jane.

The front door that leads into this part of the building has a clear glass pane in it at eye level, covered by a piece of ruffled curtain. Jane pushes aside the curtain to see just exactly what kind of potential intruders Yudi wants her to fend off.

Well, at first glance, they look like neither dope fiends nor home-invasion types, whatever that may be. They look, in fact, like two amiable young men, maybe nineteen years old, or twenty. One is a white, with longish hair, wearing a corduroy jacket over a hooded sweatshirt; the other is a gangly Asian holding a small video camera and a brown paper sack that looks like a large bag of lunch.

But what do they want at this empty time of morning, in this unimportant part of town? The house Jane lives in is on the outskirts of a small community in the middle of Long Island; on the other end of the main street is an outlet mall and on this end, a small, mismatched collection of rental housing: winterized bungalows and a few multistory private houses that were long ago shored up with aluminum siding now going gray and subdivided into apartments. These boys, Jane thinks, looking at the camera and the bag of lunch, must be lost.

So she takes a chance, though she doesn't feel like she is. She opens the door and shading her eyes against the weak spring sun, she says, "Can I help you?"

"Yeah, great," one of the boys says. Both boys smile widely and walk over to where she's standing. "We want to talk to Yehuda Guzman. He lives here, doesn't he?"

So they aren't lost at all, but their request is surprising. "Yudi?" Jane says. "Really? What do you want from him?"

"Is that what you call him?" the Asian boy says, and writes a note on a pad he has snapped briskly out of some pocket in his clothing, along with a fat green pen. It looks, Jane thinks, like he is writing with a pea pod.

"We just want to talk to him," the boy in the corduroy jacket says. "We're from Stony Brook; we both write for the university paper. We wanted to tell Yehuda—Yudi?—that Amnon Harris died yesterday. We were wondering what he thinks. I mean, after all this time."

That's a lot of information in a couple of sentences, a lot of names. Jane focuses on the one name that has some familiarity—Stony Brook. She remembers that long ago, meaning very, very long ago, she had a friend who went to film school there. That was back in the hippie days, when everybody either went to film school, if their parents had enough money to send them, or to the East Village to live in a cheap apartment and smoke hashish. Jane went the East Village route and got a job in the Post Office because in the time when everyone was still waiting around for the revolution, the P.O. was a safe haven: nobody hassled you about long hair and weird clothes, you could work night shifts that left lots of time for going outside on breaks and getting high, and besides, you had to do something in order to buy Jerusalem artichoke pasta and your weekly ration of wheat germ. It had never occurred to her, back then, that she would end up staying with the P.O. for thirty years. In other words, forever, more or less.

So this is what she finds herself thinking as she regards the boys in the brightening morning. It was a warm winter but now it's a cold spring; the grass sprouting in strips planted at the edge of the sidewalk looks knifelike in the sharp air; the few flowers look like glass. And what does she look like to these college boys with their young faces and mild eyes? Probably just like what she is, some version of that postal worker, that pensioner, retiree: a woman in her late fifties, now living at the ragged edge of herself, and dressed for it too, with her raincoat thrown over an old Grateful Dead tee shirt and pajama bottoms. Standing on the sidewalk in her stocking feet and so far along the timeline as to be irrelevant to them, except as a simple source of information.

"He's not home," Jane says to the boys. "Yehuda."

"Oh," the Asian boy says. "We had hoped to catch him. But we can come back." Unexpectedly, he holds out the brown paper sack. "Would you give this to him? It's a present."

Now Jane isn't sure what's in the sack—probably nobody's lunch. Could it be a bomb? Anything could be a bomb nowadays. Or it could be something obscene; it's become that kind of world.

She does two things at once: she both backs away and also accepts the sack, which feels like it has a harmless kind of weight to it. "Good-bye," Jane says and goes back into the building. The light in the tiny vestibule is dim, seasonless. The house is immeasurably quiet as Jane stands there, breathing.

But then Yudi opens his door to see what's going on. Jane hands him the sack and tells him it's a gift from his visitors. And she says, "They wanted me to tell you that someone named Amnon Harris died."

"Ha!" Yudi says. "He wouldn't do that."

He walks into his apartment and Jane follows him, because she wants to see what he's been given by the boys. The space where Yudi lives—it's not really an apartment—is long and narrow, but with a high tin ceiling. An industrial space heater is suspended from metal braces above their heads and there is a small bathroom with a toilet and a stall shower in the back. There is no kitchen; Yudi keeps his food in the kind of refrigerator that people in offices keep under their desk and cooks on a hotplate or in his microwave. He has a cot pushed up against one wall; nearby there is a TV resting on a discarded crate, an old portable radio on top of the TV.

Once they are inside and Yudi has closed the door, he puts the sack on a table near his cot and pulls out what's inside: an instant camera—a

Polaroid—and several packets of film. Jane hasn't seen that kind of camera in many years: after you push the button that snaps a photo, the camera pushes out a square of film that develops in a few minutes, before your eyes.

"Who brought this camera?" Yudi asks Jane suspiciously.

"Those boys," she tells him.

"Oh ho," he says. "Men in black."

"You mean like the movie?" Jane says, feeling more confused by the minute. She has spent only brief periods of time around her neighbor and while she has always thought he was odd, he has never acted quite this peculiar. Or animated; he seems charged up this morning with some kind of erratic energy, and he's saying things that don't make sense. At least they don't to Jane.

And just as she's thinking about that, he begins, again, to speak. "You know," he says, "they all used to want me to take target pictures. Hah! They'd put a picture of St. Patrick's Cathedral in an envelope, or somebody's pet Labrador retriever, and tell me to come up with the target. I could do it alright, but it was boring!" As he's talking, Yudi is unwrapping one of the packets of instant film and loading it into the camera. He does this swiftly, expertly. "So much work for some dumb dog photo," he continues. "Amnon told me not to bother about that. He said to take pictures of whatever I wanted. And so I did."

At that moment, Yudi raises the camera, points it directly at his forehead, and pushes the button to snap a photo. The camera has a built-in flash that blooms like a small fireball in the dim light of Yudi's apartment. The whole operation is a startling event that makes Jane gasp.

The camera makes an internal sound, like it's muttering to itself, and then disgorges a thin, flat rectangle of paper. Yudi rips it out of the camera and thrusts it at Jane. "Here," he says.

Jane looks down at the developing image on the piece of stiff paper. At first glance its surface is a uniform grayish brown, but almost immediately, it begins to change; like litmus paper in some childhood science experiment, patches of it begin to darken and lighten. The photograph begins to create shapes on its surface: sharp streaks of color; soft, almost translucent bubbles; multihued curtains of light. In the middle is a construction that looks like a chandelier of stars.

"What is this?" Jane asks Yudi.

"What a dope" he cackles. "That's a universe picture."

"What?" she says again. She has heard him well enough but thinks she doesn't understand what he said.

"It could be anywhere," is his reply. And then he shrugs his shoulders. "How do I know? I mean, how could I?" He walks away from Jane and stands in the middle of the floor, in the gray light. He raises his head slightly, as if he's sniffing the air, and then comes back to stand in front of his neighbor. "So he died," Yudi says. "So what?" He looks down at the photograph Jane is still holding in her hand and suddenly pokes at it with his index finger. "Yikes," he says. "That's a good one."

"I'm going to go upstairs now," Jane says, feeling she's had enough of this. She tries to give him back the photo, but he won't take it. He waves her away.

Back in her own apartment, Jane feels like what she wants to do is crawl back into bed, but it's late in the morning now and she won't let herself. She has to stay up, she has to do something with the day. First she has breakfast—a cup of coffee and a toasted corn muffin from a package—and then she takes a shower. She dries her hair. What now?

Without thinking that she's going to do it, Jane sits down at her computer, which is on a desk in her bedroom, and goes online. She summons up a search engine and types in *Yehuda Guzman.* Instantly—to her great astonishment—hundreds of links are displayed.

For the next half hour, she reads about Yudi, and what she reads sends her back into the past, to the psychedelic days, when everyone was meditating and burning candles and having their astrological chart done. Back to Carlos Castaneda and his spirit guides, to *Seth Speaks,* channeling the infinite, to Edgar Cayce and past-life regressions; back to the spooky, the spiritual, the endless *om* where everybody was looking for an answer: *What are we doing? Why are we here?* Somewhere in that time, Yudi had apparently experienced a few brief moments of notoriety for taking what were called mental photographs, which, Jane now understands, is what he was alluding to earlier. People would hide a photograph of some scene or object and Yudi would reproduce it on film, supposedly by using some thought process he couldn't explain. He also could never—or would not—explain whether he had been able to do this all his life or if it was an ability he had developed somewhere along the way. When asked to demonstrate his talent, Yudi, it seems, could be a contentious performer: sometimes he would acquiesce to take a mental photograph, sometimes he'd produce a series of them, sometimes he stubbornly refused to create any images at all. He drank a lot, sometimes he worked as a doorman, sometimes he seems to have survived as a low-level thief.

"Psychic research" was an almost respectable field to be working in back in the late 1960s, and Yudi was an interesting subject for the academics who were trying to document instances of what they believed was real psychic activity. But Yudi, as a stubborn and uncooperative subject, would probably have disappeared from the scene if not for Amnon Harris, a Harvard psychiatrist who became interested in him. A cousin, who had an apartment in a building in Manhattan where Yudi had briefly served as an overnight doorman gave Harris a photograph that Yudi had presented to his young daughter: it was, Yudi told the girl, a picture of a rough-coated pony who belonged to a similar little girl, only this one lived on a farm in Russia. He had taken the picture, Yudi told the child and her father, with his mind.

Amnon Harris studied Yudi for five years and then wrote a book about him that was published sometime around 1969 in which he declared that Yudi's ability was unquestionably real. Harris could not explain exactly how Yudi created the images that appeared on the Polaroid film—or why no other type of film or camera seemed to produce the same reliable results—but he was convinced that some true psychic process was taking place. It did not seem to matter to Harris that a few years later a famous magician, who was becoming equally famous as a professional skeptic and debunker of those who claimed to have psychic powers, had seemingly exposed Yudi as a faker. On a popular afternoon talk show that was nationally broadcast, the magician—whom Jane remembers from his appearances on a favorite childhood TV program, where he was often a sour, scowling presence, doing card tricks and holding conversations with a frightening looking clown puppet—seemingly managed to produce the same type of photographs of target objects hidden offstage. The magician explained that he used pre-treated film and skillful fakery, which is exactly what he said that Yudi was doing. To the general public, that was the end of Yudi's short reign as a cultural curiosity, but Harris stood by him. His support was so unshakeable that, in an almost unheard of move, Harvard had actually assembled a tenure review committee to see if Harris should be fired from his post. The professor survived the review and continued teaching at Harvard for three more decades, though from the Yudi days on, his reputation was irreparably tainted. Amnon Harris more or less faded back into obscurity—except on those occasions when someone once again dug up the Yehuda Guzman story for some magazine article or research paper, and asked Harris about him. *The problem was that nobody liked him*, Harris would always say. *And he didn't even seem interested in figuring out what he was really doing. But it wasn't a trick.*

In one of the numerous online obituaries of Amnon Harris, Jane finds a photograph of the professor. After looking at blurry electronic reproductions of some of Yudi's mental photographs, which pop up in different web sites devoted to psychic phenomena (everywhere, Jane sees the black Lab and the cathedral, which in their endless repetition seem to take on some unknowable symbolism of their own), she is almost surprised to see a normal picture, crisp and recognizable, of a human face. But can she read anything in the image of the professor? He is an old man with rheumy blue eyes, but the closer she looks, the more Jane is sure that the expression on his face, which she first registers as being noncommittal, is, rather, one of amusement. He looks like he's about to smile in some small but definite way. The dog, the cathedral, the inscrutable smile. *What time is it now?* Jane thinks, turning away from the computer. *Almost noon?* And she's still in her pajamas. She has to do something. Get out of the house.

She pulls on a pair of jeans, a shirt and a jacket, and walks briskly out of her apartment, out of the building, passing the silence of Yudi's locked door. She walks one block to a bus stop that will take her to the other side of town, to the library. She's carrying a small cloth bag with books she needs to return, and then she'll browse the shelves to see if anything new has come in that she wants to read.

Since she turned away from the computer, Jane has been moving automatically, performing the tasks of dressing and gathering her library books with what, if asked, she would have said was a blank mind. Nothing going on but the chemical hum of the human machine. Now, however, as she finds a seat in the nearly empty bus that travels smoothly along the town streets, under the overhanging branches of thin trees, it's as if her brain suddenly lights up again and what she's thinking about is Yudi. Specifically, how come she has never heard of him? She knows about Yuri Geller. She remembers Jeanne Dixon. She's heard of Gerard Crosiet, who could intuit people's life stories from touching objects they had owned. She's even heard of Madam Blavatsky. So why not Yehuda Guzman?

Well, Jane thinks, maybe she had heard of him long ago, when his name was rolling around in the great cultural stew that was the psychedelic days, and now just doesn't remember. That wouldn't surprise her; it's a small detail back there in the detritus of so many years, and she sometimes thinks that even the large details are slipping away. Whole parts of her life—important parts—barely seem real anymore. Her marriage, for example: Jane was married for nine years to a perfectly nice man who turned out to have a serious problem with drinking. He lost his job, went to rehab twice, and when he needed to go a third time, the insurance company wouldn't pay for it. Eventually, the marriage succumbed to the weight of its problems. That happened—what? Almost ten years ago, and sometimes Jane thinks that maybe it didn't happen at all because while she can recall incidents from the marriage—dinners, arguments, discussing the purchase of furniture, appliances—they are flat scenes when she reviews them; colorless, almost empty. They have no resonance anymore. They are stories about people she hardly knows.

Could that have something to do with getting older, she wonders? Maybe there's some connection to that timeline she had envisioned earlier, when she was talking to the boys who came looking for Yudi? Maybe as you slip further along the timeline, what you leave behind begins to dim. And then Jane has a scary thought: what if the timeline is more like a dial and guess where the needle is pointing? Closer to the end than the beginning. *Yikes*, she thinks. *Yikes, yikes, yikes.*

She tries—unsuccessfully, as it turns out—to go back into blank-mind mode as she gets off the bus and enters the library, where she wanders around in the mysteries section. She finds a couple of books she wants to read, but when she goes to the check-out desk to ask about a best-seller she's put on reserve, the librarian tells her that it hasn't come in yet. When she was working, Jane would have treated herself to the book by buying it new, but she's on a much stricter budget now. When she retired, she knew she had to move somewhere less expensive than where she had been living, so she sold her co-op in Queens and, as they had agreed, wrote a check to her ex-husband for nearly half the small profit she'd made in the declining market, which meant that all she had to live on now was what she had in the bank along with her monthly pension. This was all the money she was likely to have for the rest of her life. *For the rest of her life.* There was a concept she could never have imagined as a tangible reality. The fact that she could actually envision the rest of her life—one more package of time plopped down in front of her, ready to be opened, and then that was it—was unsettling. And what was in the package? What if it was nothing much at all?

She rides the bus home and again passes Yudi's locked door as she climbs the stairs to her apartment. She drops off most of her books, but, with the one she wants to read first in hand, decides to go up to the roof to read. It's turned into a sunny day with a freshening breeze and, with her jacket on, it will be warm enough to spend some time outside. The tenants are not supposed to go up to the roof, but there's a ladder leading to a trap door on the third floor where no one is home to hear her walking above their heads, and Jane has climbed it before. She even has a beach towel to spread out on the flat, tarry concrete.

So up she goes, and once she's on the roof, she lays out her towel, which features a multicolored parrot in a coconut tree, and makes herself comfortable. From here, she can see the peaked and shingled roofs of the white boxes, blue boxes, slate-colored and sea-green boxes that are the kind of houses that get built in mid-island towns like this that exist mostly to serve the railroad commuters, the secretaries and salesmen and middle managers who travel an hour each day into the city and an hour back. The Atlantic Ocean is to the south, but miles away; to the north, there is the deep, cold water of Long Island Sound. For the kind of rent Jane is paying in one of the few apartment buildings in her town, she is far from either body of water, but she likes the fact that she knows they're there, beyond the horizon of rooftops: water, waves, whales, fish, sailboats, and cruise ships. Sometimes even here, far from the shore, she can smell salt in the air, conjure a vision of the beach, the white sand like tiny diamonds underfoot.

The small rebellion involved in being where she shouldn't be, on the roof, helps to counteract an unfortunate image that often comes to mind when she sits down to read in her apartment: the vision of hundreds of apartments, thousands—maybe more—up and down the coasts, across the plains states, in towns at the foothills of mountains, each apartment like a cell in a vast honeycomb, and tucked into each cell, a single woman, reading her way into her old age. The only people Jane sees in the library all week, or in the larger branch, a longer bus ride away that she sometimes visits, are women her own age, and she has formed the impression that they are the last generation of readers, her solitary generation of women. At least, up here, she can look as much toward the invisible sea as to the pages of her book.

She reads for about an hour—a culinary mystery; someone has baked a pie and then committed a brutal murder—and then becomes aware that a sound she thought was a rising wind is actually a hand knocking on a door below. She puts down her book and walks over to the parapet at the edge of the roof, where she leans over to see the sidewalk below. What she sees is that the pair of boys from this morning are back, and they are knocking at Yudi's front door, the entrance on the street. Yudi is not answering, but they have spotted Jane and wave to her, as if she is an old friend.

There really is no reason for her to go downstairs, so she retreats to her beach towel, but they keep on knocking, which is annoying. She can't concentrate. Finally, she snatches up her belongings, climbs back down the ladder and descends the stairs. When she reaches the street level, she pulls open the front door of her building and says to the boys, "What do you want?" She hopes that she sounds as irritated as she feels.

They smile, both boys. The expressions on their faces are so mild and nonconfrontational that they seem practiced, and yet they are an insistent presence, this white boy and his Asian friend. They were born a world apart—or maybe just a few states, a few blocks—but they look alike, Jane thinks. Very much so.

"We know Yehuda is taking pictures again," one of them says, and Jane notes the fact that if you listen, you can hear a challenge now in the boy's carefully modulated voice, behind the blank mask that he has made of his young face. "So we thought maybe the camera we brought this morning wasn't enough. Maybe we should give him something better."

The other boy reaches into his pocket and pulls out a flat, silver-colored rectangle that Jane quickly identifies as a digital camera. A fancy, expensive one, a wafer of metal that can probably take a hundred photos at a time. A thousand, a million, and then upload them into the ether. Into the sky.

"You've been knocking," Jane says, "and he's not answering. It doesn't sound like he's home."

"But you are," the first boy says, holding out the camera. "Will you give it to him?"

Jane backs away. "No," she says.

"You'd be doing us a favor," the boys tell her.

That's what they all say, Jane thinks, and though she couldn't, at that moment, explain exactly what she means, what she is sure of is that, all of a sudden, she does not like these boys.

So, without another word, she closes the front door and goes back upstairs. Even if they keep knocking, even if they pound on both doors, she is not going down again.

In her apartment, she puts away her beach towel, puts her book on a shelf and wonders what she should do next. The late afternoon light pushes itself through the blinds and lies on the floor like bars of gold. When they fade, it will, at least, be time for dinner. Until then, time can be used by watching television; there will be some movie on one of the cable channels or she can tune into a talk show. She can tune in *something* until she's hungry and wants to eat.

Later, during the news, she microwaves something from the freezer. Afterwards, she watches a game show and a comedy, but she finds that she can't pay attention to the television. She's restless in a way she isn't used to in the evening, and thinking about going out somewhere.

There's one of those suburban restaurants nearby that serves giant steaks and burgers and usually has sports on in the bar; it's spring training season for the baseball teams, and since the bar has a satellite dish, maybe they'll be showing a rebroadcast of a game from Legends Field. Jane could use the Yankees right now, she thinks; she could use some guys in uniform to root for, some Florida sunshine at night and a draft beer.

The bar is in walking distance, and at first, when she steps inside, Jane thinks that this will help, this was the right thing to do. And indeed, there is baseball on four different television screens: hi def, liquid crystal images are being pumped out at her in hyper-sharpness; the bats make sword-slices through the humid southern air; the balls fly with atomic propulsion, white-hot as bullets, they look like they may shatter the blue-glass sky.

Jane has one beer and then another, but after a while, the bar presents the same problem as the TV: she can't focus, she doesn't feel like she has any real connection to what's going on. People are eating, talking, flirting; waitresses are gliding through the rooms with trays of icy blue drinks, heaping platters of food. This is life, Jane knows, *this is life*, or part of it, but the more she thinks of that, the more she feels like she is watching from behind a screen, and while she's watching, something is draining away. Has gone, gone, gone. She is somebody, but not who she was before. That timeline, that's the problem. It's moved further than she thought. Baseball and bars and beer. The days for that seem to have folded themselves up and moved on. Very soon—because she doesn't know what else to do—Jane is ready to go home.

She walks through the quiet streets, through the spring night. In her apartment, she watches the late news, reads her mystery for a while and then falls asleep. Outside, overhead, the night deepens. The moon rises, icy and battered. A bear made of stars paws the sky.

Keller! Jane hears in a dream. *Keller! Keller! Keller!*

But it's not a dream. Once again, it's Yudi, though this time he's not downstairs—he's knocking at her door. Jane rises quickly and then hurries to the door so he won't wake her hard-working neighbors who must be home by now and tucked into their own beds. Even in the middle of the night, in the middle of confusion—because what can he want now,

Yudi?—she is bound by her mid-century upbringing: *Be considerate of others. What will the neighbors think?*

She opens the door and Yudi rushes in. In his hands, he's holding the digital camera the pair of boys tried to give to Jane this afternoon. They must have left it behind, Jane thinks, in a bag, by Yudi's front door. Amazing that no one stole it.

"The aliens came back!" Yudi says, holding up the camera. And then, suddenly, he hurls the camera to the floor. "Junk!" he proclaims. "Who needs it?"

Jane has never, ever, seen Yudi do anything like what he's just done to the camera. He has never been violent, never broken anything—but then, really, how well does she know him? Not well at all. And now, as Yudi stands over the camera doing what? Chuckling? Is he *chuckling*? Jane is beginning to feel very uncomfortable, even disturbed. And she's on alert, waiting to see what Yudi will do next.

But he does nothing. He simply stands in Jane's living room, smiling at the broken camera. Presumably broken, because it is still in one piece, lying on the floor in some deadened state. Jane picks it up, carries it over to her trash bin, which is under the sink, and drops it in as Yudi watches her every move.

"Well," she says to him. "That's that." As if something has been resolved. "Why don't you go back downstairs now?"

"I need more film," he tells her.

He must mean that he needs it for the Polaroid. Do they even still *sell* film for that camera other than in some specialty store? "I'm sure you can find someplace that sells it in the morning."

"They have it at Walgreen's," he tells her.

She can't imagine this is true—Walgreen's, like almost every other what-used-to-be-a-drugstore has transformed itself into a phantasmagoria of digital photography: you can have digital prints made there, buy albums and accessories, upload and download to your heart's desire; you can even buy those throw-away cameras. But film for a camera that was a staple of parties in the dark ages? Why would they have that?

"The one near us is open all night," Yudi tells Jane, and by this she understands that he wants her to go and get it for him. Now. But why should she?

She is about to make all sorts of reasonable statements—it's late, she's tired—but then he holds out some money: a fanfold of bills. There must be at least a hundred dollars in Yudi's hand. Well, that's interesting; she can't imagine where he's gotten so much cash all at once, how he can spare it. Usually, as far as she knows, he's scrabbling around for a few dollars to buy groceries. What Jane is confronting here is a new development.

So, maybe just because she's been unbalanced by being told to go on an errand, right now, with a pile of money, Jane says okay, fine. And she doesn't even bother getting dressed, not really—just like this morning, she pulls on her long raincoat over a tee shirt and pajama bottoms, although this time, she also slips her feet into a pair of sneakers. She ushers Yudi out of her apartment and he disappears into his own, downstairs. And off Jane goes into the night.

In her apartment, she hadn't looked at the clock, but it seems to be very late. The moon looks small and cold now, pinned to the sky like an afterthought. Jane is the only person on the street.

It feels like a long walk, but it isn't—maybe ten minutes. And then, yes indeed, there is Walgreen's, lit up like an oasis. Like a magic planet. The end of the road. Jane moves toward it with her hand in her pocket, holding the money Yudi has given her. She still can't imagine that she's going to find what he has sent her for.

She enters the store, in which the aisles slice through the bright, brittle light like parallel roads. Music plays in the background; something rhythmic, like soft chanting. Jane walks past the aspirin and cold remedies that march down the shelves in white rows. Then there are beauty products, then diapers and toilet paper, then pet food, then stationery—and finally, she locates the photo aisle, which also bristles with related offerings such as blank CDs and headphones in plastic packages. There are a variety of computer-like machines here, too, meant to disgorge prints from digital memory sticks, create albums of vacation snapshots, or send images by e-mail to friends and relatives far away. She can buy batteries and disposable cameras that will take photos half-a-foot wide—but film? Can she buy *Polaroid* film?

And then yes, the answer, improbably, is yes. There it is. At the end of an aisle, in the middle of a nearly empty shelf down near the floor is a small stack of rectangular blue boxes with bright orange lettering. Six boxes, to be exact. Jane bends down and picks them up. Reading the price marked on one of the boxes, she realizes that the money Yudi has given her will just about exactly cover the cost of buying exactly the number of boxes that are on the shelf.

In her pajamas and raincoat, she walks to the counter and pays for the film. The money is accepted by a sleepy teenage clerk who looks like he has been randomly pierced by metal filings. He accepts the hundred-dollar bill without comment, giving Jane back just a handful of change.

She leaves the store and plunges back into the darkness of the streets. The stars look like they have retreated high into the rafters of the sky; the tiny moon has covered itself with a cloud. Jane is on a trajectory for home that is more memory than perception: *turn here, cross that street, there's the door.*

And there is the door. Now she's in the hallway of her building. Silence from Yudi's apartment, silence everywhere. She thinks she's going to just leave the film by his front door because she's tired now, really tired—isn't it, after all, some very dark hour of the night?—but instead, she sees her hand lift, form a fist, and knock. She waits, knocks again, and then the door swings open.

Inside, the cold floor of Yudi's apartment seems to be covered with litter. But then the image Jane is seeing clears itself and she realizes that what she's seeing are photographs—a hundred of them, maybe more—strewn around the floor. And Yudi is stomping around, stepping on the photographs, around them, all the while clutching the camera, which he keeps pointing at his head; each time he does, he snaps down the shutter release button and the camera spits out another damp square of photo paper, which Yudi rips out and tosses to the floor. Slowly, like a dark flower blooming, the photo develops itself into an image as it is joined by another and another and then more and more.

Jane puts down the film she's carried to Yudi and then begins to pick up photographs from the floor. Each one is similar to those he had shown her yesterday morning, but also, each one is different, showing bright beams shooting through some far, distant darkness, streaks of colored light, twisted, glowing roads of stars. There is some sort of progression to them, Jane thinks, like they are being taken from the edges of somewhere, but zeroing in, moving closer to some invisible center. One or two of the photographs Yudi has just taken and just tossed away seem to show huge orbs, fiery with color, though it's hard to tell, because these images are out of focus. But they're getting slightly clearer with each new picture Yudi produces. As he focuses in.

"That Amnon Harris," Yudi says suddenly. "He was a kidder. But you can't kid a kidder."

"What?" Jane says. "What are you talking about?"

"Dead as a doornail now," Yudi continues. "Or so they say. Ha!"

"I want to go back to sleep now," Jane says. "Maybe I'll just leave you alone."

But she doesn't move as Yudi walks over to the table where she's left the film and rips open a new package. He loads it into the camera and once again begins snapping away in a frenzy. Photos shoot out of the camera—more, Jane is sure, than each package claimed that it contained.

"No one can tell *me* what to do," Yudi says, as the photographs grow brighter and more detailed with each image. "Because no one knows what's going on. Do you?" he says to Jane. "Do you?"

He tears open yet another package of film and snaps away, but this time, instead of tossing the photos to the floor, he hands the first of his newest universe pictures to Jane. She looks down at the image he's handed her and sees that, even as it begins to develop, it promises to show very little—just darkness, barely illuminated by a faint smear of light. Wherever Yudi was, now he has moved away and is beginning again. He's refocused; he's somewhere else. But he's still looking. He's looking everywhere. He's looking like crazy.

"Do you know what's going on?"

"No," Jane admits, speaking softly. "I don't know what's going on."

"Ha!" Yehuda Guzman says, as he hands her another image that will slowly develop in her hand. "Then wake up!" he shouts at her. "Wake up!"

There's no need for him to yell, Jane thinks. She can hear him, she can hear him. Still, she doesn't look down right away at the photo she's holding because she's not sure, yet, that she's ready to. What will it be a picture of? She doesn't know and there is no time to guess. She can't imagine what she'll see.

Sand Street

"It's not good enough," Henry said. "Those flowers—they're too yellow. The cyan has to be pumped up."

"They're sunflowers," Laurel pointed out. "The yellow is supposed to be kind of electric."

Henry Martin, head of direct mail operations for what was usually described as the fifth largest health-related nonprofit organization in the U.S., continued to examine the proof sheet of decorative self-adhesive stamps and name labels. These were important products, the core of the organization's direct mail campaign for the summer. Somewhere around sixty million of them were due to start rolling off the printing presses tomorrow.

Henry held the sheet flat, balanced on his palms, and then he turned it sideways, first angled to the left and then the right. He and Laurel were in Laurel's small office—she was sitting behind her desk, he was standing in front of it—which was lit by deadly fluorescent light, so no matter how Henry held the sheet, Laurel thought the digitally printed flowers looked like they were fading fast, but she said nothing. She waited for Henry's next pronouncement.

"I'm just not satisfied," Henry said. "I mean, these are the gluebacks, right?" Laurel, who managed the organization's printing and was his subordinate, agreed with him that yes, they were. "Well, maybe they'll look alright on uncoated stock," he said, "but the self-adhesives are on a coated stock—plus they get a varnish—and you just give those babies a chance to start reflecting light and they're going to blind people."

Laurel knew all that. The organization that employed both her and Henry, and which was involved in research, public awareness campaigns, and other good works aimed at improving the lives of people with chronic diseases, had one hundred and three chapters across the United States. Over the course of the past year, she had attended eight regional meetings and participated in at least twice as many national conference calls at which the various individuals at the local and regional level involved with the organization's direct mail campaigns had chosen designs for the summer mailing (and were well into the process of doing the same for Christmas), hashed out complex issues relating to color, paper, glue-versus-self-adhesive backings (most people nowadays related better to self-adhesive stamps, but you still had your diehards who didn't believe a stamp was a stamp unless you got to lick it), costs, copyrights, high-end donor packages versus cold-mail prospects versus online tie-ins and on and on and on and on. Almost all of Laurel's counterparts on the local level had held, and had voiced, many and varied opinions about the yellow of the sunflowers that now bloomed in the digital proofs, and it had taken months to come to consensus. The saturation level of the ink in the more porous paper of the glue-backs as opposed to the smooth coated stock, where the ink would lie on the surface and gleam—or so they actually hoped—like honey, butter, or maybe liquid gold, had all been discussed. Decisions had been made and agreed upon. And Henry knew this. Henry knew it was very, very late in the game to be in Laurel's office acting unhappy about the shade of yellow (which was not really a shade or a hue but a nearly miraculous composite that computers and printing presses would create out of cyan, yellow, magenta, and black, the four values of light itself) that skilled and well-meaning people had agonized over and finally selected.

But this was something Henry did frequently—step into a project at the last minute and raise doubts. He had power and seniority, but to many in the organization, especially those at lower levels, he was an erratic, disruptive character and they resented having to account to him or to come up with answers to the questions he raised. He also yelled a lot, and could inject a personal element into his criticism of an underling's work that often crossed the line of professionalism. Laurel understood why people didn't like Henry—were even afraid of him—but she had worked for him a long time and no matter how hard he made the wind blow around her, she was usually able to remain calm enough to calm him down, too, and then to fix whatever he thought was wrong. Whether it was wrong or not. She sometimes thought that maybe her ability to handle her boss had something to do with her own difficult upbringing—she was good with monsters and crazy people. Or the years she had spent, later, wandering the hippie trail from upstate New York to California. From one commune to another, and through a dozen stays in a dozen crash pads on both coasts, she had learned a lot about making do wherever you found yourself, and about chilling out. About cooling down.

"I'm going on the press approval tomorrow," Laurel reminded Henry. "I'm flying to Duluth in the morning and staying overnight. We'll do the color corrections on press, during make-ready. I'm sure it will be fine."

"It better be," Henry said, slapping the digital proof onto her desk. "This is our second largest campaign of the year. We can't afford a mistake."

After he'd left her office, Laurel sat in her chair for a few minutes doing nothing but staring at the wall opposite her desk. A perfectly nice wall, recently painted. *How do I feel?* she asked herself and decided that actually, she felt okay. The scene with Henry hadn't been any worse than usual, and she had been ready for it.

She worked through the last hour of the afternoon and then, uncharacteristically for her, left at five—but that was office protocol. Everyone knew she had a lot of traveling ahead of her tomorrow, so although the mid- and higher-level managers usually worked until at least six, it was considered acceptable, even prudent, to leave the office earlier than usual on the day before a business trip. Who knew what you had to do at home, to prepare?

Laurel took the subway to Penn Station and then boarded a train that was headed all the way to the North Fork of Long Island. She wasn't going that far, but almost: to Shore Point, a small beach community on a sandy thumbprint of land pressed against the edge of Long Island Sound. She was still getting used to the long train ride, which she had only been taking for a few months; before that, she had been living in a railroad apartment in a brownstone in Jersey City, on just about the last block fronting the Hudson River that had not yet been turned into high-rise rentals. Manhattan had become unaffordable for many of its young professionals, so its old, industrial partner across the river, long fallen into urban ruin, had been reinvented as a suburb of apartment towers with parquet floors and city views. The tenants in Laurel's building had been told they had about a year before the wreckers came to their block to tear down the old world and build what they were assured would be a better one. She had assumed she'd just move into one of the new buildings somewhere down the line until, with nothing to do on a Sunday in early March, under a changeable sky, she'd been sitting in a park by the river, reading the paper, and had come across an ad for some new houses being built in Shore Point, far out on Long Island. She had looked at the photo in the paper of the model house and its surroundings, finished the coffee she'd been drinking from a paper cup, and then called the phone number under the ad and found out that they were showing the houses that day. About five hours later, she was writing a check for a deposit on a small two-bedroom house that still had a new paint smell lingering in the hallways.

Laurel was fifty-one years old. Through a series of relationships in which she had lived in other people's apartments and even more apartments in Queens and New Jersey that she had rented on her own, it had never before occurred to her that she could actually buy a house. That she had either the money or the credit that would allow such a purchase. Signing the deposit agreement had been like admitting something that was both bad and good at the same time: she had become an adult, a person who was not likely to drift away from home again anytime soon.

Is it ridiculous for someone her age to first be having these thoughts? Laurel had asked herself that question on the train back to the city and decided no, she was still in a long recovery from her old days as a wanderer, a worker who picked crops and worked in canning factories long past the time when the hippie tribes had disbanded and melted back into the mainstream. In her twenties, Laurel herself had returned to New York, where she had grown up, bought a skirt, two blouses and gotten a "real" job as a receptionist for an insurance company because there simply didn't seem to be anything else to do. You had to live. You had to support yourself. You needed a TV and a winter coat and the means to pay for a visit to the doctor when you got the flu.

Laurel had expected to struggle at the lower rungs of the American economy for a long time—she had no experience relevant to office work, no college degree, and no plan for how to move from a job to something that might be termed a career—but she was smart, and she was lucky. What she found out was that in a world where more people than you'd think were either lazy or incompetent or both, if you were neither, then someone might notice that and help you out because they needed someone just like you to help their enterprise thrive, whatever it was. And that was what happened to Laurel. Different bosses had shown her things, taught her, promoted her. She was good at listening and learned what she was taught the first time something was explained to her. It was at the insurance company, when she was moved from the reception desk to the department that produced the company's brochures and sales materials that she first learned about printing. She asked questions and people answered her. She had learned that even people as difficult and volatile as Henry Martin could be teachers, which was another reason that Laurel was able to tolerate him better than most. She understood that he actually did know what he was talking about, even if he conveyed what he knew in a combative fashion. If you could separate the wheat from the chaff, so to speak, listening to Henry could once in a while save you from making a big mistake, or help you do something in a way you hadn't thought of before—a better way than you might have come up with yourself.

The train was now pulling into the Shore Point station, where Laurel was one of only a few commuters to disembark. Her car, another new acquisition—you couldn't do without one this far out on Long Island—was waiting in the lot adjacent to the platform, sitting by itself in a parking lot. She had a short drive, only three miles or so to the new development where she lived. Once there, she parked her car in another lot, in the spot that had been assigned to her, though here, too, she was almost alone—there were only two other cars parked nearby.

After that, she had a brief walk, maybe five minutes along a pathway of flat wooden boards that led to her house. It was a pleasant spring evening; the air was mild and there were stars appearing in the east, like sequins sewn along the darkening edges of the sky. She knew that in the dead of winter, in the snow or sleet, even this brief trek was going to be uncomfortable, but for now it was just fine. And as for next year, well, she'd cope with it, and be glad to do it. She had no doubt about that because she absolutely loved it here.

She had loved this place from the minute she saw it: rows of houses built on a sandy bluff overlooking deep water all the way to the horizon. There were no streets here, just several rows of houses built right on the sand, with the wooden walkway serving as the only access to each one. Laurel had bought a house in the second row: the ones with an unobstructed view were much more expensive and besides, it seemed a little safer to have some barrier between her house and—what? The wind? The seasonal storms?

Whatever fleeting misgivings Laurel may have had about living in such an isolated and lonely spot—which promised to remain so; most of the other houses had been purchased as weekend getaways, so she was one of only a handful of fulltime residents—had been more than outweighed by the immediate and visceral reaction she'd had to the place. It was like some sleeping brain cell, which had taken her one happy childhood memory into safekeeping and hidden itself deep down in her subconscious, had awakened the first time she'd seen the houses set on their foundation of sand and shown her the worn, gauzy, but never-to-be-forgotten image of another place, a twin, long lost and thought never to be found again, that she had loved without remembering, until the moment it came back to her, how much. At Shore Point, she had found a sand street.

Laurel had been an only child. Her parents were unhappy people—too distant from their daughter for her to have formed any real understanding of why. She did understand, though, that they seemed to have little to say to each other and less to their child. The only time any of them seemed to get any relief from each other's company, from the daily reproach of having to spend so much time being with and either taking care or doing the bidding of people you didn't like and had little affinity for, was for a few weeks in the summer, when they rented two rooms in a boarding house on the Jersey Shore, a place they could afford because it was in what was considered an undesirable location. What made it undesirable, however, was exactly what made it attractive to Laurel's family: the boarding house and the bungalows around it were set on a street that was completely covered in sand, so that no cars or any other kind of vehicle could drive from the boulevard that paralleled one end of the block all the way to the entrance to the beach, at the other end. Because there was no traffic in the street, it was safe for children to run around outside unsupervised, day and night, so Laurel could be out of the house and away from her parents almost every minute that she wasn't in bed asleep. And because the tenants on the block knew they were the outsiders in the summer community, the lower-class renters who lived in rooms where they had to constantly sweep the floors, because the sand outside always found its way indoors, there was a sense of camaraderie among them that led them to put beach chairs outside, on the street, and leave them there for anyone to sit in—and someone was always sitting in them; if it wasn't raining, everyone was outside, it seemed, day and night—to set up barbecue grills in the middle of the street and cook more food than was necessary for one family so that anyone who was hungry (and everybody was always hungry in the summer) could have a hot dog or a burger, and to generally live outside, to talk, to drink, to play cards and mah jong and listen to baseball games outside, on the sand street. It was the sand street that gave Laurel and her parents some relief from each other.

Now, as she walked along the boards that formed a pathway across this new sand street, she was well aware of what she had done—moved to a place that reminded her of someplace else. But there were worse reasons, she imagined, for choosing a place to live. At least she *had* made a choice. She had settled somewhere.

Inside, the house still smelled of new paint. And it was still sparsely furnished: small as it was, her apartment had been smaller, and her few pieces of furniture—a couch, a chair, a television, a bed—seemed so uneasy in this bright, gleaming space that she almost expected them to tiptoe out some evening, hat in hand. (If they were magically imbued with an animate spirit. If they had hats.) The kitchen remained almost as she had found it, immaculate and virtually unused, except for the microwave. Laurel didn't cook. She had frozen dinners stacked in the freezer, so she took one out without even looking at it, and put it in the microwave to heat up.

After she changed her clothes, she took the tray of food (it turned out to be pepper steak) into the living room and turned on the TV. She was tired, which was good, because she had to get to sleep early and rise before dawn to drive to the airport. Morning flights to Duluth always left at an unreasonably early hour.

She flipped through the cable channels, not really finding anything that interested her until, suddenly, on some high-number channel where they stuck all the history, travel, and nature programs, something caught her attention. It was a picture—a crude drawing, really, scratched onto the surface of a patch of pebbled brown earth—that depicted an ellipse surrounding a filled-in circle. At one end of the ellipse, a little below and to the right of the larger circle, was what looked like a densely drawn dot.

A narrator was explaining what the drawing depicted, and Laurel found herself listening with interest: what she was looking at, apparently, was a representation of Sirius, the brightest star in the sky and a much tinier companion star, a white dwarf known as Sirius B, that followed an elliptical orbit around the larger star, making one orbital revolution every fifty years.

The narrator of the program, who had a kind of antique English accent meant, Laurel supposed, to underscore the authority of his information, went on to explain that the Dogon, a fairly primitive tribe by modern standards, who lived in a remote corner of the African nation of Mali—and who had no technology and certainly no telescopes—had based their entire societal structure, including birth, death, and marriage rituals, on the relationship between these two stars. It might not be surprising to involve Sirius in one's cultural infrastructure the narrator continued, as grainy film of the Dogon dancing in a circle, wearing tall wooden masks that looked like coal-colored chimneys topped by a two-tiered cross—

after all, it dominates the night sky—but what was inexplicable was that Sirius B, the immensely heavy dwarf star, was actually at the heart of the Dogon beliefs. Why was this so extraordinary? Because Digitaria, as the Dogon called Sirius B (after a tiny seed indigenous to their territory), was invisible to the naked eye; it hadn't been discovered until 1871, and no photograph had been taken of it until 1970—yet the Dogon had incorporated Sirius B into their beliefs for countless generations before that. As it lurks in the interstellar darkness—cold and nearly dead, though not quite, not yet—the white dwarf, with its super density and powerful gravitational pull (factors that added to the evidence that it was once more massive and luminous than Sirius itself) affects everything about Sirius, including how it oscillates on its axis and what, ultimately, will be its fate.

So how did the Dogon know about Sirius B? Well, they said, they had been told about it by the Nommos—beings who had come to earth thousands of years ago from a planet somewhere in the Sirius system. The Nommos had not been seen or heard from for millenia, but the Dogon didn't seem to be bothered by this; it made the knowledge they had left behind no less important to them and certainly, no less true. They went on celebrating tiny, invisible Digitaria as if it was their best friend in the universe. Or maybe they were just interested in keeping on the good side of such a powerful force.

Beyond such speculation, there was something that seemed familiar to Laurel about the Sirius story—not the specifics, but the sense of mystery, of mysterious lore and hidden meanings. That was a feature of the psychedelic years: when she was younger, almost everyone she knew either read the Tarot cards or consulted the I-Ching before making a decision of any importance, and as much time as she and her friends had spent debating politics had been devoted to speculating about the power of crystals, the messages hidden in the measurements of the Great Pyramid and whether peyote-fueled wolf visions in the western deserts were simple drug dreams or manifestations of some deeper genetic imprint. She remembered all this again the next morning when she woke before dawn, dressed, and went out to her car while the stars should have still been visible, but looking up, interested in pinpointing the position of Sirius in the sky, Laurel saw only a skin of night-dimmed clouds. It was going to be a chilly, overcast morning.

She had a long drive to the airport, but traffic was light and, as a bonus, her plane actually took off on time. She went back to sleep on the flight and arrived in Duluth, as she always did, confused about whether to set her watch backwards or forwards and, as always, just left it alone. Terry Becker, one of the owners of the printing company, met her as she walked off the plane and greeted her with a hug. Laurel's organization was the company's biggest client, but his affectionate greeting was genuine: Laurel had known Terry for years, now, and considered him a friend.

"So," he said, as they settled into his car and moved smoothly into the stream of traffic bound for the industrial edge of the city, "What's Henry's problem this time?" Laurel had not called Terry yesterday to tell him that Henry was concerned about anything, but he always was, so Terry's question was asked with a grin.

"Whether we can hold the color evenly on the matte stamps and the coated stock," Laurel replied.

"You know we can," Terry told her.

"Sure," Laurel said. "But aren't you at least supposed to pretend to be concerned about it?"

"I am concerned about it," Terry answered, still smiling. "But not that much."

At the printing plant—which was really several huge buildings set back to back to back, including a temperature-controlled warehouse stocked with paper and cans of ink substrates to make custom-blended colors—Terry ushered Laurel into a conference room where enough sandwiches and beverages to satisfy a crowd of people were laid out on a sideboard. Was it lunchtime? Laurel wasn't sure, but she was hungry, so she filled a plate and sat down at the end of the gleaming conference table to eat. It had been her experience that this was what printers always did when a client came to the plant on a press approval: they fed them all day, maybe on the theory that a person stuffed with enough cold cuts was likely to be easy to please. And perhaps it was true.

Since everyone at the plant knew that this was the custom, from time to time throughout the afternoon both secretaries and press operators—most of them, people Laurel knew—would stop by to grab a sandwich and say hello. Terry, also, returned to the conference room many times over the course of the afternoon, sometimes accompanied by Chris Johnson, the production manager, to show Laurel press samples of her stamps and name labels. There were actually six different designs in the flower series, so she inspected the coloration of roses, lilacs, lilies, daisies, gladiolas, and the troublesome sunflowers. Consulting with Terry and Chris, she did ask for some adjustments. At one point, she laid the latest sample of sunflower sheets next to the make-ready run—the early sheets that had come off the press while the color was still being calibrated—and realized that Henry had a point in questioning the quality of the yellow. But he was off the mark a little because she could now see that the yellow was fine; it was the browns and greens of the plant stems surrounding the flower petals that were muddy and that was affecting the way the yellow appeared, by contrast. Terry and Chris agreed, so they spent half-an-hour with the technician who adjusted the computers that controlled the printing presses and finally produced what Laurel declared was a perfect sheet.

After she had been hanging around the conference room for a few hours, Laurel decided to stroll out to the pressroom floor to watch the mixed sheets of stamps and labels as they came off the presses. These were massive machines, monsters of steel a block long, studded with enormous cylinders and roller beds that pulled huge rolls of paper, at high speed, into and over the rubber blankets and etched plates that would produce the image of Laurel's flowers. Men with stoppers in their ears stood at different spots along both sides of the three different presses that were running Laurel's job, making adjustments at computer stations that controlled different parts of the process. It was always impressive, this much roaring industry, this much sheer size wedded to complex technology. And at the end of the process, sliding smoothly onto wooden palettes, there they were: roses, lilacs, lilies, daisies, gladiolas, and perfect sunflowers.

As she watched the production line, Laurel's attention was suddenly diverted by three men who walked past her, wearing what appeared to be white lab coats. Their faces were serious, almost professorial. Clearly engrossed in their own conversation, they paid no attention to Laurel, who became curious about what they were saying to each other. She couldn't quite hear them—it was noisy in the plant—but she did quickly realize that they weren't speaking English. What language, then, were they conversing in? Could it be German?

"Yup," Terry said, answering the question she asked him when he had come to stand beside her. "German. They're here to service the Kleindorf presses." He pointed to a distant part of the plant. "I told you, didn't I? We bought two of them. Half a million dollars apiece, but they're high-end digital, direct-to-plate and can run night and day for weeks without a problem. Of course, if you buy them, you also have to buy a service contract from Kleindorf because they won't sell you the maintenance or service manuals; they're proprietary. That's why we have to let the Nazis visit every six months; they're the only ones who know how to keep their babies humming."

Laurel started walking along a row of palettes, selecting samples of the stamps and labels to give to Henry. Terry followed her. "I can't believe they won't teach your technicians how to service your own presses," Laurel said to him.

"They won't even let us into that part of the plant when they're working," Terry told her. "But," he said, leaning over to whisper, theatrically, in her ear with a fake German accent, "vee have our vays."

"Your ways to do what?" Laurel asked, whispering back.

"I'll tell you later," he said. "So how about we all go out to dinner? I think we've got everything right now, don't you?"

Yes, Laurel agreed, the color on the sheets couldn't be better and she had even tested the glue samples when she was in the conference room—she and one of the secretaries who came in for a couple of cookies had spent ten minutes licking sample name labels and placing them on envelopes Terry had supplied. The next stop for the label sheets would be a mail house on the other side of Duluth, where another set of monster machines would inkjet the names and addresses of millions of people onto the labels and send them out into the U.S. postal system, along with an appeal for donations. In millions of homes, people would either throw them out or put them aside to use later. Some people would like them; some people would think they were no better than junk mail. Probably no one would turn to anybody else and say, *Look at that lovely yellow. How did they manage to create such a wonderful color?*

Laurel selected samples of the different sheets and put them in a Fed Ex package for Henry so he would get them first thing in the morning. She was staying over tonight, in a hotel near the airport and wouldn't be back in New York until the afternoon. Therefore, she wasn't planning to go to the office; she was awarding herself part of the day off and intended to head straight home.

After they dropped off the package at a Fed Ex office, Terry, Chris, and two of the plant managers took Laurel to dinner at a suburban restaurant with a colonial theme. There was a fireplace, fat, waxy candles on the tables, and the beer came in silver tankards. Everyone agreed that tonight, the hell with cholesterol and wavering blood sugar levels: they ordered appetizers stuffed with cheese and meat dishes as entrees, all around.

Laurel always enjoyed these evenings with what she thought of as a group of grown-up Midwestern boys who were all about the same age as she was. The stories they shared tended to start with getting high in someone's basement and then progressed to details about the antics that ensued. Laurel's favorite was a mostly true tale about a time when airports were places as bland and meaningless as parking lots; fueled by methedrine, she and a pack of friends had piled into someone's older brother's Mustang and driven onto the runway of a small airport on Long Island to race the twin-engines taking off into the night. Terry had once told the group about a frigid midwinter evening when he and a buddy stripped down to nothing and streaked through the front door—and then out the back—of a local VFW post, chased by a pack of elderly veterans who were still spry enough to have beaten the boys bloody if they'd been caught. *See?* The moral of these stories all seemed to be, *New York and Minnesota: back then, it was all the same.*

Tonight though, the conversation went in another direction: something—maybe the silver tankards and foamy steins of beer—reminded them of the German technicians back at the plant and their guarded behavior.

"What are you doing?" Laurel asked. "Photographing their secret documents at night when they're asleep?"

"We would if we could," Terry said, "but we don't have to. Someone's doing it for us."

"Page by page," Chris Johnson added. "The service manuals, the schematics; they're all turning up on the web."

"And in chat rooms," one of the plant managers said, pausing to speak while he still had a healthy chunk of plank steak on his fork. "All you have to do is ask. I mean, if you know who to ask, and where."

"Chat rooms?" Laurel said incredulously. "Printers have chat rooms where they pass trade secrets to each other?"

"Of course," Terry said, with feigned indignance. "This is important stuff. We have a need to know."

"Right," Chris said. "What if something happens to those presses between the regular maintenance checkups? We're supposed to wait for someone to fly in from Germany with their magic toolkit? Nope," he said. "That's not the American way."

The next morning, after rising again in the chilly, predawn darkness, Laurel spent six hours traveling; she was either in the air or waiting at the airport in Minneapolis to change planes. She slept for the first leg of her journey, but spent much of the second half looking out the window at the icy blue sky and the clouds rolling beneath the wings of the plane like an airborne sea.

When she landed in New York, it was warmer than it had been in the Midwest, but below the clouds the sky was gray. As she walked toward her car, Laurel retrieved her cell phone from her purse and turned it on; she had switched it off on the plane but wanted to call Henry now, to see if he had received his samples.

The phone lit up with bars and pulsing icons; one of them meant that she had a message. She assumed that it was Henry calling her, but it wasn't; it was her friend Maureen. *Hi, Laurel,* she heard as she unlocked her car and slid in, behind the wheel. *Dad had trouble breathing last night, and chest pain, so I called an ambulance and they took him to St. John's. Can you come? He's asking for you.* There was a pause; a silence in which the message could have ended, but it did not. Maureen went on: *I mean, I know he's always asking for you. But he's very agitated and it might calm him down if he could see you.*

Laurel started her car, but let it idle where it was parked. From where she sat, she could see the signs leading out of the parking lot: after she paid the overnight charge, turning left would take her to the Long Island Expressway and home. Turning right, and then right again, would lead to the maze of roads and parkways—endlessly under construction; blinking with detour signs and warnings of congestion—that would eventually let her slip off into the side streets of Brooklyn. St. John's Hospital was in Bay Ridge, just a few blocks from where Maureen and her father lived.

She allowed herself to hesitate for a minute or so before pulling out of her parking spot, but once she'd paid the fee at the booth guarding the gate out of the lot, she turned right, heading for Brooklyn. She called Henry from somewhere in Queens and he told her yes, he'd gotten the samples and yes, they were much better than the proofs had been. She'd done a good job, he told her before they hung up, which was also something that made it possible for Laurel to work for Henry as long as she had—he knew when something had been done right, and he knew how to say so.

An hour later, in Brooklyn, she prowled the old streets of squat brick apartment buildings and weary looking trees, trying to find a place to park near the hospital. This was her old neighborhood—the place her family had left every summer, to go down the shore. There were other families who had done the same, usually with a grandmother or maiden aunt in tow to help pay the summer rent at one of the boarding houses. In Laurel's family there had been the occasional cousin or uncle who had slept on a cot in the kitchen. When she told people about that now, they seemed to think she was describing something from another century.

After she finally found a spot, she walked the few blocks to the hospital and then started looking for her friend. Maureen had given her a room number but the hospital was vast: one gray-tiled corridor led to another. And the lighting was bad, the hallways smelled of bleach.

Laurel finally found Maureen sitting in a family waiting room under a television that looked like it was skewered to the wall. Onscreen, one of the afternoon soaps was winding its way through some sort of confrontation scene—a woman in an evening dress was making wild gestures at a man in a tux, holding a drink—but the sound had been turned off. There was no one in the room but Maureen.

Laurel sat down beside her. "How is he?" she asked.

Maureen shrugged. "I don't know," she said. "The doctor is supposed to come and talk to me."

She looked exhausted—more so than usual, Laurel thought. It was always something of a trial for Laurel to see Maureen. They were the same age—had, in fact, grown up together in separate apartment buildings nearby—but Laurel, feeling bad about it all the while, sincerely hoped that in Maureen she was not seeing a reflection of some possible, discomfiting direction that her own life might unthinkably take. She wasn't even sure what she meant by that: almost everything about the way they lived was completely different, so how could they end up in the same place? Until about five years ago, they hadn't even had contact with each other for almost three decades, until Maureen's father had gotten sick and she had found Laurel's phone number in an online white pages. Maureen was a parochial school teacher who was either in the classroom or at home, taking care of her father; she was always tired, and dogged by depression and money worries (there was no insurance in the world that covered all her father's medical expenses). The situation she found herself in never seemed to improve.

"Would you go in and see my dad?" Maureen said to Laurel. "He seems even more upset now than when they brought him in. And of course, he doesn't stop asking for you."

"I'll go right now," Laurel said.

Maureen's father was in a room with two other men; his bed was by the window, which faced a wall—another wing of the hospital—where rows of windows looked back. On both sides the glass was grimy, so it was impossible to tell if there was someone across the way who was also staring out the window but, Laurel thought, presumably there was. Presumably there was an infinity of patients looking out of windows, at nothing. At more windows and walls.

She walked over to the bed where Maureen's father was laying and tapped him on the arm. "Hello, Mr. Farrelly," she said.

He was an old man—somewhere in his late eighties—thin and age spotted. He suffered from advanced Alzheimer's, along with whatever else was wrong with him now, and he was always restless. At the moment, he was smacking his lips, making the damp, mumbling sounds that comprised one variety of his communications, and his hands gripped the bed sheets, twisting the edges into tight cones, letting them unravel, and then twisting them again.

But something in him changed when he realized that Laurel was standing beside his bed. Something always did. No one could explain why, out of all the thousands of people he'd known in his life, including some, like his daughter, he had undoubtedly deeply loved, he now recognized not one of them—with the single exception of Laurel. He seemed to see her as she was in the present day, because once or twice, since she had started visiting him at Maureen's request, he had remarked on something she was wearing, yet the Laurel he spoke to also seemed to be the child who had occasionally passed through his life decades ago—through his kitchen, where his wife had handed out cookies; his living room, where he had watched television shows from a couch where the slipcovers were changed from a plaid to a flower pattern as the seasons changed—when she and Maureen had been friends. It was the fact that after the onset of his disease he had started asking for her, for Laurel, that had prompted Maureen to find her. On the phone, Maureen had said to Laurel, *Do you remember me? Do you remember my Dad? Because he seems to remember you.*

Now, Mr. Farrelly fixed his eyes on Laurel, and she could almost see him trying to focus, to connect the image seeping into his cloudy mind with whatever information about the world was left to him, and then find the words to comment. Finally, he did. "Laurie," he said, in a raspy voice, "Laurie. What are they doing to me?"

Though he was impaled on the bed by a tangle of tubes and wires, including a hollow, rubberized band that went around his head and was feeding oxygen to him through his nose, what he said was not necessarily a reference to his current situation—it was one of a handful of questions he often greeted Laurel with.

"Don't worry," she told him, which was one of her stock answers. "You're fine. Nothing bad is happening."

Probably, this time, that wasn't true, but what would be the point of telling him that he had a reason to be agitated? If he would even understand her explanation. He reached out to grasp her hand with the thin rails of his fingers. Who was she now to him, Laurel wondered? Some composite of people he would have trusted? Hoped would help him, wherever in his mind he thought he was?

"Whap, whap, whap," Mr. Farrelly said, which was another set of sounds he often made. Then he just started saying her name over and over again. "Laurie, Laurie, Laurie, Laurie." It should have been irritating, Laurel knew, but it wasn't. It sounded like a mantra. *Om mane padme hum.*

After a while, Laurel let go of his hand and got up from the bedside chair where she had seated herself. She thought she should go outside and see how Maureen was doing, but as she started to walk away, Mr. Farrelly became agitated. "Don't go!" he cried after her, as if she were his last hope in the world. It was something that always happened when she tried to leave him, even when he was at home.

She walked back to his bed, past the other old men lying quietly in their own tangle of sheets. Again, she took his hand. "I'll just be outside," she told him. "I'm not leaving."

This time he let her go, but he started making the *whap, whap, whap* sounds louder and faster.

In the waiting room, she sat down beside Maureen, who looked at her with tired eyes. Above their heads, on the television, a talk show was now being broadcast. Someone vaguely famous was being interviewed by someone else on a blue set; blue chairs, blue lights, the projected image of a city behind them, seen in the soft blue distance.

"How is he?" Maureen asked.

"He's him," Laurel said. "You know."

"I'm so hungry," Maureen said. "But I can't eat anything. I keep thinking of things I want to eat, but I just can't."

"Maybe we can go to Viggio's later," Laurel said, naming a neighborhood restaurant that had been around since before she and Maureen were born. They served big, comforting plates of food and brought wine to the table in brightly decorated carafes.

"That sounds good," Maureen agreed. "Yes. Let's go there."

For a moment or two, then, Maureen rested her head on Laurel's shoulder, an unexpectedly intimate gesture. They weren't that kind of friends: maybe they had been when they were kids, but not now, not really. How could they be? As adults, they had little in common—topics they both knew not to go anywhere near when they were around each other included most of the big ones: religion, politics, social mores—and yet, more seemed to bind them together than the fact that the only person in the world Maureen's father remembered was her childhood playmate. Maybe it was the neighborhood. Maybe it was something else. Laurel remembered that in the summers, when they were separated, Maureen used to write her letters that included a list of what songs their favorite radio station had counted down as the top ten for the week, as if, on her sand street at the Jersey Shore, Laurel might not be able to hear that station and so be deprived of what, at the time, was critical information.

"Miss Farrelly?"

Both Laurel and Maureen looked up to see a doctor standing before them, a handsome man much younger than them both. He was holding a sheaf of papers in his hands, and frowning.

"I'm Doctor Kelvin," the young man said. He briskly shook hands with Maureen and then started to speak, seemingly addressing the papers, not her. "Your father has a coronary artery blockage," he explained. "That's why he was having chest pains. It could cause a clot, and that could kill him. I'm sending him for surgery immediately."

"What?" Maureen said to this unexpected news. "What?"

"The surgeon will try to come and talk to you beforehand," Dr. Kelvin continued. "But he may not be able to. We're very busy tonight," he concluded, and Laurel thought he sounded like he was describing an overflowing diner. With a nod of his head, then—having completed his duty to report to the family—the young doctor walked out of the room.

Maureen turned to Laurel, her face ashen. "Did I hear him right? He said he's sending Dad to surgery right now?" When Laurel confirmed that was exactly what seemed to be planned, Maureen said, "Well, he can't do that yet. I've got to call my brother."

She pulled her cell phone out of her purse but then put it back again and strode swiftly out of the waiting room, heading in the direction that Dr. Kelvin had taken. Laurel followed her.

They found him standing at the nurse's station, still frowning as he scribbled notes on someone's chart. Maureen stood beside him, but he never looked up at her though he hardly could have missed the fact that she was there, waiting to talk to him. Finally, she said. "Excuse me, Dr. Kelvin. Can we talk about the surgery, please?"

He clicked his pen and slowly, with what seemed like a deliberate flourish, and laid it down on top of the papers. "What is it?" he asked.

"Is the operation dangerous?" Maureen asked.

"Any surgery has risks," Dr. Kelvin replied.

"I mean for my father, specifically," Maureen persisted.

"Your father, *specifically*," said Dr. Kelvin, who was making it clear that he did not like being questioned, "is going to throw a clot if we don't get him into surgery and then there's no going back. We won't be able to save him."

Maureen looked at the doctor, long and hard. Watching her, Laurel thought that must have been her schoolteacher look—the flat, questioning expression she presented to a student who was being difficult. "Okay," she said, "I get it. But right now my dad seems to be holding his own, so maybe we could wait a few hours? If there's a possibility that he might not make it through an operation, we have to wait until my brother can get here. I called him earlier and he said to tell him if there was any immediate danger. He wants a chance to see his father before anything happens."

"Where would he be coming from?" Dr. Kelvin asked.

"Delaware," Maureen told him. "It will take about six hours to drive here."

"Impossible," Dr. Kelvin said. "For one thing, I've already spoken to the surgeon and the operating room has been reserved. The arrangements can't be changed at this point."

"But you didn't ask me," Maureen pointed out.

"You're the health care proxy for your father, right? That's what it says in his chart," Dr. Kelvin pointed out.

"Yes," Maureen agreed.

"And you signed a surgical release form in the emergency room when he was admitted."

"Yes," Maureen said again. "But I didn't realize...I mean, I guess I just signed whatever they told me to. I was scared for my dad."

Listening to her friend continue to try to argue with the doctor, Laurel could hear the sound of defeat beginning to tear at the edges of her voice. The doctor and the hospital had already made their decision and set it in motion. What power did she have against these great forces?

Dr. Kelvin picked up his pen and put it in the pocket of his white jacket. Then he took a stethoscope that had been on the counter and wound it around his neck; after that, he lifted the sheaf of papers and a clipboard that was beneath them and wrapped his arms around them. Thus armed, he swiveled around and pointed himself at Maureen. "Do you understand," he said to her, "that if we don't do anything, your father is going to die?"

"Of course he's going to die," Maureen said softly. "He's an old man. But his son wants to see him, so we're going to wait."

"I'm sorry," Dr. Kelvin said. "I told you, the arrangements have been made." Carrying his papers and equipment, he walked around the counter that separated the nurses from anyone who might come to talk to them and sat down, signaling the end of their conversation.

"Do you believe this?" Maureen said to Laurel as they walked back to the waiting room. "I have to call Benny." She got out her cell phone and started to dial. Following behind her, Laurel listened to Maureen's side of the conversation as she reached her brother and explained to him what was going on.

Laurel hadn't seen Benny since they were kids, but she remembered him—Maureen's older brother, a tall, tough, blue-eyed boy with dark hair. He muscled his way around the neighborhood with a pack of friends who wore white tee shirts, black jeans, and were always smoking. Those were the years when it was cool to smoke. When it was cool to be that kind of tough guy—harmless, really, when Laurel thought about it now. They hung around. They made remarks when girls passed by. He had ended up working for the transit authority, Laurel recalled, and Maureen had once mentioned that he was retired now; that's why he had moved to Delaware: no sales tax, no property tax. It was a relatively inexpensive place for a retired person to live.

She was having trouble picturing Benny Farrelly as an AARP member when Maureen suddenly handed her the phone. "He wants to talk to you for a minute," Maureen said.

"I should have called you before this," Benny said when Laurel got on the phone. "I should have thanked you for visiting my father the way you have been."

"It's not really any trouble for me," Laurel told him.

"But this is trouble now, isn't it?" Benny said. "Even if my dad doesn't know I'm there, I want to be. I mean, he's my father." Benny paused for a moment, observing the rule that never changes: boys try to never let girls know that they have feelings. When he had composed himself again, Benny said, "Maureen told me that this Dr. Kelvin is about twelve."

"He is young," Laurel replied, and had the sense that they had made a transition to the kind of conversation that went on at lots of levels all at the same time: in this case, right now, *young* meant, *What does he know? Nothing. He doesn't understand a thing. Not yet.*

"There must be someone in that hospital we can talk to," Benny said. "I can get in my car right now."

"Then you know what?" Laurel said to him. "Start driving. You're right. There's got to be someone."

She hung up the phone and handed it back to Maureen who said, "You have an idea?"

"I don't know," Laurel replied. "Maybe."

Somewhere behind the scenes, while she was talking to Benny, or maybe before, when she was listening to Maureen argue with Dr. Kelvin, some little bubble of a thought had begun to float a little closer to the surface, some small idea had begun to get a little bigger. There was a reason Laurel had been in Duluth looking at sunflower stamps; it was because the organization she worked for used the stamps to raise money. And one of the things they did with that money was support research. And one of the places that did this research—a place they gave a lot of money to—was a hospital in Manhattan. Maybe someone at that hospital would know how to deal with a problem at this one?

Laurel had no idea who to call there, but she did know who might. Twenty minutes later, after she had talked to the hospital's development officer, who had told her to speak to a particular administrator, who had then directed her to the patient advocate at his hospital, who had told her to call the New York State Department of Mental Health, Mental Hygiene Legal Services (because, the advocate explained, if a person with Alzheimer's is not mentally competent to make decisions about his own health care, under the mental health laws of New York State, a physician can't necessarily override the wishes of his family no matter who has signed what; it all depends on the circumstances), Laurel found herself dialing the cell phone number of a man named Mark Gerritson who, she had been told, was an attorney who worked for the Department of Mental Health and might be able to advise her.

Laurel thought it was a long shot that he'd actually answer the call—it had been a long afternoon, and when she glanced at her watch, she realized it was well after five o'clock—but he did. Trying to condense everything into a few brief sentences, Laurel told him how she'd gotten his number and began to explain the situation, while Maureen sat beside her, watching her talk into her cell phone. Miles and miles away, Benny was probably starting out on his journey, heading up the highway to New York.

It seemed that Mark Gerritson, too, was on the road. "I'll tell you what," he said, interrupting Laurel's story, "I'm in my car. Let me pull over."

"I didn't realize you were driving," she said. "I'm sorry."

"I was on my way home," the lawyer told her. "Hold on a minute."

In the pause that followed, Laurel listened to—what? The wind? An electronic hum? The pulse of infinity sailing through the tiny circuits of her phone?—as she waited for the lawyer to speak to her again. Finally, he came on the line again. "Okay," he said. "I'm back."

"I really apologize for bothering you like this after hours," Laurel said.

"It's not a problem," the lawyer told her, and Laurel thought he was telling the truth. He sounded relaxed, even cheerful. The other people she had spoken to this afternoon had been helpful enough as she traded her access to the fundraising office for names and information, but also blunt and matter-of-fact. This man, Laurel thought, sounded different. He sounded like a human being. "It's actually pretty nice here," he continued. "I was on Ocean Parkway, on Long Island. I pulled off the road near Gilgo Beach, and now I'm looking out over the dunes, at the water. Things could be worse. So," he continued. "Go on. Tell me about your friend's father."

While Maureen listened, Laurel explained the situation with Dr. Kelvin. "He seems to think he has the right to decide what to do, even though it's not what his patient's son and daughter want."

"Well," Mark Gerritson said, "if he feels it's a life-and-death emergency, he's not necessarily wrong, especially since your friend signed a release form when her dad was admitted, but I still think he might be interpreting the rules a little too strictly. And he certainly could be a little gentler in the way he's presenting his case to your friend. In any event, it sounds to me like there's some room here to work with. Let me try to call some people."

"It's already after five," Laurel reminded him, worried that it was too late to do anything.

"Oh, that's alright," the lawyer told her. He had a smooth voice, confident and serene. The voice of a man looking out at the ocean on a spring night. A man who apparently felt sure enough of himself to sound almost playful as he said, "I have everyone's secret phone numbers."

When they had come back into the waiting room, Laurel and Maureen had seated themselves in a different set of chairs than before. Now, they were facing the television, where the early news broadcast had begun, but Laurel realized that they could also see the nurses' station down the hall. Dr. Kelvin was still there, plowing through his paperwork.

Half an hour went by, then forty-five minutes. Laurel told Maureen that she was going to check on her father, so she went down the corridor to his room. Outside, it was getting dark; the room was in darkness, too, except for the nightlights above each patient's bed, which didn't seem to be disturbing any of the old men. They were all peacefully asleep. And

Laurel saw no evidence, yet, that anyone had done anything to prepare Mr. Farrelly to be moved.

On the way down the corridor, Laurel had passed Dr. Kelvin, who continued to scribble away. Now, as she headed back toward the waiting room, she had to walk by him again. He hadn't looked up the first time she went by and he didn't look up now; Laurel was just another figure drifting through his peripheral vision—if he even saw her at all.

Just as she was approaching the nurses' station, meaning only to march on quickly by, Laurel heard a phone ring. The phones here had been ringing all afternoon, but it had gotten quieter at the dinner hour, so the sound seemed to break the calm that had descended on this busy place. It seemed very loud and very urgent.

A nurse sitting near the phone picked it up, listened for just a few moments, and then handed the receiver to Dr. Kelvin. If he spoke, Laurel couldn't hear him, but she could tell from the way his eyes narrowed and his back stiffened that somebody—some Nommo, she found herself thinking, with a secret phone number—was probably giving him an earful.

When Laurel sat down again, Maureen said, "Benny just called. He's made it almost to Wilmington. Depending on the traffic, in another hour or so he'll be in Jersey."

"That's good," Laurel replied. From where she was sitting now—Maureen had changed their seats again, looking for a comfortable spot to camp out for the next few hours—Laurel couldn't see Dr. Kelvin any longer, which was also good, because she didn't want to watch him frowning at the phone as he slammed it back into its cradle, which is what she assumed was happening right now. Instead, she preferred to picture something better: Benny, obviously still ready to rock and roll if he had already been able to put so many miles behind him. Above him, the stars were probably just starting to come out. All night long, some of them would be visible to the naked eye. Some would not—but that doesn't mean they aren't there. That you can't figure out things about them, or, once in a while, however unexpectedly, find that you are being told.

Edison Park

The board at the front of the control room showed the eHorizons IPS network radiating out from northern New Jersey like a starburst, bright and steady, but that was just for show; the computer terminals in front of Jeanne and Avram—who were standing almost side by side in the control room, drawn out of their offices by the emergency—told the real story, which was not good. Not good at all.

"Shit," Avram said. "Shit, shit, shit. Here it comes again."

He put down the mug of cold coffee he'd been nursing to focus his full attention on the screens before him, which were monitoring the Internet traffic flowing across the router connections managed by a phalanx of servers and IBM RS/6000 supercomputers in the vast, temperature-controlled data center locked behind a fireproof door down the hall.

eHorizons had its own proprietary programs that measured Internet volume twenty-four hours a day, seven days a week; Avram, the company's head of IT security, was following the real-time information they were charting while he also watched the public monitoring sites. All the programs—as they had yesterday and every day for nearly two weeks before—were showing a significant increase in traffic over the course of a few minutes and that was growing. If the increase followed previous patterns, it would swell to over ten times the normal volume in the next hour. Neither Avram nor Jeanne, who ran eHorizons' customer service department, had any idea what an untenable percentage jump would be. Other than theoretical models that various researchers had been floating for the past few weeks, probably no one did.

"What do you think?" Jeanne asked Avram. "Script kiddies?" She was hoping for copycats or pranksters, but knew that what they were seeing on the monitors was something more.

"Not this time," Avram replied as they watched their company's software try to trace the surge back to its source. "The zombies are in Europe: France, Germany; one in Turkey. Right now, the trace ends there." He shook his head in frustration: for days now, he had been trying to ramp up the program, give it an almost forensic capability to analyze paths and patterns that might lead beyond the computers—the unwitting zombies—that were being remotely seized by parties unknown to launch the cyber attacks they were experiencing, but so far, nothing was working. "This is definitely another DOS attack," he added, pointing to a separate monitor that displayed the customer complaint logs that were constantly being updated by Jeanne's staff. There were already dozens of sites reporting problems that were clearly resulting from a massive denial of service attack focused on major hosts and Internet Service Providers in North America.

"Can we handle the volume?" Jeanne asked Avram.

"For the time being, yes," he told her, "but I'm starting through the trouble levels. We'll begin at six."

Level six meant Avram had deployed a filter that could distinguish between legitimate and bogus traffic to a site; it would help to keep the sites operational but it would also reduce their response time. If they had to move up the levels, launch stronger filtering programs, and raise additional firewalls, response time would become correspondingly sluggish. For the brokerage houses, banks, auction sites, booksellers, and myriad other commercial ventures that lived on eHorizons' servers, that could mean hefty revenue losses. Avram and Jeanne's joint priority was to keep the sites working with as few interruptions as possible.

Avram pulled up a new screen shot on his monitor, typed some swift commands on his keyboard and then said something to Jeanne that she didn't understand.

"English, English," she said to him. Jeanne had worked with Avram for more than five years and in all that time, this was the only absent-minded thing she ever saw him do: when he was particularly focused on something, he tended to lapse into Hebrew without being aware of it.

"Hebrew is better," he told her. "You should learn."

"It's a little late for that," Jeanne replied.

"Never too late to learn your own language."

"I *am* speaking my own language. I was born in New York City."

"New Yowk," Avram drawled, making fun of an accent that Jeanne firmly believed she did not have.

She looked over at him, ready to complain about the teasing, then she decided not to. Despite the joking, he looked very serious—but then, that was how he always looked, she thought: serious, almost scary, with his dark eyes and deep scowl. All the Israelis she met looked like that to her: striking, often handsome, and always seeming to be on the verge of anger. Even the women. It was like they had sprung up on a different planet, carried different genes. The mild people she had grown up with, polite, working-class Jews with roots in the ghettos of Russia and Eastern Europe, would have been terrified of this new species.

As Jeanne watched Avram work, a nearby phone rang. Its LCD panel did not display a number, which meant the caller was using an encrypted line, which meant that Jeanne knew who it was. She groaned; this just wasn't the best time to be having the conversation she was afraid she would be in for.

Hearing her reaction, Avram said, "Is that the brainiac?"

"Don't worry," Jeanne said. "He won't want to talk to you. He's afraid of you."

Jeanne picked up the phone and, as she expected, was connected to John Ettinger, an agent with the FBI's cybercrime division. Jeanne had been speaking to him on an almost daily basis since the DOS attacks had started. eHorizons was the largest web host in the U.S., as well as a major provider of web tools and applications, so it was likely that millions—billions?—of the message packets being sent to North America in an attempt to choke off Internet traffic were going across the company's networks; the FBI, therefore, had asked for their cooperation in trying to track down where the attacks were coming from. eHorizons' corporate bosses had directed the agency to Avram and the FBI had then appeared at the data center in the person of Special Agent Ettinger, who was probably in his twenties but looked like a teenager in a business suit. Avram—not the most patient of people under any circumstances—had talked to the Special Agent for ten minutes, concluded, as he told Jeanne, that the guy was an idiot, and passed him on to her. Jeanne's assessment was a bit kinder: she thought Ettinger was probably an amateur hacker, recruited out of college, who had decided it would be safer to work for the government than to be chased by them. Worms, viruses, defacements, and distributed denial of service attacks: for a hacker, they were probably interesting to play with but frustrating when you were the suit trying to defeat them because each was a puzzle, a string of complex code that had to be unraveled and then treated with an antidote—another string of code—or else blocked by some kind of filter or shield.

As far as Jeanne could tell, Avram's problem with Ettinger stemmed from the fact that the agent was equally concerned with finding out who was marshalling the attacks and developing evidence against them as with how to counteract the assaults; Avram, an ex-soldier, though twenty-some-odd years removed from his military service, still had a soldier's bitter mentality: he no longer cared much about the who or why of the enemy—it was enough to know that there *was* an enemy that had to be defeated. Evil was snaking its way along the international networks and he wanted to crush it. He didn't want to engage in long discussions about why the attacks were happening, who was behind them, or how far they intended to go. He just wanted to win.

Jeanne understood what Ettinger had to do, but she sympathized with Avram, so she had resigned herself to being her colleague's message bearer. The agent asked her how they were holding up under the attack and Jeanne reported that so far, their sites remained operational.

"Miss Wocek?" Ettinger said, as the conversation neared its end. "You'll be at the meeting tomorrow?"

"Yes," Jeanne replied.

Ettinger cleared his throat. "And Mr. Guzman?" he said finally. "He has to come."

"I'll do my best, Special Agent," Jeanne said. Using that title was the only part of the conversation she enjoyed: it was like talking to someone in a comic book. Besides, she was a forty-two-year-old woman, she felt funny calling anyone so much younger than her "mister" anything, no matter who he was.

"What did he want?" Avram asked when Jeanne hung up the phone.

"He was worried that you won't come to the meeting tomorrow."

"It's a waste of time. They can't tell us anything and we've already told them everything we know."

"We have to go," Jeanne told him. "Corporate agreed that we'd cooperate, so we have to play nice. Reps from all the other major hosts and ISPs in the northeast will be there. Besides, it's only for the morning."

"But it starts at eight fucking o'clock on a Saturday. Whose idea was that?"

"Government time, I guess," Jeanne said and went back to watching her trouble logs.

The next time Jeanne's phone rang, it was a good call because it was her girlfriend, Julie, a surgical nurse at St. Vincent's in Manhattan. Julie told Jeanne that she would be late for a dinner date they had planned with another couple, old friends the two women lovingly referred to as their boyfriends, Joe and Robbie. That was okay, Jeanne told Julie, because she was probably going to be late herself, and filled Julie in on what was happening. Julie asked Jeanne to call the boys because she had to scrub for a procedure, so Jeanne clicked off and dialed Robbie, a dressmaker who had a shop in the city, in the East 60s. Don't worry, Robbie told Jeanne, he had a vintage Chanel he was restoring for a witch of a client and the more he got done today the better, and as for Joe—a senior partner in a downtown law firm—you could never pry him out of his office anyway, so why didn't they shoot for eight o'clock on the Jersey side, at the marina near where the two couples lived, only blocks apart. Robbie would corral Joe and Julie and then the three of them would come over on the ferry. So they agreed: that was their plan.

When Jeanne hung up the phone after her conversation with Robby, Avram said, "This is what you do? In the middle of disaster, you arrange your social life?"

"We're not having a disaster," Jeanne said. "We're preventing one. And besides, it's not my fault that you don't have a girlfriend. Or any friends at all, really." She turned to Avram then and smiled wide. "Except for us, of course. We're your cross to bear, so to speak." Avram made a grunting sound, which Jeanne took as a sign that he was trying not to laugh, so she went on. "And just to reinforce the fact that the only people who can stand to socialize with you are four very tolerant gay people, why don't you eat with us tonight? We'll drop you off at the ferry afterwards."

"What makes you think we're even going to get out of here tonight?" Avram said.

Before she replied, Jeanne glanced from one screen to another, checking that all the tracking programs they were watching verified each other's reports. "Because," she said, "the volume's only up by fourteen percent across North America, which is not much different than the last couple of times this happened, so I'm going to guess it's all going to peter out by late afternoon. It always does, once the main zombies are identified and taken off line."

"What if it's different this time?" Avram said. "It's going to happen, you know. One day, these brute force packet flood attacks are going to morph into something a lot more sophisticated that filters and firewalls won't stop."

"Well, let's hope that doesn't happen today," Jeanne replied, "because I'm really looking forward to sitting out on a deck by the river and having a couple of glasses of wine before the world comes crashing down around my head."

For the next few hours, Avram and Jeanne remained together in the control room, watching the progress of the attack. By late afternoon, as Jeanne predicted, the assault, which had been created with software, was being stymied by other software programs being sent out to the edges of individual networks and groups of networks working together in the hope that they could take back control of the zombies that were flooding the Internet with blind, meaningless traffic. Eventually, the strategy started to have a palliative effect and the threat of overload began to ebb.

By six o'clock in the evening, everything seemed to be back to normal. The DOS attack appeared to be over and the only fractional increase in volume that the eHorizons tracking program could measure was the nightly homework blip that occurred when kids across the U.S. logged on, to be followed, later at night, by the porno blip, as the older crowd went online to prowl for some fun. Jeanne was even thinking about trying to talk Avram into leaving a little early in case they hit traffic on the turnpike, when one of the techs sitting a few stations down from where she was standing called her name.

"Jeanne?" he said, and she immediately registered the tension in his voice. "Avram? Pull up our homepage. Now."

At separate computer terminals, both immediately called up the homepage of eHorizons own web site, where visitors could access information about the company and customers could interact with online tools that allowed them to manipulate features on their own sites. As soon as the page appeared, both Jeanne and Avram said the same thing at the same time: *Fuck.*

Despite the fact that it should have been impossible—or nearly so—someone had hacked their site. The eHorizons homepage was visible on the screen, but superimposed on top of it was the big, round, golden yellow happy face with two button-sized eyes and symmetrical grin that had become an icon of good-natured joy. But as Jeanne and Avram stared at it—in the moment it was taking them to register that the defacement of their site was real—the grin opened wide to reveal a mouthful of pointed fangs.

Gotcha. Ha-ha. Gotcha. Ha-ha.

Everyone in the control room shivered as a squeaky, cartoonish voice came out of multiple computer speakers, repeating that phrase over and over again.

Gotcha. Ha-ha. Gotcha. Ha-ha.

"Mute that," Jeanne said to the tech who had first reported the defacement.

"And capture the page," Avram added. "Then replace it, immediately."

He sounded calm, but Jeanne knew better, so she decided to do the job herself. She took a screen shot of the page, saved the source code, which would contain the foreign program that had been inserted into their own scripting to create and animate the face, and replaced it with a stored copy of their home page. She then took the additional step of e-mailing the hacked source code to the FBI as well as to a number of other hosts, ISPs and site managers to report what had happened to eHorizons and find out whether others had been victimized, too. Answers came back quickly. *No*, everyone said. *No.*

"Just us," Jeanne reported to Avram.

"Fabulous," he said grimly. "Cancel dinner. I'm not going."

"Yes, you are," Jeanne told him. "There are at least four other people in this room who can figure out how the hacker got in and then block him. If anyone needs us, they'll get in touch."

It took another half-hour of persuading, but Avram finally gave in. He made sure that everyone had the numbers for their cell phones and their home phones, which of course, they did, but he also got the number of the bar at the marina where they were headed and gave that out, too. Only then was he willing to leave.

Avram lived in the city, in the East Village. Since the data center where he and Jeanne worked was housed in a deliberately nondescript warehouse building near Port Elizabeth, New Jersey, he usually took a ferry across the Hudson to the Jersey side and then boarded a commuter bus that dropped him close to the office. On his way home, he made the reverse commute. Tonight, though, he got into Jeanne's car and drove with her to Jersey City, an old, industrial town that had once been notable primarily for its ravaged waterfront; the city and the riverfront had been dying together until a developer had hit upon the idea that maybe middle-income urban types would like to live at the edge of the Hudson in apartments with spectacular views of Manhattan, even if that meant their address would be in New Jersey. They would, they did. The Jersey Gold Coast, as the area had come to be known, studded with terraced high-rises and the corporate headquarters of business and industry, now stretched as far north as the George Washington Bridge and south to a state park near the Statue of Liberty in the New York harbor. Across from the southern tip of Manhattan, off exit 14C of the Jersey Turnpike, was a marina that had berthing slips for yachts and sailboats but also housed a huge lightship permanently moored in the middle of the ship channel; the vessel doubled as both the marina office and a summer bar/restaurant. It was one of Jeanne's favorite places; she could sit on the lightship deck, at a table under an umbrella, and gaze at a view that included her own apartment building across the channel to the north, and to the east, the wide river and the towers of the city.

By the time they got to the marina, night was beginning to fall. The river was turning from blue to a color somewhere between slate and sapphire; ferries floated like lanterns across the water, from New York to New Jersey and then back the other way. Ever since the World Trade Center had been destroyed, taking with it the cross-Hudson train station beneath it, many of the sixty thousand or so people who used that rail line to get to work had taken to the ferries, which had multiplied in number. The sight of the ferries calmly sailing back and forth between the river coasts—some of them docking on the New York side in a cove just city blocks away from Ground Zero—always made Jeanne think optimistic thoughts about the resiliency of human beings.

She said something about that to Avram as they sat down at a table near the lightship bar and ordered drinks. He didn't reply, except to hold up a newspaper that someone had left on a chair by the next table. The headline was about suicide bombings in Israel. Many people had been killed.

"Okay," Jeanne said to him. "You win. There's no hope."

Just then, her cell phone rang. It was Julie, calling from one of the ferries. Joe and Robbie were with her. "We just left the dock," Julie told Jeanne. "Where are you?"

"We're already at the marina."

"Great. Can you see us?"

"Sure," Jeanne told her, waving at all the lights on all the boats moving along the river. "But tell the captain to make the boat go faster. Avram's full of doom and gloom and I need someone to tell him jokes."

Julie repeated that to Robbie, who then got on the phone. "Hey, sweetie. Tell Avram to listen in." Jeanne told Avram to pull his chair close to hers, so they could both hear Robbie.

"Avram?" Robbie said. "Remember, I'm a bar mitzvah boy too, so don't get mad at me."

"Go ahead," Avram said. "Make me laugh."

"How many Jews does it take to screw in a light bulb?" Robbie asked.

"I don't know," Avram said.

"Ten. One to screw it in and nine to argue about how to do it."

"Nope," Avram said. "Not funny."

"Okay. Did you hear what Kraft Foods is going to call its new factory in Israel?"

"What?"

"Cheeses of Nazareth."

Avram almost smiled. "Closer," he said.

"I'll try to think of some more," Robbie told him, and clicked off.

A few minutes later, the ferry docked at a slip beneath the bow of the lightship. Julie was the first person off the boat, a thin woman with red hair, still wearing the top of her hospital scrubs above a pair of jeans. Joe came next, a burly man with an impressive suit and weighty briefcase. He was followed by Robbie, who jumped off the boat, carrying a long cardboard tube that he was twirling around like a baton. Robbie, with his spikey gray hair and reading glasses bouncing around his neck on a sparkly chain, he looked exactly like who he was—a handsome boy beginning to grow old.

Of the trio, Robbie was actually the person that Jeanne had known the longest. They had met in the gay bars in the Village years ago and had become friends: Jeanne was the steady, serious one, working her way through a succession of information technology jobs when the field was first opening up and everyone was figuring things out as they went along. Robbie, a theatrical costume designer, was the golden-haired, all-night partier (fond of running around in a tee shirt that said *Kiss Me! I'm a Queer Jew!*) who often ended up in Jeanne's tiny kitchen in the middle of the night, relating some story about love, sex, and intrigue in which he was a featured player. He had settled down some when he decided to open his own dressmaking shop and had become almost domestic as he approached his forties, when he met Joe, who was a few years older and ready for a quiet, comfortable life. When Jeanne met Julie—also Jeanne's opposite; flirty, funny, a rambunctious girl from a big Irish family—the four formed a supportive social circle. Both couples had recently joined the other urban exiles who had made the move from Manhattan to the Jersey side of the Hudson. After some initial trepidation about their decision, all four had finally decided that the view of the river made the move worthwhile. Making dinner, Robbie would sometimes call Jeanne and say, *Look out the window, sweetie: there's a cruise ship going by. Look at the sunset, look at the stars.*

After everyone was assembled at the table on the lightship deck and more drinks and food had been ordered, Joe turned to Avram and started asking about the DOS attack; he'd had difficulty getting online all day and was wondering why.

Avram gave him a quick rundown of what had happened and how eHorizons was handling the packet flood attack. Then he said, "There's been a network security conference scheduled in the city at the Marriott for weeks. The FBI decided to commandeer the morning session to discuss all the attacks that have been taking place lately, and *she's* making me go." He finished up by dramatically pointing across the table at Jeanne.

"Do we really have to go through this again?" Jeanne sighed. Laying her head on Julie's shoulder, she said, "Can you tell me why he's so stubborn?"

"He's not just stubborn," Julie said, "he's argumentative."

"Oh, I see," Avram said. "The Jews are argumentative. I mean, it's more than a joke. The Irish, for example, aren't?"

"Nope," Julie told him. "We like a good, clean fistfight in a bar and then roll on home, happy as Leprechauns."

"Ethnic stereotypes," Joe said. "Now *there's* something we need more of."

"What's the matter Mr. DiCicco?" Robbie said. "Touchy?"

"Listen, *boychik*," Joe said. "Don't even start. You're way out of your league."

"You think that's a Yiddish accent?" Avram said to Joe. "It's awful."

"Well at least we stopped talking about computers," Robbie said. Grabbing Julie's hand and raising it in the air, along with his own, he added, "Some people here don't care at all about the damn Internet."

"Robbie's right," Jeanne said. "Enough with work." Pointing to the cardboard tube leaning against Robbie's chair, she said, "I want to know what's in that."

"It's something I've wanted for a long time," Robbie said as he picked up the long tube and popped open the plastic plug on the end. "A friend of mine bought it a couple of years ago and I've always admired it. He's producing an off-Broadway review now and needed some costumes; I said I'd help him out and take this print in trade. It's a Maxfield Parrish." Slowly, he pulled what was apparently a rolled-up art print out of the tube and stood up so he could unfurl it. "Isn't it beautiful?" he said, holding it open.

The print, which was actually a large poster, showed a dreamy eyed, half-naked woman draped in gauzy scarves and holding aloft a softly glowing lamp as she stood by a pool of greeney blue water. Little winged nymphs flitted around her feet, like half-human fireflies.

"I'm so in love with her," Robbie said.

"Who is she?" Julie asked.

"She's Psyche," Robbie said, "shining the light of knowledge on a dreary world."

"But why does it say 'Edison Mazda' on the bottom?" Julie persisted.

"Mazda is part of the Persian name for the god of light," Robbie explained, warming to a subject he was apparently familiar with because of his interest in the print. "In the early 1900s, Edison Mazda—part of General Electric—commissioned Maxfield Parrish to create calendar illustrations and ads promoting its Mazda line of light bulbs. This is one of the calendar illustrations."

Avram had been silently studying the print. When Robbie finished his explanation, he said, "I think I've seen this before."

"Really?" Robbie said, sounding surprised. "It's one of the rarest of Parrish's prints. Hard to find."

"Not the print," Avram said. "I saw the statue. A bronze."

"That can't be," Robbie told him. "I've done a lot of research about this print and I never found anything about the image being based on a statue—or made into one."

Avram shrugged. "Well, it's there. And I'm sure it's exactly the same."

"It's where?" Robbie asked.

Avram answered, "In Edison Park."

The name was familiar to Jeanne, but it took a few moments for her to remember why. Finally, she said to Avram, "You've told me about that, right? Edison? Isn't that the name of the pencil factory where you used to work?"

Julie laughed. "Avram," she said, "You worked in a pencil factory? I just can't picture it."

"It was a long time ago," he said, "when I first came here. I was living in the Bronx and going to grad school. At night, I was the watchman at the Edison Pencil Company. It was in a town called Boylersville, about an hour out of the city. I had an old junker, and I'd drive up after school."

"It's hard to imagine that a pencil factory in a town called Boylersville would need a night watchman," Julie said.

"Well, I guess they didn't really," Avram said, "which worked out fine for me; I used to sleep most of the night after I made my rounds. In the morning, if the weather was nice, sometimes I'd get a donut and coffee and eat breakfast in this little park before I drove home. Edison Park," he added, almost belligerently, in case Robbie still didn't believe him. "That's where the statue was."

"And you're sure it was *my* Psyche?"

"I'm sure it was the same figure. I saw it enough times to remember."

"I'd love to go see it," Robbie said.

"Well, then, Avram," Julie said, "you should show it to him sometime."

"Yeah," Avram said with a shrug. "Whatever."

"How about tomorrow?" Jeanne suggested.

"Great. You've already got me doing one stupid thing on a Saturday. Now you want me to do two?"

"You just said you'd show Robbie the statue."

"When did I say that?"

"We can go in the afternoon," Jeanne said. "I was already planning to drive in. How hard will it be to shoot right up the Saw Mill? The conference is supposed to be over by noon, so we could go right afterwards."

"That would be great," Robbie said. "I was going to go to the shop in the morning, so you can pick me up."

Julie had to work and Joe wanted to watch a baseball game—the Yankees were heading to the playoffs and he was convinced that if he didn't watch, they'd lose—so in the end, it was decided that it would be just Jeanne, Avram, and Robbie who would make the trip to go look for Edison Park.

The next morning, Jeanne decided to sit out on the terrace for a while and watch morning come to the river. It was a rainy day that was forecast to be sunny later: behind the gray clouds and weak sun was a deeper blush of light and the promise of fresh breezes. Finishing her coffee, she thought about where she was going to be headed in a little while: it was a gathering of the clan, of sorts, a convocation of all the geeks and nerds and ex-cracker/hackers, all the babies and the baldies, all the Linux rebels and the grownup Game Boy cowboys and Atari pioneers from up and down the northeast corridor; even the ex-secretaries like herself would be coming, the ex-file clerks and typists, office drones who'd changed careers when they found they had an affinity for a technology that had barely existed when they were kids. All these people were going to gather to try to figure out how to stop the world they had created out of computers and electricity—first for fun and then for business—from being invaded and possibly permanently corrupted. It was, Jeanne knew, entirely possible that finding a way to do that would be a long way off.

Half an hour later she said goodbye to Julie, who was just getting up, got her car out of the garage and started into the city through the Holland Tunnel, an easy drive on an early Saturday. She crossed lower Manhattan, heading for the East Village, a neighborhood she had always known as a warren of wrecked tenements and drug-infested streets, but in the past decade—as was always happening in the city—the area had changed character and become gentrified: four-hundred-dollar-a-month rents for an apartment with a bathtub in the kitchen had given way to half-million-dollar condos with terraces overlooking Tompkins Square Park, where the hippies and the yippies used to get high. Avram had managed to find one of the few blocks in the neighborhood that had resisted transformation: he lived in a drafty loft filled with computers and electronic equipment three doors down from the New York headquarters of the Hell's Angels. The block had a bad reputation but apparently, so did Avram: walking with him to his apartment on a spring day last year, Jeanne had heard one of the bikers hanging around outside call him *Commando.*

"What do those guys think you did in the army?" she'd asked him when they were out of earshot. "Do they know you programmed computers?"

"Those computers launched missiles," he answered testily, "not video games."

Jeanne had simply nodded then, and fallen silent. *Soldier Jews,* she remembered thinking. Where *had* these people come from?

Avram was waiting for her downstairs, sitting on the stoop. He got into the car and Jeanne started heading uptown, but she'd only gone a few blocks when she noticed that there was something very wrong with the traffic signals: they were out of sync. Usually, if you timed things right, you could sail through at least a couple of green lights before you hit a yellow or red, but this morning, they seemed to be randomly changing color—some weren't even changing at all. The weekend traffic was relatively light, but even so, the erratic signals were making for a lot of near-accidents and horn honking since no one could anticipate what signal they might encounter at the next intersection.

Jeanne pointed this out to Avram and then turned on the radio; in a few minutes the local news reported that the computer system controlling the traffic signals in Manhattan had failed; the far west side was somehow not affected but traffic in midtown and the east side below the 59th Street

Bridge was a mess. The problem was going to have to be solved by traffic agents going out into the streets and resetting individual junction boxes around the city. The radio announcer said that clearing up the problem was likely to take all day.

Proceeding at a crawl, Jeanne managed to steer the car up toward Seventh Avenue, where she parked in a garage near the Marriott. She and Avram made it to the hotel and found the conference room they wanted just as the meeting was about to start. Hurriedly, they both grabbed some breakfast snacks that had been set out on a side table along with urns of coffee and then settled themselves into a pair of empty seats.

At the front of the room, John Ettinger was already seated on the podium, at a table draped with a white cloth. There were a few other men perched beside him, partially hidden from the audience by an array of microphones, water glasses, and heavy silver-colored pitchers.

The room grew quiet quickly. The FBI agent stood and began speaking, opening his remarks by thanking everyone for coming. Then, after clearing his throat, he made a surprising announcement.

"Those of you who drove here today know that the traffic signals around town aren't working properly. We've been informed by the city that the problem isn't the result of an accident. Apparently, early this morning, someone hacked the city's traffic control network and partially disabled it. As a result, a great deal of the integrated programming has been disrupted."

After giving everyone a moment to absorb the news, Ettinger went on. "There have been other attacks in recent days directed at specific networks and companies. Some have been minor annoyances, some near disasters. eHorizons was hacked yesterday, a problem that was handled quickly and effectively, but early in the day, the Berne-Zeiss E-trade site was taken down for six hours, which affected thousands of stocktraders. The list goes on. These narrow-focus attacks, of course, are in addition to the ongoing DOS packet flood. So, taken together, what we're all experiencing is a major, orchestrated, and ongoing cyberterrorism assault on the North American networks, engineered by some person or persons unknown, using a variety of methods that, taken together, are affecting the entire web."

Ettinger talked on for some time longer, but after a while, Jeanne stopped listening. She was as frustrated as she was disappointed to hear the FBI more or less admit that they had developed no new information about the problem and had no new leads. Which was the gist of what the next speaker said, as well: representatives of the government/university consortium involved in setting up Internet2 reported that their lightning-speed networks were faring no better in warding off the attacks.

After the presentations, the floor was opened for discussion, which allowed the assembled techies to do what they had really come for: to talk to each other. For over an hour, people stood up to ask questions or explain what they were doing to deal with the attacks and suggest how their methods might be adapted to others' needs. The discussion was orderly and collegial until someone stood up in the back of the room—a latecomer to the meeting who, unlike everyone else who had spoken so far, did not introduce himself as being affiliated with any company or service—and interjected his own ideas.

"You know," he said, "you're all spending so much time trying to figure out how to deal with the problem that you're forgetting that we have to think about why it's happening. And we all know why: it's because of the Jews. The Jews have taken over the land of Palestine, they're directing our foreign policy, and they have to be stopped. If we end the Jewish domination of America and the Holy Land, I guarantee that we can end terrorism against the rest of us, who've been dragged into a fight that we didn't ask for."

For a moment, there was dead silence in the room. Everyone—including Jeanne—was apparently so shocked by what had been said that it seemed no one had a reply. That is, until a donut suddenly went sailing through the air toward the speaker, who was still standing, and hit him on the side of his head. The sugary projectile left a small, powdery mark on his cheek, just below his eye.

Jeanne started to turn her head to see where the donut had come from, but she realized that she knew before she even looked around: it was Avram. Understanding that, she found herself thinking another oddly disconnected thought: where had he gotten a donut? She hadn't noticed any laid out on the table with the coffee.

Then a bagel went flying by. *Those* Jeanne had seen a lot of stacked up near the coffee. The bagel also hit the speaker and left a little smear of cream cheese on his shoulder. More bagels were soon flying across the conference room. Jeanne had only a napkin in her hand, but she decided to join the spontaneous protest—one that the guy who'd made the anti-Jewish remarks should have expected, she decided; this was New York, an information technology meeting attended by a lot of ex- and current smart-ass computer types, so a good percentage of the people in the room *were* Jewish (well, she thought, some cliché's do hold true)—so she wadded up the napkin and flung it in the same direction as the flying bagels.

Once all the available breakfast food had been sent soaring, people started booing. Ettinger rushed from the stage, joined by some other agents who had apparently been seeded throughout the audience and began to drag the speaker out of the room. He didn't go easily. Shouting some sort of statements Jeanne couldn't hear about the rising din, he strained against the agents' efforts to remove him.

Finally, they managed to maneuver the troublemaker out of the room and after that, the meeting started to break up. People drifted out of the conference room in small groups, exchanging business cards and phone numbers. It was eleven o'clock in the morning; the meeting had been scheduled to last until noon.

Together, Jeanne and Avram left the Marriott, got Jeanne's car out of the garage and started uptown. Jeanne went west first, so she could travel along avenues not affected by the crazed traffic lights, which the radio news reported were still behaving erratically. She called Robbie at his shop to tell him they might be a little earlier than planned and started to explain why the meeting had broken up ahead of schedule, but as she did, Avram gestured for her to give him the cell phone.

"It's because of the Jews," Avram told Robbie. "We're the cause of all the problems of the modern world."

"You know," Robbie said to Avram, who, laughing, repeated his answer to Jeanne, "my mother always told me there were people who believed that, but I thought she meant everything was my fault. Specifically, me."

Jeanne took the phone back from Avram. "How many Jewish mothers does it take to screw in a light bulb?" she asked Robbie. When he obligingly replied that he didn't know, she said, in what she hoped was a decent imitation of her grandmother's Yiddish accent, "Don't even bother with it darling, I'll just sit here in the dark."

When she finally hung up on Robbie, Avram said, "What is it with all of you? You're compiling an encyclopedia of Jewish jokes?"

"Define 'all of you,'" Jeanne said to him.

"You know what I mean."

"You grew up in Jerusalem," she said to him. "I gather it's not a funny city. Robbie and I grew up right here. In New Yowk," she drawled, "What can I tell you? It's a great place to pick up jokes."

Jeanne doubled-parked in front of Robbie's shop and ran inside to get him. He spent just a few minutes locking up and soon they were heading up the Saw Mill River Parkway, which paralleled the Hudson. They drove past exit signs for one historic, picturesque town after another: Sleepy

Hollow, Tarrytown, Ardsley, Dobbs Ferry. Boylersville, though—an hour north of the Bronx—was a different kind of place entirely, as was clear as soon as they left the parkway and followed a number of twists and turns along connecting roads that finally led to Alva Street, the town's main thoroughfare.

"Alva?" Robbie said to Avram. "As in Thomas Alva?"

"As in Thomas Alva," Avram agreed. "This is a company town. A man named Herman Schlager built the pencil factory and he built the town around it. He admired Edison, so he named everything after him. Even the pencils."

"So why isn't the town called Edison?" Robbie asked.

Avram shrugged. "I guess it was already a place named Boylersville before Schlager got here. But he made it bigger."

"And ugly," Robbie said, looking out the window.

Jeanne agreed. The place looked downtrodden, worn out; a town built to serve a business that had died. There were shops on Alva Street—a diner, a grocery, a check-cashing service—and people walking around, but even in the brightening afternoon sunlight, there was no energy in the pedestrians' steps, no open doors inviting commerce into the stores. The town of small brick buildings and clapboard houses seemed to have little in common with its upscale suburban neighbors, reminding Jeanne more of the dying towns to the north, in the valleys of the Catskills, towns haunted by a past century, by trains that didn't run anymore and visitors who had stopped coming.

"It doesn't look like pencils are such a hot item these days," Robbie observed.

"I heard that the factory closed down a couple of years ago," Avram said. "I don't think there's really much other work around here."

A few minutes later, already past the town center, they were driving by the shuttered factory, a hulking, multistoried building of dark red brick. Along one windowless outside wall, in three-foot high letters that were probably once an orangey-yellow as bright as a crayon, was the name, "Edison Pencils."

"Where's the park?" Robbie asked. "Did we pass it already?"

"No," Avram said. "It's just ahead."

And so it was. A little way down the road, with "Edison Pencils" still visible in her rearview mirror, Jeanne saw a rustic wooden sign that said, "Edison Park." Here, she pulled into a small, gravelly parking lot and turned off the engine.

"Okay," she said to Avram as they all climbed out of the car. "Lead on."

The place Avram had brought them to was one of those experiments in civic planning that had been popular in the first half of the twentieth century, when kings of commerce, believing themselves to be enlightened—and fearing the growing power of both unions and public education to cause unrest—had tried to create environments that created contented workers. The park, which Avram said he'd been told had once included a carousel and a skating rink, even a manicured green suitable for candlepin bowling—now all long gone—was still maintained by the town, but seemingly without much enthusiasm. Perhaps as a result, it didn't seem like a place that got much use: as Jeanne, Avram, and Robbie walked down a cobbled path lined on both sides with linden trees just turning from green to gold, they saw no one else, heard nothing but the sound of quarreling birds. Still, it was a pretty walk: wildflowers had grown up along the path and the glimpse of sky through the canopy of rustling leaves was now a bright, cloudless blue.

When they finally reached the end of the path, they found themselves walking across an expanse of meadow dotted with dandelions that ringed a small, still lake. In the middle of the lake was a little island, overgrown with brush and vines.

"Here it is," Avram said, stopping at the edge of the lake.

"Where?" Robbie said, peering out at the water. "I don't see it."

But Jeanne did. It was in the center of the island, a dark and delicate bronze figure holding a bronze lamp. "Put on your glasses," Jeanne said to Robbie.

"I just use these for reading," he said, touching the little silver half-glasses hanging from a chain around his neck.

"Well, what do you use for actually *seeing* anything?" Jeanne asked.

He didn't answer, just walked toward the lake's muddy shore and squinted. "Oh," he said. "Oh my." Annoyed now, he turned to Avram. "Why didn't you say something about it being in the middle of an ocean?"

"That?" Avram said. "That's a little tiny lake."

"Don't tell me," Robbie said. "Edison Lake, right?"

"Of course," Avram said. But even as he spoke, he looked distracted, glancing back and forth between the lake and the shore. "There used to be a footbridge around here somewhere," he said. "You could walk over to the island and back." He started wandering along the shore, following the grassy edge line that encircled the lake, stopping, finally, to point at some wooden pilings topped by broken boards that were jutting out of the mud and extended a few feet into the water. "There it is," Avram said. "I guess it must have collapsed."

"Is there any other way to get over there?" Robbie asked. "I really would like to be able to see it up close. How deep is the water?"

"How would I know?" Avram replied to both questions.

"Robbie?" Jeanne said. "It does look like the same figure as the one in your picture."

"It does," Robbie said. "It looks just like the Maxfield Parrish. But that's so strange—Parrish wasn't a sculptor. And he certainly never did any bronzes."

Before anyone could suggest that it might be dangerous, Robbie had climbed up onto the pilings. Crawling out to the edge of one of the last, large boards that had once been part of the footbridge put him about twenty feet closer to the island, but another fifty feet or so of water still separated him from the statue.

Now, with his glasses perched on the end of his nose, he called back to Jeanne and Avram, "It's Psyche alright. I think I can even see the little fairies—and don't anybody make any comments about that word!—at the base of the statue, between the weeds." After a few more minutes of clinging to the broken footbridge, he climbed off the pilings and plopped himself down on the grass, facing the island. Jeanne sat beside him, followed by Avram.

"It's a wonderful sculpture," Robbie said. "But a real puzzle. Who made it? Is it a copy of the original Maxfield Parrish, or did Parrish copy this scene? The lagoon in the print could be this lake."

Compared to the problems that Jeanne and Avram had been dealing with in recent days, Robbie's mystery seemed monumentally unimportant, part of an old story that didn't deserve any new speculation. But that was also what made it so comfortably intriguing: if it went unsolved, it didn't matter. Nothing would be affected, nothing changed.

Which seemed to suit Avram, who was willing, at least, to consider clues. "You know," he said, "I never actually saw it on, but I bet that lamp used to be lit up at night. I think I saw a junction box back there near the path." He stood up and walked quickly into the thick stand of broad-leafed lindens and returned to the lakeshore a few minutes later.

"Well," he reported, as he sat down again beside Jeanne and Robbie, "there is a box back there, all right, and it's still got juice. If there's a cable buried under the lake, that lamp might still work."

"You mean it might just need a bulb?" Robbie said.

"It's possible," Avram replied .

"Well, I'd sure like to know what the story is here," Robbie said, but Avram had no other information to offer him.

They stayed in the park just a little while longer and then drove back to the city, where it seemed that the traffic lights had finally been fixed. Jeanne dropped off Avram, drove herself and Robbie to New Jersey, and was back in her apartment around dinnertime. She made herself a sandwich and later fell asleep on the couch; later than that, Julie came home and woke her up, but just to point her toward the bedroom, where she quickly fell back to sleep again.

Hours later, when she heard the telephone ringing, she was deep in a dream and thought it was still the middle of the night but it wasn't; it was seven-thirty on Sunday morning. She picked up the extension by the bed and heard Avram's voice.

"I'm in a cab on my way to the ferry," he said. "Meet me in twenty minutes."

"What?" Jeanne said, still waking up. "Why?"

"Somebody's trying to take down the whole fucking web," Avram said. "Half our sites are down."

"Nobody called me," Jeanne said.

"*I'm* calling you," Avram shouted. "Hurry up."

Julie was also awake by now and Jeanne tried to explain to her what had happened, though she wasn't completely sure herself. She took a quick shower, threw on her clothes and then, without even drying her hair, ran to the building's garage, started the car, and raced through the quiet streets of Jersey City to the ferry dock just as a boat pulled up to the pier. Three people disembarked, and the first one off was Avram; as soon as she saw him, Jeanne also noticed that he was carrying an overnight bag. *Okay*, she thought, *so it's going to be that bad.*

Avram grunted something that sounded like hello and jumped into the car. Jeanne started the engine up again, negotiated the local streets and got them onto the turnpike before she asked Avram for more details about what was going on.

"Apparently another attack started about five a.m.," he told her. "I got a call about an hour later when the weekend crew realized they were being overrun and couldn't stop it. Whoever launched the attack created a worm that got past everyone's firewalls; what it seems to do is find a router connection to use as a portal, opens it up and that allows for remote programming. What *that* means is someone's been able to get into thousands—thousands and thousands—of servers, including ours, and use them to send out billions of message packets."

Jeanne understood what he was saying, impossible as it seemed. "You mean we're being attacked by our own computers?"

"I should have seen it coming," Avram said. "And on top of that, a lot of the messages contain viruses. New ones we haven't seen before. God knows what they're programmed to do."

"Okay," Jeanne said as they came up on the exit for Port Elizabeth. "What do we do now?"

"What you're going to do," Avram told her, "is set up a local network between at least two of our IBM 6000s and purge them of anything they're running now—I want them dedicated to one job: I'm going to reprogram them to cycle through the packets, look for our own IP addresses and destroy any messages with our IPs as a header. That might let enough real traffic through to let us get our sites back online without crashing from the bogus traffic flood. And I'm going to call that jerk at the FBI and suggest that he suggest that everyone else who can should do the same thing. More fingers in the dike," he explained. "Everyone's going to have to cooperate to stop an attack of this magnitude. It's unbelievable. You'll see," he said. "Wait till you get to the office and look at the logs."

"What about the viruses?"

"That's what we pay our subscription services for. Hopefully, someone got them out of bed at five a.m., too."

He got on his cell phone then and started making calls. Jeanne turned her full attention to the road and concentrated on driving.

As soon as they arrived at the data center, Jeanne plunged into work. She created the LAN that Avram wanted set up and was then drawn into other tasks: eHorizons dealt with a number of companies that provided secure financial services, and they were all hysterical. Because of the magnitude of the DOS attack—all across the country, people were finding it impossible to get online, even those using high-speed broadband connections—the story had made the morning news, so besides those trying to log onto the web, everyone who turned on the TV or radio heard about it. Even the talking heads on the Sunday morning shows knew about it: after a pundit on one of these programs reported that a virus component of the packet flood was attacking credit card information, stealing or replicating millions of card numbers, all of eHorizons' phone lines lit up. Even on an early Sunday morning, people were trying to check their bank balances, apply for a home equity loan, or get an early jump on their Christmas shopping. When they couldn't do these things, they called someone, somewhere, to complain, and that someone, it seemed to Jeanne, ended up calling her.

Eventually, she arranged for other staff members to deal with the calls coming in and started sifting through the reports being generated by the servers, but nothing made much sense. There were literally millions of lines of meaningless, garbled code to try to read through and to Jeanne, surrounded by printouts and spreadsheets, it felt like she was stuck in the middle of a giant mound of glue. She'd look up every now and then and see Avram flash by with a phone still stuck in his ear: he looked angrier and angrier, she thought, every time she focused on his face.

By the afternoon, they had antidotes to some of the viruses, but the packet flood kept coming. Avram's fix made it possible to get their crashed sites back online but this wasn't doing much good, because ninety percent of the time, customers were still blocked from reaching them by all the bogus traffic streaming in, which went on through the afternoon and into the night. Jeanne never even considered going home; around seven p.m. she called Julie and told her she was staying at the data center overnight, though she wasn't really sure that she'd be getting home tomorrow, either.

She slept for only a couple of hours that night, sprawled on a couch in her office, and then went back to work as Avram slept. In the interim, Sunday's tech crew went home and new staff arrived Monday morning with new ideas about how to speed up the software's ability to divert or destroy the spam traffic. Avram was soon back in the control room again and he tried everything that anyone suggested, making incremental progress with each new fix. Still, none of eHorizons' sites were functioning at anything near a normal level; their colleagues and competitors reported the same situation up and down the line.

The packet flood continued unabated all through Monday, with Jeanne and Avram watching helplessly as their own servers—which they could not completely wrest from outside control—continued to churn out data that was adding to the traffic clogging the Internet. In the afternoon, on a conference call with another host company—one of their main competitors, located in Florida—and a number of FBI cybercrime agents, including John Ettinger, one of the agents raised the possibility of simply shutting down all the affected computers and servers across the United States.

"That might work," Avram said, "but there's a problem. What if we couldn't get them back up again?"

Ettinger seemed startled by that suggestion and asked the security director of the other company for his opinion. "Well," came the answer, "Avram could be right. It wouldn't exactly be like turning off a toaster and then turning it on again and having toast pop right out. Everything's connected to everything else. Everyone's made millions of adjustments, calibrations, set up millions of connections in specific ways to send and receive data. Theoretically, sure, if we 'turn everything off,' we should be able to turn everything on again just as easily, but who knows? A million—a zillion—things might have to be reset. It could take weeks. Months."

"Alright," Ettinger said. "We'll table the idea for now. But we might have to come back to it later."

When they got off the call, Jeanne asked Avram, "Do you think they can make us shut down?"

"I don't think they can *make* us," Avram said, "But they certainly could apply a lot of pressure."

"Why do I feel like if we did that, it would be like killing the computers?" Jeanne said.

"Because you've been around them too long," Avram told her. "And because you're a woman. Women romanticize everything."

"Do I tell you often enough," Jeanne said to him, "that you're a pig?"

"Oink, oink," he said, and went back to punching strings of code into his computer.

Later, Jeanne decided that she had to go home just long enough to shower and change. She was back at the data center in ninety minutes and found that little had improved. The web was still alive, but barely—slowly, it was choking to death on its own traffic.

And then, on Tuesday afternoon at 2:15, the attack stopped. It was like watching the waters of an electronic sea recede beyond the far horizon and disappear. Gone. Vanished: in less than a few minutes, disappeared. All the monitors showing traffic levels reaching into red zones, all the software showing web capacity going off the charts dropped back to normal as Jeanne, Avram, and all the staff in the data center looked on in astonishment.

"What happened?" someone asked.

"It's just...gone," Jeanne replied, sounding, even to herself, like she was spouting dialogue in a monster movie. *Is it still out there? No, thank God, it's gone for now.* "Avram?" she said, turning to him for confirmation.

"That's what it looks like," he agreed. "Someone pulled the plug on their end."

"But why?"

Avram shook his head. He had absolutely no idea.

He got back on the phone, but no one else had any answers either, nor was anyone any closer to figuring out who was behind the attack. No one was taking responsibility and there still seemed to be no clues about whom to blame.

As she lifted herself out of her chair in the control room and started toward her office, feeling stiff and sore, Jeanne's intention was just to retrieve her jacket and then go out to her car and head directly to her apartment. But habit—and the inability to leave things undone—made her pick up a pile of faxes that had fallen off the holding tray of the machine in her office and, unread for days, had spilled onto the floor. She leafed through them quickly, thankfully finding nothing important enough for her to have to deal with immediately until, completely unexpectedly, she came across one from Robbie that was dated just that morning. She couldn't imagine why he would be sending her a fax, of all things, so she sat down at her desk to read it and was soon engrossed.

There were three pages in the fax. The first was just a cover note from Robbie, on his shop stationery, that said, "Dear Jeanne: I'm sure this is the last thing you've got time for right now, but when things calm down, I thought you might enjoy this little story. On Monday morning, I called the library in Boylersville to see if they had any information about Edison Park and the statue—and look what the librarian sent me. A nice lady named Enid. When you finally get home (Julie says you've been living at your office), curl up with a cup of tea and a teddy bear and then call me. Love, Robbie."

It sounded like a really tempting thing to do—Jeanne thought she even really did have a teddy bear somewhere at home—but she was more than eager for any diversion from the stress of the past few days so she started to read the few pages that the librarian had typed out for Robbie, apparently after going through some town records.

As Avram had said, Herman Schlager was an admirer of Thomas Edison and had written to tell him so. Thereafter, Edison and Schlager had developed an ongoing correspondence in which Schlager revealed to Edison that not only had he named the pencil company after him, he had also incorporated many of Edison's ideas and designs into the operation of the factory and the construction of employees' houses, built for them by the company, which were among the first outside of a large urban area to have indoor electricity included in their original plans. Edison was impressed enough to visit the Edison Pencil Company sometime around 1920, during the height of the Maxfield Parrish-inspired advertising campaign for Edison Mazda bulbs, and apparently presented Schlager with print #1 of the Psyche image, which had been originally given to Edison as a gift by Parrish himself. To commemorate Edison's visit, Schlager had a statue erected in the new park he had just built for the town he was populating with pencil factory workers and their families: that statue was the Psyche in the lake, which had been cast in bronze by Yussel Gittelman, a Jewish sculptor who had fled the turmoil in Europe during World War I and found work as a foreman in the Edison Pencil Company.

"Jews just turn up everywhere," Jeanne murmured to herself as she went on reading.

In answer to your question, the librarian had written to Robbie, *our records indicate that the statue's lamp was indeed meant to be lit at night.* And, Jeanne read, it seemed that the lamp had stayed lit until sometime in the 1960s when the town could no longer find the special, old-fashioned electric sign bulbs with a triple tungsten coil that the lamp required. There had been discussion for years about converting the lamp to accommodate modern bulbs, but it had never been done and now, in the town's reduced circumstances, it was unlikely that it ever would.

Jeanne folded the fax pages, put them in her pocket and then started tidying up her desk, but soon decided that she was too tired to care about what her office looked like. She went to look for Avram to tell him that she was leaving and found him in his office, poring over reams of data printouts.

Impulsively, she took the pages out of her pocket and handed them to him. "Here," she said, "read something else for a while. Robbie found the answers to all your questions about Edison Park."

"I didn't have any questions," he said, but she was already out the door.

She drove straight home and slept from four in the afternoon until almost eight the next morning. When she finally got up, Julie was just getting ready for work, so they were able to have breakfast together, a rare occurrence lately. After Julie left, Jeanne was still taking her time, figuring she deserved to go to work late if she wanted to, but her dreamy progress through showering and dressing was interrupted by the telephone.

She answered it with dread, thinking, of course, *Here we go again*, but it was only Robbie.

"Hey," he said. "Did you read my fax yesterday?" When Jeanne told him she had, he said, "Well, guess what? I think that I actually found the right bulb."

"Robbie," Jeanne said, not really connecting to what he was telling her, "what are you talking about?"

"The bulb for Yussel's lamp. I found one that I think will work." And then he added, "I actually do know how to use the web, you know. There are a whole bunch of online sites that sell antique bulbs, and I found one this morning. It only took me fifteen minutes. Of course, I had to wait a couple of days until you people fixed the Internet, so thank you for that."

"I'm sorry to disappoint you," Jeanne replied, "but I didn't have a hand in fixing anything. On this one, I'm just one more face in the crowd, watching the world fall apart. It's very frustrating, actually. Even Avram couldn't do much—which I think has been driving him crazy."

"Well, I've got something he can do," Robbie said. "You, too. You can help me light Yussel's lamp."

"Why would we want to do that?"

"Because it's been out for a long time."

"Robbie..."

"Because it's a beautiful thing that's fallen into disrepair and it can be fixed. Because it's like a fabulous dress that you can refurbish instead of throwing it away so you can wear it to one more fabulous party. Come on," Robbie coaxed. "I know that I can talk you into this. Think about it," he said. "Yussel would have come here about the same time that your grandparents did. And mine. Think about how much less they had than we do. How much they lost. This guy was a sculptor, for heaven's sake, and he ended up working in a pencil factory."

"So because all these people suffered we should dedicate ourselves to repairing their lighting fixtures? That'll right all the wrongs?"

"Something like that. Do you think you can get Avram to come?"

"No. Besides, why do you need him?"

"What if some electrical things need to be connected or something?" Robbie said.

"Then I think you'd better witch up Thomas Edison," Jeanne told him. "Avram is not an electrician."

"But he's the closest thing we've got. He has to come."

Jeanne waited a week before she even broached the subject with Avram. At work, they both went about their business in an orderly and seemingly normal fashion, but, like the rest of the staff, they were constantly on the alert for the next attack. The tension of waiting for it to come—and every night when she went home, Jeanne counted up the days that it didn't: *two, three, four, five, six*—was, Jeanne thought, more exhausting than fighting it when it did. They didn't talk about it much, but Jeanne assumed that Avram felt the same way: he was at the data center early, stayed late, and was short-tempered with everyone, even her.

Because his behavior was so unpleasant, Jeanne felt that she was doing him a big favor by agreeing to spend an extra day at work with him—a Saturday, no less—helping him install and program a new supercomputer that he wanted to set up as, essentially, a guardian at the gate: like a great electronic sieve, it was going to sift through every single message packet addressed to any web site on the eHorizons servers and attempt to screen out bogus traffic. It was also going to play a version of a war game that Avram had come up with: the computer itself was going to create viruses and then develop antidotes to its own poisons in the hope that once it had amassed a large enough collection of homegrown fixes, it would be able to apply them, or at least quickly adapt them—to any new virus that an outside attacker tried to launch at the eHorizons system.

To Jeanne's surprise, Avram was actually in a relaxed, almost cheerful mood as they worked together on the computer. It was a relatively quiet day at the data center and Jeanne found the work interesting. Avram also seemed to enjoy teaching her as they went along, explaining how he was setting up the virus-producing program, keeping it isolated from the computer's other functions, and how the program would catalogue the various properties of the antidotes it would invent so that it would eventually be able to select from thousands of different pieces of code and quickly string its choices together in order to produce an effective remedy when it encountered a virus it hadn't dealt with before.

Late in the afternoon, when they were finally finished and the computer was apparently doing everything exactly the way Avram wanted it to, he seemed pleased—so much so that he was even able to say thank-you to Jeanne, words she didn't hear from him very often.

"The work wouldn't have gone so quickly without your help," he told her. "You doing the backup checks saved a lot of time."

"Well, good," Jeanne said. "I'm glad. But if you really want to thank me," she said, thinking fast, "you can take me out to dinner."

"Sure," Avram agreed. "I can do that." Still in a jocular mood, he said, "What's the matter? Are you on your own again tonight?"

"Julie's working her last Saturday night for a month," Jeanne told him. "Thank goodness. There are just so many episodes of *Cops* I can watch."

"So where do you want to go?" Avram asked.

"Boylersville," Jeanne told him.

"Ah. Boylersville," Avram repeated slowly. "Because you suddenly found out that one of those dinky little diners we passed serves the world's greatest hamburgers?"

Jeanne sighed. "It's Robbie's idea," she told him. "He wants to light Yussel's lamp."

"What?"

"I'm supposed to play on your sympathies," Jeanne went on. "I'm supposed to tell you a sad story about this poor Jew who could have been a great sculptor but only created this one work and then, for some reason, just stopped."

"Well, we don't know that really," Avram said, "but it probably does end up being a sad story. He came here from some town in Poland, all by himself, when he was twenty-two and ended up in a pencil factory in upstate New York. God knows what horror brought him here—or what happened to him later. He quit the pencil factory just after he completed the Psyche and then, nothing. He just disappeared."

"You looked him up, didn't you?" Jeanne said.

"Well, it's not like it took any great effort," Avram told her. "The Mormons have half the world's genealogical records online. And then there are tax records, census counts..." he shrugged. "So I was curious. So what?"

"So you were also twenty-two when you came here," Jeanne said. "I remember you telling me that."

"I was. But I also had parents at home who I still go back to see once a year, and a dozen cousins living in New York. If I ever got really desperate, there was always someone to turn to for help."

Jeanne looked at him. He looked back at her.

"Alright," he said finally. "You got me. Let's go light Yussel's lamp."

Jeanne called Robbie and told him—whispering into the phone in her office—that it was now or never; Avram was willing to go tonight so they'd better take advantage of his compliant state of mind. But Robbie didn't need any encouragement: the Yankees had made it to the playoffs; game one was tonight and Joe wasn't going to budge from his post on the couch in front of the TV. Jeanne told Robbie that they'd pick him up in half an hour.

When they got to his building it was in the blue hour of a silky, late September dusk. Robbie was waiting downstairs, holding several canvas bags secured with drawstrings. When Jeanne pulled up to the curb he motioned to her to pop the trunk and as he stowed away the bags, Avram asked him what he'd brought.

"Rafts and a foot pump," Robbie told him. "We need some way to get over to the island."

This time, going north, they drove up the Hudson on the Jersey side and crossed over to New York via the George Washington Bridge, which proved to be a much quicker route than the one they'd taken last time. Still, night had fallen by the time they were driving through Boylersville, and once past the pencil factory, the road was so dark that they almost missed their turnoff. When they finally had the car safely parked, they took the canvas bags out of the trunk and Jeanne grabbed a flashlight, which they needed as they walked along the path to the lake. A harvest moon was rising quickly in the night sky, turning from the color of honey to a darker, rusty hue as it climbed higher into the stars. That was the only other light available until they emerged into the meadow: the paved path around the lake was lit by streetlights, old wrought iron fixtures topped by finials in the shape of oversize acorns. The light they gave off, though, was weak and provided little illumination beyond the few benches surrounding the water. In the center of the lake, Psyche and her island were lost in darkness.

Robbie dropped the canvas bags on the grass and started opening them, one by one. With the foot pump, he quickly filled the first two rafts, five-foot-long rectangles of clear plastic decorated with a pattern of colorful seahorses and dancing clams. Jeanne recognized these as pool furniture that Robbie and Joe had bought last summer and used at a house they'd rented on Fire Island.

She was telling Avram about this as Robbie opened the third bag; when she saw what fell out of it, she recognized that, too, and started to laugh.

"Whoops," Robbie said. "I thought that was another raft."

"No," Jeanne told him, "it's that stupid pool chair you and Julie kept fighting over last July, when we came to visit you."

"She can be a very stubborn girl," Robbie said as he began to pump up the chair. "I'm sure you're aware of that."

When he was finished, sitting on the grass before them were two plastic rafts displaying an aquarium's-worth of giddy sea life and what looked like one fat, puffed up armchair of clear pink plastic.

"So look what we've got here," Jeanne said. "It's the gay armada."

"You can just imagine how comfortable that makes *me* feel," Avram said. Then, turning to Robbie, he asked, "Where's the light bulb? We do have it with us, don't we?"

"Sure," Robbie told him. "It's in one of the bags."

Avram was the one who found it, swaddled in a mound of bubble wrap and tucked into the end of the first canvas bag. It was too big to fit into even a jacket pocket, so Avram stuffed it inside his denim shirt and started dragging one of the rafts toward the edge of the water. Jeanne took the other and Robbie, the pink chair.

Stopping for a moment, they all pulled off their sneakers and socks, rolled up the legs of their jeans and then their shirtsleeves, climbed onto their chosen watercraft and launched themselves onto the calm, dark lake.

Lying on the plastic rafts, Jeanne and Avram were able to move steadily forward by paddling with their hands and feet, but Robbie quickly found that the armchair was not so easily directed. It was meant to hold a lazy dreamer who wanted nothing more than to float aimlessly around a waveless pool; any attempt to steer it in a particular direction caused it to bob up and down and then tip wildly from side to side. Still, Robbie kept trying, kicking his feet and fanning his hands through the cool lake water.

Jeanne slowed down to wait for him while Avram paddled on ahead. Robbie had managed to make it to a point about halfway between the shore and the island when Jeanne, watching Robbie rocking around on the water suddenly knew exactly what was going to happen next.

In an effort to make the chair move a little faster, Robbie kicked the water just a little harder, and the forward motion, disturbing his own balance as well as the chair's, sent him head first into the lake.

As Jeanne heard him yell, *Shit!* and saw a spray of water rise into the air, glittering like tinsel, she couldn't help but marvel at how well orchestrated the whole accident had seemed: the chair had actually appeared to tip forward intentionally, like a malevolent acrobat getting rid of an ungraceful partner—but just as she started to giggle about this, a wave caused by Robbie's splashdown caught her, too, and she rolled right off the raft into the water.

She was a good swimmer so she didn't panic; she righted herself quickly and was prepared to start dog paddling around so she could find Robbie, who was hopeless in the water, but to her surprise, her toes immediately touched the bottom. It was soft and slippery beneath her feet, but the lake actually turned out to be relatively shallow; they had probably fallen in at its deepest point and yet she was still only standing in water up to her chest.

Immediately, she saw Robbie flailing around in the water, not ten feet away. He was frantically windmilling his arms up and down and screaming something that sounded like, *Frogs! Frogs!*

Jeanne made her way over to him, half walking, half swimming, and grabbed his tee shirt.

"Robbie!" she yelled at him. "Stop it. Stop screaming. You can stand here. Do you hear me? It's not deep. You can stand."

"I know that!" he shouted. "But something bit me! A frog bit me!"

"No, honey, no," Jeanne soothed, deciding that he must be hysterical. What made him believe it was, of all things, a frog? "I don't think so."

"I saw him when I was under. A fat frog with teeth."

"I don't think frogs *have* teeth," Jeanne told him, but the fact that she clearly wasn't taking him seriously only made him yell louder.

"There is some animal down there!" he insisted.

"Okay, okay," Jeanne said. "If there is, I'm sure you scared him away."

By now, Avram had paddled back to where they were standing in the murky water.

"Ahoy there," he said. "Should I send up a flare?"

"You know," Jeanne said to him as she tried to push her cold, dripping hair back from her face, "this might not be as funny as you think. We're both soaked. And the water's like ice."

"And something bit me," Robbie complained, though at least he did seem to have calmed down enough to catch his breath.

"Then I'm sure you're going to die," Avram informed him and, grinning, quickly paddled away.

Jeanne had managed to hold onto the flashlight when she fell off the raft and luckily, it somehow still worked. She turned it on and lit the way as she and Robbie struggled toward the island's pebbly shore, where Avram was now waiting for them. They dragged the raft and pool chair behind them, beaching them safely at the edge of the island.

And then, there she was, behind a low ring of bushes and viney plants: Psyche, the soul, with her dreamy Maxfield Parrish expression. Seen close up, it was apparent that she had been transformed by the sculptor into a figure with a more steadfast gaze than in the print; her posture had been made straighter, her features set in a more fearless configuration, and even the way she held high her now-extinguished lamp with a taut arm, a bronze grip, seeming to imply a more fierce determination than the printmaker had suggested to banish the darkness, to light the way into the future and bring the clarity of knowledge to bear upon human events.

Robbie took the flashlight from Jeanne and brushed away the tangles of ivy growing around the base of the statue, searching for some kind of inscription. "Look," he said at last, pointing the narrow beam of light at the name struck into the bronze rock upon which Psyche stood. "There's his name," Robbie said. "Yussel Gittelman."

"Well, Yussel," Avram said, "wherever you are, I hope you're watching this."

He took the package out of his shirt and gave it to Jeanne to unwrap as he climbed onto the statue's base to get to the lamp. She pulled off the bubble wrap and found herself holding a clear glass bulb so large she couldn't actually get her hands around it. Through thc thin, crystalline glass she could see three delicate-looking, intertwined tungsten loops that were the bulb's filament, and above them, etched on the outside of the glass, a logo she could just about make out in the moonlight: it said, *GE National Mazda.* The oddest thing about the bulb, other than its size, was its extremely narrow base: it was like holding a fat glass balloon with a tiny brass tail.

Avram had brought a set of screwdrivers with him, tucked into his back pocket; he had removed one and was now using it to chip away at the rust and grime around the bottom of the lamp's cage. With his left arm wrapped around the statue's wrist for balance, he set about unscrewing the fittings that held the lamp in place.

Watching him, Robbie said, "That's something I never thought of bringing—a screwdriver."

As he worked his way around the bottom of the lamp, Avram suddenly stopped for a moment. Looking down at Jeanne and Robbie, he said, "So tell me. How many Jews *does* it take to screw in a light bulb?"

Jeanne smiled back at him. "Three, apparently. One to drive the car, one to fall in the lake, and one who was smart enough to bring tools."

"Hey! How come I'm the dumb one in the story?" Robbie complained.

"You're not the dumb one," Jeanne told him. "You're the one who makes it funny."

Avram had finally freed the heavy glass lamp cage from its base and carefully handed it down to Robbie; Jeanne then handed up the bulb.

"Does it fit?" she asked. "Does it work?"

"Just hold on a minute," Avram told her. "Cross your fingers."

Jeanne and Robbie watched him place the clear, round bulb inside the lamp and nervously eyed every movement he made as he turned the bulb around in the socket, maybe a quarter of an inch at a time.

And then it went on. For what seemed like just a split second—so brief a time it could have been an illusion—only the three coiled loops of the tungsten filament glowed yellow-white, like the unexpected result of some primitive science experiment—and then, suddenly, the lamp filled up with radiant light. The antique bulb had turned into a golden moon, a small orb-shaped companion to its golden twin now grown small and distant, hanging high overhead in the September sky.

Without a word, Robbie handed the top of the lamp cage back to Avram, who fitted it carefully over the bulb and screwed it back in place. Then he climbed down off the statue and stood beside Jeanne and Robbie, looking up at the bright lamp.

Finally, Jeanne said to Robbie, "You were right. It is beautiful."

They only stayed on the island for a short while because the undergrowth was too thick to actually sit down and rest anywhere, so they started back to shore. Avram used the same raft and Jeanne used hers, but this time she tied the raft's neon-colored tow line to the pool chair and dragged it along behind her as she paddled, with Robbie safely enthroned in the chair's pink plastic clutches and under strict instructions not to move around.

Once they were back at the edge of the meadow, Jeanne and Robbie both started to shiver—the warm night was turning chill—but they were all reluctant to leave. Still, they couldn't linger: it was getting late and two of them, at least, were expected home. So they began walking slowly toward the path that would lead them to the car, all the while turning back to look at the light showering on the lake, on the leaves and the linden trees, and saying to each other, *We should come back, we should take pictures, we should bring Joe and Julie, we should do it soon.* And then the path made a turn, so they could no longer see the lamp they had lit in Edison Park. Just a few minutes later, they were driving home.

There are thirteen root servers housed in separate facilities in different countries around the globe and these devices, essentially, control the Internet by managing the domain names and addresses of all the web sites online, everywhere. Three days after their trip to Edison Park, when Jeanne and Avram were back at work, eleven of these servers were knocked out by a massive, catastrophic denial of service attack launched by an unknown number of computers under the control of unknown persons operating from a location, or locations, that no one could identify. In North and South America, in Europe, and parts of Asia, online commerce, chat, conversation, trading, browsing, bidding, research, reporting, publishing, teaching, and learning simply stopped. This was, by far, the worst attack yet because it was so concentrated and aimed directly at the super-servers that every single online site depended on. If those servers could not be rescued soon, it was impossible to predict whether the Internet itself could be restored to full working order. That morning, as Jeanne looked around the control room of the data center at the dozens of computer monitors all displaying *Page Not Found* errors or just blank white screens—the bare, empty nothing of a virtual nowhere—she felt a real sense of dread. Something she had always thought could not happen, had: it was like a healthy heart had suddenly stopped beating. Like an entire world had just winked out.

Across the room, she could see Avram shouting into the telephone, fighting already, rallying anyone he could get hold of to the cause of pushing back the oncoming tide of woe. And then her phone rang—actually, all the lights lit up at once—and she answered one randomly, expecting the caller to be a frantic customer but instead, it was Robbie. Without realizing it, she had picked up the outside extension of her own private line.

Everyone seemed to be yelling now; people were running around, more phones were ringing, and standing in the middle of all this confusion, Jeanne was having a hard time concentrating on what her friend was saying to her. Finally, though, she sorted it out. He wanted to know if next weekend was good—maybe on Saturday they could go back to Edison Park?

Jeanne told him she didn't know about that: all hell had broken loose at work and she didn't think she would be able to plan anything for a while. Okay, Robbie said, but he told her they should try to make the trip soon; the bulb he had bought was a used one and he didn't know how long it would last.

Oh? Jeanne said. She could hear Avram calling her name now, could see even the monitors connected to computers that were working off local networks—the ones supposedly safely barricaded behind impenetrable firewalls—beginning to go blank. *So tell me,* she said, even though she knew the answer to her question would only be a guess, a stab in the dark, *what are we talking about here? How much time do you think we've got left?*

About the Author

Eleanor Lerman is a writer who lives in New York. Her first book of poetry, *Armed Love* (Wesleyan University Press, 1973), published when she was twenty-one, was nominated for a National Book Award. She has since published three other award-winning collections of poetry—*Come the Sweet By and By* (University of Massachusetts Press, 1975); *The Mystery of Meteors* (Sarabande Books, 2001); and *Our Post-Soviet History Unfolds* (Sarabande Books, 2005); along with *Observers and Other Stories* (Artemis Press), a collection of short stories. She was the recipient of the 2006 Milton Dorfman Poetry Prize; was awarded the 2006 Lenore Marshall Poetry Prize from the Academy of American Poets and the Nation magazine for the year's most outstanding book of poetry for *Our Post-Soviet History Unfolds*, and received a 2007 Poetry Fellowship from the National Endowment for the Arts. Most recently, she received a grant from the Puffin Foundation to support a novel based on the life of Carlos Castaneda.

Other Recent Titles from Mayapple Press:

Sophia Rivkin, *The Valise*, 2008
Paper, 38 pp, $12.95 plus s&h
ISBN 978-0932412-720
Alice George, *This Must Be the Place*, 2008
Paper, 48 pp, $12.95 plus s&h
ISBN 978-0932412-713
Angela Williams, *Live from the Tiki Lounge*, 2008
Paper, 48 pp, $12.95 plus s&h
ISBN 978-0932412-706
Claire Keyes, *The Question of Rapture*, 2008
Paper, 72 pp, $14.95 plus s&h
ISBN 978-0932412-690
Judith Kerman and Amee Schmidt, eds., *Greenhouse: The First 5 Years of the Rustbelt Roethke Writers' Workshop*, 2008
Paper, 78 pp, $14.95 plus s&h
ISBN 978-0932412-683
Cati Porter, *Seven Floors Up*, 2008
Paper, 66 pp, $14.95 plus s&h
ISBN 978-0932412-676
Rabbi Manes Kogan, *Fables from the Jewish Tradition*, 2008
Paper, 104 pp, $19.95 plus s&h
ISBN 978-0932412-669
Joy Gaines-Friedler, *Like Vapor*, 2008
Paper, 64 pp, $14.95 plus s&h
ISBN 978-0932412-652
Jane Piirto, *Saunas*, 2008
Paper, 100 pp, $15.95 plus s&h
ISBN 978-0932412-645
Joel Thomas Katz, *Away*, 2008
Paper, 42 pp, $12.95 plus s&h
ISBN 978-0932412-638
Tenea D. Johnson, *Starting Friction*, 2008
Paper, 38 pp, $12.95 plus s&h
ISBN 978-0932412-621
Brian Aldiss, *The Prehistory of Mind*, 2008
Paper, 76 pp, $14.95 plus s&h
ISBN 978-0932412-614

For a complete catalog of Mayapple Press publications, please visit our website at *www.mayapplepress.com*. Books can be ordered direct from our website with secure on-line payment using PayPal, or by mail (check or money order). Or order through your local bookseller.